OTHER BOOKS BY LINCOLN JAMES

Vintage Thrillers • Modern Nightmares

Coming Spring 2026

All We Wanted
A Supernatural Thriller

They make your dreams come true. Then you disappear.

Spring Formal, 1982—a weekend of open bars, rented tuxedos, and bad
decisions at a luxury resort in Las Vegas.
But the casino has unveiled something new.
Buried behind the lobby stands a glass display case housing three
mummified figures adorned in gold:
a ring, a tooth, an eyepatch.
By day, they're on display. By night, they hunt.
They slip into borrowed skin.
They feed on desire, envy, regret.
All they need is one phrase.
I wish.
Because in this hotel, dreams don't come true.
They come for you.

<u>Now Available</u>

We Are Human
A Gripping Sci-Fi Thriller

They said it was evolution... He knew it was murder.

In 2040, Tyler Alcaster disappears.
When he wakes, his reflection isn't his own.
His skin is flawless. His pulse is wrong.
His memories—fractured.
They tell him he's special. Reborn. Immortal.
But Ty knows something still hurts. Still remembers. Still dreams.
Now he's trapped in a facility where nothing dies.
The people around him aren't people anymore—
a girl with glass eyes who never blinks,
a woman sewn together like a secret.
They all whisper the same question in the dark:
What are we becoming?
Because immortality isn't a gift.
It's the end of everything human.

Available in print and ebook.

Written Just For You
A Romantic Psychological Thriller

Some love stories are written in the stars. This one was written in blood.

Will wasn't supposed to stay in town. Jean wasn't supposed to meet
him. And the book she gave him? It wasn't meant to be read.
Depoe Bay is a place of whispers—where the fog clings too close and
stories go unfinished. The town says Jean is a ghost, a siren, a memory
that never made it out of the water.
But Will knows she's real. He's seen her. Heard her laugh.
Felt something shift.

And now that he's read her words...He can't let her go.
As the town turns colder, the secrets grow louder—about
the past, the dead, and what love refuses to bury.
Some girls don't make it out of their stories...
But Will's about to make sure this one does.

Available in print and ebook.

All the Time
A Coming-of-Age Sci-Fi Thriller

The past isn't just a memory... It's a trap.

When Carter sets out to reconnect with his dying mother, he never
expects to arrive at her house years before he was born. Stuck in
the past with nothing but his car, a bag of clothes, and a barely
working iPhone, Carter faces an impossible question: how did he
get here—
and how can he get back?
Time is slipping through his fingers, and every moment spent in the
past pulls him further from the future he's desperate to return to.
Caught between what was and what could be, Carter begins to
question if time is something you can outrun...
or if it's already run out.

Available in print and ebook.

Devils Like Us
A Tense, Gritty, Chase Thriller

Some devils hide in the shadows. Others look just like us.

Jason Murich thought he was heading home for a quiet weekend—
until two desperate runaways hijacked his car.
Now he's hurtling through the underbelly of 1990s Los Angeles on a
high-stakes chase that spirals into chaos.

As secrets surface and loyalties blur, Jason is forced to confront just how far he'll go to survive.

Gripping and raw, *Devils Like Us* is a taut psychological thriller that will keep you holding your breath until the final page.

Available in print and ebook.

The Vanishing Eight
A Pulse-Pounding Survival Thriller

Disappearing was only the beginning.

Eight friends. One missing.

The town of Piedmont had always whispered about them—
too close, too wild, too perfect.

Then Roy disappeared.

Now, Jonathan is racing to hold what's left of their group together. But the deeper he digs, the more he realizes: Roy's not the first to go missing. And if Jon's not careful...

He won't be the last.

In a town built on secrets, nothing stays hidden forever.

And some friendships don't survive the truth.

Available in print, ebook, and audiobook.

FOREWORD

Content Note

This story contains depictions of claustrophobia, violence, psychological distress, and scenes set in confined underground spaces. Reader discretion is advised.

A Note on the Descent

The Ninth Layer began with a simple question:

How far would you go for answers?

Beneath every campus, every town, every carefully built institution, there are foundations. And beneath those foundations—sometimes— there are things we were never meant to disturb.

This story explores fear in its most primal form: the dark, the unknown, and the unsettling realization that the ground beneath you may not be as stable as it seems. It is about survival, yes—but also about curiosity, guilt, loyalty, and the quiet pull of something calling from below.

Some doors open inward.

Some only open down.

Thank You

To every reader who dares to descend—thank you. And to those who have ever felt the pressure of the dark closing in, who have heard something breathing just beyond the edge of the light—this one is for you.

Respectfully Yours,

Lincoln James

THE NINTH LAYER

LINCOLN JAMES

ISBN 979-8-9985731-7-0 (hardcover)

ISBN 979-8-9985731-8-7 (paperback)

ISBN 979-8-9985731-9-4 (ebook)

Library of Congress Control Number: 2026903189

This is a work of fiction. Names, characters, organizations, places, events, and incidents are either the product of the author's imagination or used fictitiously. Any resemblance to actual persons, living or dead, or actual events is purely coincidental.

Published by Lincoln James

P.O. Box 10660 Page Ave # PO 4034

Fairfax, VA 22038-4034

www.thelincolnjames.com

Edited by E. Lee Caleca

First edition, February 2026

Printed in the United States of America

CHAPTER ONE

I SHOULD HAVE WALKED past the bulletin board.

I didn't know that yet, of course. At the time, Bennington, Vermont just looked the way a sigh feels—a little tired, a little dramatic, and definitely overdue for a spa day. After the rain, the whole town glistened in that "we did our best" kind of way: puddles everywhere, steam curling from brick buildings like they were auditioning for an artsy commercial. And behind all of it, the Green Mountains loomed—ancient and quiet, supervising us like bored giants.

April 12th, 2002.

Mud Season.

Exactly what it sounds like: the time of year when the ground collectively gives up and turns to soup. The locals say it proudly, like it's a regional celebration. Meanwhile, everything I owned smelled faintly of wet wool, and I haven't been properly warm since September. By this point though, we were caught in the days where it was forty-eight in the morning and sixty-eight by noon. No one knew what to wear. Still—spring was creeping in, and that was enough to put me in a halfway decent mood.

I was still dry when I left my on-campus apartment that morning, but I knew it wouldn't last long.

The elevator ride down was slow and familiar. It was the kind that rattled just enough to make you wonder how often it was inspected without ever actually feeling dangerous. A handful of students rode with me, half-awake, backpacks slung over shoulders, no one speaking. The air smelled faintly of detergent and old carpet, and someone had pressed the wrong button because we stopped on the second floor for no reason at all.

By the time I stepped outside, I was hit with cold and wet; the illusion of dryness was already gone. The hoodie I'd thrown on sagged heavy with moisture, sleeves stretched over my hands the way they always did, blond hair already curling damp against my forehead. The quad glistened under weak skylight, puddles reflecting the clouds like broken mirrors. I cut across campus toward the Geosciences Building, careful where I stepped.

I made it inside a little early—which surprised me enough that I checked the time twice. The clocktower hadn't gone off yet. No bells, no rush. Just that quiet stretch where campus felt like it was holding its breath between semesters while it waited for fresh, young, unwitting people to fill it up... or consume.

The lobby smelled like wet stone and paper—earthy, academic, comforting in a way only a building full of old books and questionable wiring could be. I slowed near the door to my lecture hall, fishing my notebook out of my bag, already running through what I remembered about last week's lecture.

That's when the bulletin board caught my eye.

I sloshed closer to it, dripping onto the tile like a malfunctioning fountain. It was the same board I passed every day without really looking at it. It was its usual collage of campus chaos—band flyers, roommate pleas, a tutor claiming he could "guarantee success," *sure buddy*, a poster for a film club screening that was already two weeks past.

But there was one flyer that didn't match anything else. Didn't seem to fit.

Centered. Perfectly pinned. Pristine, like it had been printed by someone who ironed their socks. Like it had been placed carefully, thoughtfully and with purpose—unlike everything else around it.

PAID RESEARCH OPPORTUNITY
GEOLOGY STUDENTS NEEDED
Document subsurface mineral formations.
Supervised fieldwork.
Sponsored by the
Bennington Subsurface Research Initiative.

No contact name.

No end date.

The paper didn't even have tear-off tabs. However it got here, it wasn't student-made. It didn't look... casual.

At the bottom was an embossed triangle—clean, sharp, official.

No slogan. No university seal.

Just the symbol.

I leaned in, scanning it again, trying to place the unease crawling up my spine.

The emblem felt familiar in the way old paperwork does—like something I'd seen once in passing and filed away without context.

It reminded me of the boxes my dad kept taped shut in the back of his office, the ones labeled in careful handwriting and never opened in front of me.

Research materials, he'd always said.

Nothing you'd be interested in.

He would've loved this, I thought. The phrasing alone sounded like him. It felt like a conversation I'd finally been invited into.

Before I could chase that thought anywhere useful, a paper cup bumped gently into my chest.

"Fuel," Brandon said. "For your underpaid academic journey."

I looked up. He stood a good head taller than me, jacket half-zipped, dark hair doing that permanently tired thing it only did when he hadn't slept enough to pretend otherwise. He looked like someone who belonged in hallways like this—comfortable, unbothered, already acting like he had permission.

"How long have you been standing there?" I asked.

"Long enough to watch you stare at that thing like it owes you money."

I took the coffee, sniffed it suspiciously, and took a sip.

Regretted it immediately.

"Why does this taste like metal?"

"Because the old machine downstairs is powered by spite," Brandon said. "Anyway, Alex—you're doing it, right?"

"Doing what?"

He nodded at the flyer with his chin. "The cave thing."

I glanced back at it. "Since when is there a cave thing?"

"Since approximately"—he checked his watch—"twelve hours ago."

I frowned. "Wait. What—what are you—" I stammered. "How are you even standing here? I thought you were asleep when I left. Knocked on your door and everything."

"Incorrect," he said. "I crashed in the grad lounge. Very glamorous. Concrete floors. Endless emails. I woke up to this whole situation."

I eyed him. "You're telling me you just... forgot to mention you were running an underground expedition?"

"*Running* is a strong word," he said quickly. "More like gently guiding. With a clipboard."

"So you either hid this from me, or I'm a terrible roommate. How did I not know about this?"

He smirked, spreading his hands. "What, like I can't have a little mystery?"

I studied him for a second. Brandon had that look—the one he got when he'd stumbled into something exciting and was already halfway convinced it was destiny.

I rolled my eyes. "When did you find out?"

"Last night," he said. "Email came in late. Grad consortium. Very hush-hush. Very *you up?* energy."

"And you didn't think to tell me?"

"I knew you were probably asleep," he said again. "And the way you bolt for your class in the morning like a responsible citizen is... pretty adorable."

I snorted. "Yeah, well, you're not even in my classes anymore to see it. Not since you upgraded to grad school."

"Correct," he said proudly. "I've ascended," he said. "Basement labs.

Coffee at illegal hours. You know—where they keep the stuff they don't want undergrads asking about."

I looked back at the flyer. Clean. Crisp. Too official for something students were supposed to casually sign up for between lectures.

"There's no professor listed," I said.

"Yeah," Brandon shrugged. "It's a group thing. Departments sharing toys. They needed someone with clearance who wouldn't panic underground. Couple of kids already signed up who... honestly, shouldn't be down there unsupervised."

"And they picked *you?*"

"They picked competence," he said. "Me and a few others from my cohort."

I raised an eyebrow and huffed a small laugh. "They really don't know you at all. So, which group are you overseeing?"

"The first," he nodded. "Helmet. Flashlight. I say things like *'please don't touch that.'* Very authoritative."

I smiled despite myself. That was Brandon—confidence first, questions later, optimism doing most of the heavy lifting.

"And you're *sure* this is legit? We're not just breaking into the campus tunnels? Because that sounds like a great way to get kicked out."

"As sure as anything around here ever is," he said. "We'll be the first students in decades to explore the quarry tunnels, sealed since the sixties. University wants updated data. Grants. Science. Adventure." He said it like he was advertising a theme park.

"Adventure," I echoed.

He grinned. "See? You're already sold."

I wasn't.

But I also wasn't *not.*

Something was tugging at me—like that itch you get when life offers you a door with your name on it that you didn't know existed. Like the partial vision you have when you can't actually see something but you know it's there. Part déjà vu, part dream. In your mind. In the part of the universe that pulls us into an unknown that we're sure we've experienced before. Familiar yet not.

It wasn't danger I wanted. It was proof that something bigger than lectures and midterms existed—and that I might be brave enough to step into.

"And you just found out last night," I said again, mostly to myself.

"Brand new," Brandon said. "Fresh flyer smell and everything."

I looked at the triangle at the bottom of the page. The imprint caught the light just right, a beacon beckoning me.

"Alright," I said. "I'm in."

Brandon lit up like I'd just agreed to rob a bank with him.

"Yes! Excellent. Fantastic. I knew you'd make the right choice."

As he clapped me on the shoulder, I had the strange, fleeting thought that this—standing in a hallway, coffee in hand, agreeing to go underground—felt like the start of something... almost fun.

Something unplanned.

Something you fall into.

AFTER CLASS, the campus outside was doing its typical impression of normal life—a little too chipper, a touch too coordinated. Someone's boombox blasted Ashanti out a dorm window—tinny, hopeful. A Frisbee skidded across the quad, splattering a freshman who barely complained.

Normally, I loved this stuff—the chaotic spring energy, the sense that the whole place was waking up with me.

But today it all felt... half a beat off. Like the shadow of a mouse pointer leaving a trail.

Maybe it was the early hour.

Maybe it was the cave sign-up burning a hole in my thoughts.

Still, it was Bennington's version of spring:

Mud. Regret. And occasional sunshine if you said "please."

Notebook tucked under my arm, Nokia knocking against my leg, I followed the brick path toward the library like a scarecrow on his way to Oz. The ground was soft and loud beneath me—every step making that squelch that was one bad choice away from becoming quicksand.

The walkway cracks were worse after the rain, filled with water so still it reflected the sky in tiny broken pieces. A maintenance crew worked near the fountain; orange cones circled them like they were performing a ritual. One of them muttered something about a "subsidence cavity," which, from the tone translated to: *Stuff is shifting under our feet, and we don't love it.*

Still, I knew it wasn't fatal.

Somewhere behind me, a guy leaning against the Geosciences steps overheard it and immediately launched into a correction, using words like *karst* and *load-bearing strata* like he'd been waiting all morning for an excuse to spout his unwavering wisdom and knowledge.

I avoided that confrontation like the plague, veering toward the overlook beside the athletics field—aka my unofficial introvert refuge. It sat on the edge of campus overlooking a stretch of nothing that felt like everything: the mountains, the track, the old part of town, complete with a cemetery and all the ghosts of Christmases past. It was a whole lot of quiet, and far enough from everyone pretending not to be stressed about midterms.

I leaned on the cold railing, breath fogging in front of me.

The metal vibrated faintly under my palm. Just a soft hum—barely there.

Probably nothing.

I pressed again.

Still there—steady, patient—but when I tightened my grip, the vibration vanished.

I glanced back to the Geosciences Building. Light hit the windows wrong, making them look like they were glowing from inside.

Definitely my imagination. Spring tends to bring that out. And the mold.

Only a little weird, I admitted inwardly. Just enough to raise an eyebrow.

And then—

Laughter.

Bright, unbothered, chasing away the mood like someone cracking open a window.

I turned.

It was Jennifer Weiss and her orbit—Stacy and Marissa—walking across the pavement like they were enchanted objects immune to dirt.

Their jeans were pristine. Their sneakers clicked politely. Even the rainwater avoided them out of respect.

If a campus brochure ever needed *"effortlessly put-together future leaders of America,"* the photographer could've just yelled, *"Hey! You three!"* and been done in five minutes.

But Jennifer still managed to stand out.

Dark hair pulled back tight, wearing a soft rose-colored sweater against the gray morning, she had that calm, open expression that made people feel like she'd listen—even if she didn't agree.

Stacy was mid-sentence about how she'd *"totally been down there before,"* waving off Marissa's look like rules were optional if you sounded confident enough. She was taller than both of them, red hair gleaming even under overcast skies, dressed like the rules of the season didn't apply to her.

Marissa trailed slightly behind, smaller, bundled in layers, dark hair also pulled back like a sycophant, like she'd dressed for comfort over presentation—and hadn't apologized for it.

Jen stepped around a shallow puddle without looking down, shoe skimming the edge, and only then glanced up.

And she definitely recognized me.

Not from parties—I didn't go to those. Not from socials—she lived in a world where mixers existed; I lived in a world where ramen and microwaves existed.

No, she recognized me from last semester's Earth Systems lab. Her best friend Stacy had sat beside me all term, all long legs, confident posture, and a smile that always looked like it definitely wanted the test answers. And Jen would wait for her after class, pretending she wasn't eavesdropping.

She and I had never talked. But we had the hallway nod down to an art—

The subtle, *"Yep, your face is familiar and neither of us hates that"* acknowledgment.

We'd probably shared maybe five nods total.

Solid nods.

Reliable nods.

Today, she upgraded to a wave.

A small wave.

A warm wave.

And I waved back, immediately regretting the lack of committee approval.

For some reason, I thought of the flyer again.

"—Jesus Christ."

Brandon's voice hit my left ear at the exact moment I realized he was suddenly there, and I jumped hard enough that my notebook nearly became airborne.

"What is wrong with you?" I snapped, clutching it to my chest. "Do you take classes in stealth or is this a natural gift?"

He grinned, completely unrepentant. "I said your name. Twice. You were too busy having a moment."

"I was *not* having a moment."

"Uh-huh."

He followed my line of sight just in time to see Jennifer Weiss laughing at something Stacy said as they walked ahead of us toward the quad. The sound carried—light, warm, effortless. The kind of laugh people wrote bad poetry about and then deleted out of shame.

Jennifer glanced back. Just once.

Quick. Curious. Just like she'd noticed me.

I told myself it meant nothing.

But I did *not* believe myself.

Then the three of them rounded the corner and disappeared into the morning crowd, leaving behind a faint trace of expensive perfume and general competence.

Brandon let out a low whistle—the kind that usually preceded him saying something deeply unhelpful.

"Dude."

I started walking toward the library, because if I stood still, this would become a 'conversation'.

"What."

"You waved."

"I acknowledged her existence. It's called politeness. Some cultures even encourage it."

"Uh-huh." He stretched the word like he was pulling taffy. "And she waved like she already knows your favorite band, your hometown, and your social security number."

"Yeah, totally," I said, unconvinced, but the heat crawling up my neck was basically screaming, *you have no chill and everyone can see it*.

"Just saying," he muttered. "If Stacy's crush wasn't obvious before, it's basically neon signage now."

"Stacy's fine," I said. "We talked about sediment layers and chalk dust. That's not—"

"It was absolutely a thing," he said, waggling his eyebrows like a cartoon detective. "Trust me, I'm a grad student. I can spot academic thirst from a mile away."

I groaned. "Please never say that again. For the sake of humanity."

He slung an arm over my shoulder, steering us toward the library steps. "Relax. You don't have to date a sorority girl. But you should at least admit you're interested."

I wasn't.

...Maybe.

...Probably.

...Okay, fine, she has nice eyes. And a nice smile. And a nice wave. And—

Nope. Not going there.

Someone jogged past wearing a motorcycle helmet clipped to his backpack like an accessory, bragging into his phone about *"restricted access"* and *"finding the old levels."*

Guess the expedition was the talk of the school.

I rested my palm against the metal railing beside the library door, expecting the cool shock to settle me. It didn't. The unease stayed and I couldn't put my finger on why.

A vibration rolled up my arm again, the kind of thing most people would chalk up to machinery. Except that machinery didn't usually feel like it was throbbing.

It felt wrong. Like maybe they were drilling somewhere on the grounds.

That moment I had with Jennifer, though?

Shockingly, *that* was the weirdest thing to happen all morning, and I still hadn't recovered.

Everything else—the cracked sidewalks, the tremors, the campus buzzing with too much energy—that almost seemed normal. And normal problems?

Bring them on.

Whatever was happening between me and her? If anything *was* happening...

That was new territory.

THAT NIGHT, our apartment smelled exactly like every other night in early spring: a cursed combination of abandoned pizza boxes, wet laundry that had given up on ever being dry again, and the faint burnt-dust scent rising off the space heater we absolutely were not supposed to own. The whole place had this vibe like it needed a good exorcism, or at least a strong breeze.

Brandon's desk lamp in the living room was the only real light source—glowing like a dim, heroic beacon in a sea of geological despair. He sat hunched over his desktop, typing survey numbers with the kind of focus usually reserved for defusing bombs or leveling up in RPGs. His long frame folded awkwardly into the desk chair, sleeves pushed up, hair falling into his eyes as the screen's glow caught sharp angles in his face, making him look like a young Doc Brown formulating the DeLorean time machine. The computer tower wheezed beneath his desk like it was on life support.

"Tomorrow morning," he said without bothering to look up. "Seven sharp. We take the freight elevator in Geosciences."

I frowned. "Seven in the morning? On a *Saturday*? And when did we get a freight elevator?"

"It's basement access only," he said. "Left over from the mining days. Very vintage. Very *please don't sue us*."

I peeled the label off a soda bottle, slow and methodical, in the therapeutic the way I always did when something didn't quite sit right.

"Isn't that... kind of sketchy?" I asked. "I mean, with everything going on lately?"

He paused—just for half a second—then kept typing.

"Define 'everything'."

"The tremors," I said. "The microquakes. You felt the one last week, right? The one that rattled the lab sinks?"

"That was barely a two-point," Brandon said, waving a hand. "Glacial rebound plus mud season. Happens every spring."

"Yeah," I said. "But this year's been weird. Subsidence near the quad, cracks by the fountain—"

"Alex," he cut in gently, finally turning in his chair. "We're geology majors in Vermont. If we panicked every time the ground made a noise, we'd never leave the house."

"That's not what I'm saying."

He grinned. "It's exactly what you're saying."

I huffed. "I'm just saying—mines, old tunnels, thawing ground—those things don't love each other. And human intervention does not bode well either."

"They tolerate each other," he said. "Like us."

"That's not comforting."

"It shouldn't be," he replied cheerfully. "It's accurate."

I glanced at the open textbook on the coffee table—*Updated Geology*, swollen from humidity, its spine cracked like it had opinions about our life choices. When I picked it up, the cover caught the light.

By Dr. H. Mercer.

My dad's name. Faded. Familiar.

He'd given me the book freshman year, saying something like, *"It'll make more sense when you're older."*

Still waiting on that part. He'd said it like a warning. Or a promise. I've never been sure which. All it was to me was a textbook with outdated findings, and theories that felt more like science fiction. I thought maybe I could find something about the humming but... no dice.

I tossed the book back onto my desk with a thud that felt metaphorical.

Brandon followed my gaze. "Your dad's book again?"

"Yeah. Dad used to say caves were honest places. They didn't hide what they were doing — they just took their time."

"Man," he said. "Between the two of us, we're basically a walking encyclopedia."

"Low bar," I said.

He snorted and spun back to his screen. "Look, I get it. You're thinking like a structural analyst. Stress points, collapse risk, liability nightmares."

"And you're not?"

"I'm thinking like someone who needs field hours and a thesis topic that doesn't involve staring at thin sections of rock under a microscope until I forget my own name," he said. "Plus, the tunnels we're using were reinforced back in the day. Concrete lining, steel supports. This isn't some wildcat shaft from 1890."

I hesitated. "And the tremors?"

"Snowmelt gets into everything. Freeze-thaw cycles loosen rock. It settles. It groans. It complains."

He flashed that grin again—the one that said *I've weighed the risks and decided optimism is cheaper*. He stood, stretching, arms overhead. "Come on. This is *literally* what we study. Rock does stuff. We write it down. We get paid."

"So, what's the catch?" I asked.

"No catch," Brandon insisted. "We're mapping mineral deposits so the university can chase some grant money. You get field hours, I pad my thesis, everyone's happy."

He pointed a pencil at me like a royal decree.

"I'll be the supervisor. You'll be my charming assistant. And I promise—absolutely nothing sketch."

"You sure?"

He gave the world's laziest salute.

"As your superior, I order you to relax."

I shook my head. "You're right. I'm overreacting."

But the words stuck with me like a sinister interlude:

Old mine shaft.

Sealed since the sixties.

Totally safe.

Yeah, no. Those words felt like the opening lines of a cautionary tale featuring a haunting and at least one missing person.

When Brandon finally called it a night, silence settled over the living room like a blanket someone forgot to wash. Brandon's computer tower kept whirring—an old, dying rhythm that made the fan click every few seconds like bones shifting in a crypt. A tiny orange LED blinked from the power button, steady and eerie, like a heartbeat trapped inside a machine.

I laid back on our sofa, staring at Dad's book while the night drifted in through the cracked window. The usual campus sounds rolled across the dark—laughter somewhere near the quad, a car thumping over the speed bumps, the irritated caw of the crow that had apparently claimed our apartment building as prime real estate. It was ordinary noise, the kind that filled the background of every night and didn't mean anything.

But then I heard it again.

The hum.

At first it barely registered as sound—more rhythm than noise, something low and steady that seemed to settle beneath everything else. It was the kind of vibration a person could ignore if they wanted to, the sort you could blame on heating pipes or old floorboards, except this one carried a strange sense of intention, like it was choosing to be noticed.

I pushed myself upright slowly, as though the air itself might crack if I moved too fast. It definitely wasn't coming from the window. It wasn't drifting through the hallway either. The walls felt too still for that. No—the noise came from deeper. From somewhere beneath the building, beneath the concrete foundation, beneath whatever this campus had been built over long before students filled its lecture halls.

It felt like the earth had something to say.

I pressed my palm against the wall. A faint vibration pulsed through the brick, traveling up my arm and along the delicate pathways of my nerves until it settled behind my eyes—a soft thrum, steady and patient, a rippling energy that felt like it was connecting me to something. A heartbeat that wasn't mine.

But still, I didn't pull back.

CHAPTER TWO

BRANDON WAS ALREADY GONE when my alarm went off at 6:45am.

His bedroom door was half open, and the room looked like it had been ransacked by a raccoon with a caffeine addiction—lecture notes scattered across every available surface, highlighted printouts curling at the edges, empty coffee cups stacked into what I could only assume was a shrine to academic desperation. A granola bar sat abandoned on the dresser with one bite taken out of it, like Brandon had chewed, reconsidered his life choices, and walked away mid-snack, leaving the lonely remnant in the aftermath.

If grad school had an aesthetic, this was it: chaos, but with confidence. The kind of mess that says *I swear I know where everything is* even when that is clearly a lie.

Outside the dorm window, the morning sky hovered in that in-between state Vermont specialized in—gray, washed out, undecided. The clouds clung low to the Green Mountains, dragging long shadows across the slopes like slow-moving bruises. It looked less like dawn and more like the world reluctantly waking up after a fitful night.

I looked back toward my side of the apartment and spotted a folded piece of paper sitting dead center on my desk, addressed:

To My Charming Assistant.

Brandon's handwriting had never been neat, but this looked especially aggressive—like the pen had been fighting him the whole time.

I couldn't sleep.
Meet me in the Geosciences basement.
Bring your old textbook.
Don't be late — the elevator's temperamental.
Hit B8.

I reread *Temperamental* twice.
That was Brandon talk for *Dangerous*.
And *Danger* could wait five more minutes.
It was 7:30 by the time I got up, but the building still felt half-asleep like no one got the message it was daytime.

I stood in front of my open closet longer than necessary, staring at a pile of damp hoodies and wrinkled shirts that smelled faintly of regret. Laundry day had been postponed one too many times, and now it was collecting interest.

In the end, I went with the only things that were both clean and dry: a lightly stained white polo and my khakis. Respectable. Neutral. The kind of outfit that said *I am not prepared for this adventure, but I'm totally okay with getting a little messy.*

I pulled on my sneakers, threw my textbook in my backpack, and checked Brandon's room one last time out of habit—still empty, still chaotic—before heading out. The sneakers were already damp at the edges, soles whispering against the floor like they knew better than I did.

Outside, campus felt muted—like the volume had been turned down on everything except the cold. The air smelled of thawing earth and pine sap, and the sidewalks shone faintly where last night's rain hadn't quite drained away. Students crossed the quad in loose clusters, coffee cups clutched like lifelines, conversations low and unfinished. Everyone looked like they were moving through fog, mentally if not physically.

I crossed the brick path toward Geosciences, slipping slightly on the damp stone. The cuffs of my khakis darkened with moisture where they brushed the ground, and I tugged the hem of the polo down out of habit, like neatness might somehow pass for preparedness. The building rose ahead of me, squat and old, its red brick exterior darkened by moisture. Steam curled faintly from a vent near the foundation, disappearing into the gray morning like a sigh.

Inside, the building was quieter than the rest of campus—no chatter, no people, just the echo of my footsteps and the distant vibration of machinery buried somewhere in the walls. The hallways were still waking up as I stepped into them. Fluorescent lights buzzed overhead with that tired, electric rattling they make right before they give up entirely, flickering just enough to feel passive-aggressive. The floor tiles were still damp from the janitors' early rounds, the sharp chemical smell of cleaning solution mixing with wet cement and the acridity of old heaters. Someone had tracked muddy boot prints down the hall toward the stairwell. The impressions were still crisp around the edges, like the mud hadn't decided whether it wanted to dry yet. I passed the bulletin board near the stairwell without stopping this time, the flyer still pinned there, pristine and watchful, like it knew I had already committed.

The stairwell itself smelled foul, like dust and old paint, rancid from the overgrowth of bacteria in the walls. Each step down felt heavier than the last, like the air thickened the farther I went, the musty atmosphere pressing in around my shoulders.

The basement door loomed at the bottom of the steps, marked **AUTHORIZED PERSONNEL ONLY** in peeling red paint. Someone had scratched their initials into the concrete beside it—old enough that the letters had softened at the edges. I wondered how many students had ignored that sign before it finally started to matter.

The door was slightly ajar, propped open with a rock about the size of a grapefruit.

That's got Brandon's name all over it.

I stepped through, and the temperature dropped immediately. It smelled like dust had been sitting untouched for decades and didn't appreciate the disturbance. The concrete walls swallowed sound, turning my footsteps into something smaller, duller.

The elevator sat at the far end of the basement, past rows of closed doors, wedged into the wall like the building had grown around it instead of it being installed. Rust crawled along the metal grates. Dust hovered in the air, suspended in that unnatural stillness you only find underground, like it was waiting for permission to fall.

I pressed the call button.

Nothing happened.

For a long second, I wondered if that was it—if the elevator had finally decided it had done enough in this life and retired without notice.

Then, somewhere far below, something shifted.

A low rumble echoed up through the shaft, followed by a metallic screech that set my teeth on edge. Cables strained, creaking like they held a grudge against the work they were being asked to do. Gears ground against each other in further protest, a union formed from decades of abuse.

The elevator was moving—slowly, with the patience of something old.

It didn't sound like a machine doing its job. It sounded like something waking up and resenting the effort.

When the doors finally lurched open, I found myself holding my breath without realizing it. Half of me expected—ridiculously—to see a face staring back at me through the dust. Some forgotten miner, pale and unmoving, waiting patiently for company.

Instead, there was just the elevator car.

Empty.

Stale air pooled inside it, heavy and unmoving. Shadows clung to the corners like they didn't trust the dusty overhead light.

I stepped in anyway.

The walls were cold enough to sting through my shirt. I reached for the panel and pressed the button marked **B8**.

The doors closed with a tired groan, and the elevator began its descent.

That's when I heard it.

The hum.

Like the one from the apartment walls— close enough to make my jaw tighten. The same low sound that used to live beneath my dad's late-night typing, steady enough that I'd learned to sleep through it. A low vibration that settled into my bones instead of my ears, like the sound was traveling through me rather than around me. My teeth felt sensitive, like they had ears of their own and didn't like the sound's taste. I clenched my jaw, the collar of my polo damp with sweat now despite the cold.

The elevator kept sinking.

No lights flicked across the panel. No reassuring dings to mark passing levels. Just the steady sensation of moving deeper, farther from anything that felt like surface or safety.

Dark rock slid past the caged window—too fast, too close to study.

The doors opened with a reluctant hiss, a testament to the persistence of their hydraulics.

Brandon stood in the center of the staging chamber like he owned the place. Goggles pushed up into his dark hair, work jacket zipped to the collar, boots already dusted pale with limestone, he looked less like a grad student and more like someone who'd been down here long enough to stop asking permission. Or, more accurately, like he'd decided ownership was mostly a state of mind and no one had challenged him on it yet.

The room felt enormous, the stripped-down skeleton of something once important. Standing lamps dotted the floor in a loose grid, each one casting a pale circle of light that barely held its shape before dissolving into shadow. Thick black cables ran between them, looping and tangling like roots that had given up on finding soil and settled for stone instead.

"About time," Brandon said. Music leaked faintly from his headphones as he lowered the band around his neck—something poppy and aggressively upbeat, the kind of song meant for treadmills and optimism. It felt wildly out of place here. "Tried to wake you, but you could sleep through an earthquake."

I stepped out of the elevator, rolling my shoulders as the cooler air settled on me. "Yeah, well, when they actually keep happening on campus, you stop registering them as emergencies. Where is everyone?"

"They won't be here till eight," Brandon said. "But I figured I'd get set up early. Plus"—he gestured around us—"it's kind of nice having the place to ourselves. You should've seen it before the school cleaned it up," he added. "Beer cans fossilized into the floor. Cigarette butts in the sediment layers. Real dignified stuff—or so I've heard."

"One hell of a place for a frat party."

"Yeah. Pendleton spent a fortune clearing out old vandalism before they reopened it," Brandon said. "Apparently kids used to sneak down here in the eighties. Like it was a rite of passage."

I could see why. The place was unreal. The chamber swallowed sound the way deep water does. Our voices didn't echo so much as disappear, like the walls were politely absorbing them. Thin mineral teeth hung from the ceiling in places the lamps barely reached—stalactites snapped short and blunted, like someone had broken them off decades ago and forgotten to finish the job. Below them, stubby stalagmites rose from the floor in uneven clusters, some old and scarred, others just beginning again, pale and delicate, the stone slowly trying to remember what it used to be. Was supposed to be. Or wanted to be.

Rows of old ceiling fixtures hung from rusted chains high above us, bulbs long dead. They sagged slightly, frozen mid-collapse, as if they remembered light but no longer believed in it. A length of chain had been twisted into a crude knot, like someone once swung from it and thought of leaving proof.

"Those still hooked up?" I asked, craning my neck.

"Leftovers from the mining days," Brandon said, following my gaze. "Power's shot. Too expensive to replace. Standing lamps only."

"Ah," I said. "Vintage danger."

He tapped his clipboard against his leg. "Relax. We're not going deep, if that's what you're worried about."

I looked back at him. "We're not?" I looked around me as if to say *I thought we already were.*

"Nope." He leaned on the clipboard like it was a cane. "Old tunnels are sealed. What's left of them probably collapsed years ago. We stick to the newer sections."

Even relaxed, he took up space—long frame loose, confident, like the chamber had already decided he belonged in it.

"And by *newer*," I said, smiling despite myself, "you mean—"

"The parts that won't collapse on us," he finished brightly.

That *did* help.

While Brandon sorted clipboards and checked battery packs with the exaggerated seriousness of someone pretending this wasn't extremely cool, I wandered toward the nearest wall. Up close, the stone wasn't rough the way I expected. It had a faint glassiness to it, like heat had once pressed against it hard enough to soften the surface before retreating. Ground and sealed like screed.

Tiny orange flecks threaded through the rock here too, caught in fractures and seams like sparks frozen mid-flight.

I brushed my fingers over one.

Warm. Just enough to notice—like a rock that had been sitting in sunlight. *But there was no sunlight anywhere near this place.*

"Huh," I murmured, more impressed than concerned.

"You seeing that stuff?" Brandon called from across the chamber.

"Yeah," I said. "It's... different. Kinda cool, actually."

My sleeves were already smudged with gray and orange dust, the semi-clean lines of my outfit giving up faster than I'd expected, while Brandon barely seemed to notice the grime collecting on his boots.

He nodded without looking up, flipping a page on his clipboard. "Ghostglass, I think. Or—uh—Eurydium. Something like that. You bring your book? Your dad used to talk about it."

That landed differently than I expected. Familiar.

"My dad?" I echoed.

"Yeah," Brandon said casually. "Dr. Mercer's research is half the reason we even got clearance to come down here. Toss it over?"

I slipped my backpack off and pulled the book free, its spine worn smooth from years of use. "Careful," I said, handing it to him. "It's... kind of sentimental."

"For a geology major, you're surprisingly protective of paper," Brandon said, flipping it open.

I smiled to myself.

Dad would've loved this place. The space. The structure. The way the stone told a story if you knew how to listen. Growing up, he'd taught me that geology wasn't just about rocks—it was about time, pressure, and patience. About how something ordinary could become extraordinary if you gave it enough time.

Standing there, boots on cold stone, lamps buzzing softly around us, I felt that same quiet thrill he used to talk about—the feeling that you were standing somewhere you weren't supposed to be yet. Like sacred ground meant for those who understood it.

And maybe that was exactly the point.

Brandon flipped the book open, skimming until he found what he was looking for.

"Here we go," he said, adopting his best mock-professor voice. *"Eurydium—otherwise known as Ghostglass. A quartz-adjacent mineral characterized by its glassy orange sheen."*

He squinted, then kept reading. *"Found in scattered deposits worldwide. Largely understudied."* He looked up, grinning. "Which is academic speak for *someone should really do something about this.*"

"Guess that's why we're here."

"Bingo!" He snapped the book shut and handed it back to me.

I took it, sliding it carefully into my bag. "Yeah. I know that page." I glanced toward the wall again, unable to help myself. "He's mentioned it before. Not a lot—just in passing. But I've never actually seen it in person."

Up close, the stone felt unreal. It caught the light in a way that made it feel... awake. Alive. I stepped a little closer, more curious than cautious.

"I bet he wishes he could be here," I said. "He'd lose his mind."

Brandon leaned back against a crate. "Where is he, anyway? You guys usually talk more. At least, you used to."

I shrugged. "Probably home. Working. He always is." After a beat, I added, "Does he know about this?"

"I assume so," Brandon said. "But he wasn't the one who emailed me. Came straight from the BSRI."

"Someone official?"

"Official enough to have an email signature longer than my thesis proposal."

"Huh." I nodded, then smiled to myself. "Still. I might try to snag a rock or two. You know—purely sentimental theft. I think it'd make his whole year."

Brandon cleared his throat loudly.

"Ahem. As acting authority figure down here, I must inform you that you absolutely cannot disturb the tunnel's natural ecosystem." He paused, nodding solemnly. "And you absolutely cannot take a rock."

I laughed. "What, you think there are cameras hidden in the walls?"

"Nah," he said. "But you never know. Someone could be wearing a wire."

I snorted. "This isn't *Law & Order*. It's PBS at best."

Brandon was like that—easygoing, generous with space, never pushing when I didn't offer. Sometimes I wondered if I should tell him more. About my dad. About the moves. About how being raised by a brilliant, distracted scientist meant learning independence early.

But I liked that Brandon didn't ask.

He didn't know about the woman in the hospital room back in '82 —the mother I never met, the one my father never talked about except in pauses.

He didn't know what it felt like to grow up in houses that always felt temporary—Burbank, Fairfax, then Vermont—each move framed as 'just for a while', each one quietly orbiting whatever my dad was chasing next.

He didn't know what it was like to be raised by someone who could diagram a crystal lattice from memory but struggled to answer *How was your day?* without drifting somewhere else.

And he definitely didn't know how relieved I'd felt when college gave me a reason to put a little distance between us.

Or how guilty that relief made me.

"Hey," Brandon said suddenly, snapping me back.

He thrust a clipboard and pencil into my hands. The paper clipped to it bore the same sharp-edged triangle from the flyer—the triangle logo clean and official against the grime of the cavern.

"You log the deposits on the map," he said. "I'll finish setting up the lights."

He crouched beside one of the standing lamps, tugging at a cable—

—and the lamp flickered.

Once.

Then went dark.

Half the chamber vanished into shadow, like something had reached out and taken the light.

I tightened my grip on the clipboard, the darkness pressing in.

And for the first time since stepping off the elevator, the thrill in my chest shifted—only slightly—into something I couldn't quite name yet.

Brandon tugged one of the standing lamps upright, gave it a sharp shake, and light rushed back into the chamber. The darkness retreated just enough to feel managed again.

"There we go," he said. "The rest of the group should be here in fifteen. You can get started on the rest of your work if you want, before it turns into a full-on field trip."

I nodded. That part I could handle.

I MOVED along the wall with my clipboard tucked under my arm, my shadow skimming the stone as I went. Thin orange flecks ran through the limestone in shallow fractures, catching the light when I shifted my head. It reflected in a way that felt different. Deep. Like the color wasn't on the surface so much as inside it. "Bioluminescent," I whispered. *But that was not possible. Was it?*

I stopped without really meaning to.

"Hey," I called over, tapping the wall lightly with my knuckle. "This stuff's kind of incredible." I waited for him to come look. Like it wouldn't be real until he saw it too.

Brandon glanced up from his notes. "Yeah? Your dad's miracle rock?"

I smiled despite myself. "I don't know about *miracle*. And maybe it's just my imagination, but it seems to glow more the closer I get to it."

I leaned closer, squinting at the seams. "I've only seen it in diagrams. And, like... one bad black-and-white photo in his old book." I hesitated, searching for the right words. "But it never looked like this."

Brandon stepped closer. "I'm still not too sure what to call it. Ghostglass. *Eurydium*. I don't know what's official, just what your dad renamed it to."

"Yeah," I said. "He never liked *Ghostglass*. Said it made people stop asking questions."

I traced the edge of one fracture with my eyes, careful not to touch it again. "All I really know is that it's... *weird*. Doesn't behave the way it's supposed to. That's what he used to say, anyway."

Brandon snorted. "And we both know how much he *loves* that."

I laughed softly. "Yeah... He just likes answers. Kind of goes along with being a scientist."

"He wrote about it like it was unfinished," I went on. "Like geology, physics, and chemistry had skipped a step somewhere. Not dangerous. Just... unanswered."

Brandon raised an eyebrow. "And now you're standing next to it."

"Yeah," I said quietly. "Which feels unreal."

"Well, believe it." Brandon continued. "Syenite, calcite... fluorescent. They absorb UV light then re-emit it so they can *seem* bioluminescent. But they're actually not. Just reflecting back. I imagine this one's no different."

"Yeah, but that's *only* UV light. These overhead lamps might have had enough power at one time to do that but... it's doubtful. And since they've been dimmed for so long, how are these rocks still reflecting light?"

Brandon was momentarily speechless as the sentence hung in the air.

I straightened, glancing back at the chamber. "Honestly, I think my dad would be jealous."

"That's allowed," Brandon said. "You're living every academic parent's dream right now."

I smiled, but it came with a tug in my chest. "He'd probably want samples. Charts. Six months alone with it and no interruptions."

Brandon pointed at me with his pen. "Say it with me: *I will not steal a rock.*"

I held up my hands. "Hey, innocent til proven guilty."

"The chamber has eyes, and so do I."

"Apparently," I said, looking back at the glowing walls.

"Besides, it would *really* complicate my paperwork if I had to write you up."

I waved him off, jotting a few notes I barely trusted myself to write —*orange inclusions present, nonuniform distribution, surface feels warmer than expected*—nothing definitive. Just impressions.

But even as I wrote, I couldn't shake the feeling that I was standing in front of something my dad had spent years circling without ever quite reaching.

A door cracked open, maybe one he expected me to step through. A scientific breakthrough still waiting to happen.

Something faint carried beneath my feet. Easy to ignore if I stayed busy. I told myself it was the world above, or maybe power lines. Just another oddity. Another thing geology didn't have a clean answer for yet.

The air smelled faintly metallic, sharp enough to notice. A single droplet fell from somewhere above us and splashed onto my clipboard. The ink bled outward in a thin, wavering line, darkening until it looked almost like a tear sliding down the page.

"Brandon, you feel that?" I asked, nodding toward the floor.

Brandon slid his headphones down around his neck again, rubbing at his jaw with the back of his hand like he'd just remembered it was there. "Generator," he said easily. "Or construction starting up again upstairs. I think we're somewhere below the fountain."

"You think we'd hear that this far down?"

"Who knows. Vibrations travel, and pressure does weird things underground," Brandon said. "Ears. Jaw. Totally normal."

"Right," I said. That made sense.

Every time the vibration passed through the room, the mineral flecks caught the light again—quick flashes, gone as soon as I noticed them.

A strange chill slid up my spine, brief but easy to shake off.

I ran my tongue along my teeth, suddenly aware of how tight I'd been holding myself all morning. One of the molars in the back. And it...clicked. Just wrong enough to be irritating.

Dentist, I told myself. *That's a future-me problem.* There were worse things than a loose molar. Like missing out.

Brandon was humming along to whatever song was playing in his headphones, blissfully unaware. When he looked up, I straightened instinctively.

"So what do you think? Creepy place, huh?" he said, grinning.

I shrugged. "Kind of cool, actually."

He clicked on a flashlight and swept it toward the far end of the chamber. The beam sliced through the dark, revealing the mouth of another tunnel half-hidden behind rock and shadow.

"Wait till you see the next chamber," he said. "It's beautiful."

His flashlight beam caught the dust swirling around his boots, then swept back across my own scuffed sneakers and dirt-streaked khakis— proof that whatever this place was, it was already leaving its mark.

I wasn't sure *beautiful* was the word I would've chosen for this place, but I nodded anyway.

Because whatever this place was, it wasn't done showing itself yet— and a part of me, the stupid adventurous part, wanted to see what came next.

CHAPTER THREE

THE ELEVATOR ROARED BACK to life—a full-bodied, metallic bellow that shook dust loose from the ceiling and sent it drifting down in lazy spirals. The grated cage rattled like it had opinions about being disturbed, and the standing lamps flickered in protest, angry over the energy theft.

I jumped.

Didn't mean to. Didn't *love* that I did.

"Is it supposed to do that?" I asked.

Brandon didn't even look up. He was hunched over his clipboard, headphones still hooked around his neck, still leaking tinny beats that barely traveled in the cavern.

"Yep," he said. "Failsafe. In case of a cave-in, it automatically returns to the top level. Keeps the shaft accessible for rescue teams. Either that, or our company has arrived."

I stared at the elevator shaft as the noise stretched upward, thinning as it climbed.

"Comforting," I said, even though the word came out a little crooked.

"Hey," Brandon said, finally glancing up, "nothing says '*safety*' like a machine whose main feature is *abandonment*. Builds character."

The sound faded slowly, like something retreating into sleep. Or pretending to. Like a ghost whose time had not yet come, waiting in the shadows.

"You ever think about..." I started, then stopped.

Brandon finally glanced up. "About?"

"How much trust we put in rusty machinery that predates color television."

He smirked. "You're saying that like it's philosophy. It's a freight elevator, not God."

"Bold of you to assume God doesn't also creak ominously," I said.

That got a laugh out of him. "I'd put my trust in something mechanical sooner than I would in something computerized."

The air down here felt thick—like it had weight. Water dripped somewhere in the distance, slow and deliberate, each drop landing with a soft *plink*. And underneath it all was that hum, steady enough to become part of the background, thoughtful and unhurried; the percussion part of the symphony.

Brandon adjusted his goggles, squinting at me. "You're looking a little ghostly. And not in the fun, tragic, Victorian-orphan way."

"Haven't eaten," I said. "My dad always said I'd starve myself to death before anything else got the chance."

Brandon snorted. "Your dad says a lot of things. I once skimmed his notes. I'm pretty sure he could write a twelve-page paper on dust and somehow make it threatening."

I smiled, but it didn't quite stick.

Every time my father came up, something inside me tightened— just enough to be noticeable. Like a rope being pulled through a pulley, testing the tension.

"You still talk to him?" Brandon asked, casual.

"Yeah," I said. "Just... not as much as I probably should."

He nodded.

"I mean," he gestured vaguely upward, "he's not exactly far. His office is basically right above us."

I shrugged. "I'm trying *not* to live in his shadow. That's kind of the point of being here. Geology instead of Physics. Rocks instead of equations."

"And then he switched departments," Brandon said, grinning.

"Yeah."

"Man's got impeccable timing," Brandon said. "Really committing to the bit." He laughed, louder than necessary. Too bright. Like he was turning up the volume so neither of us would hear the echoes of the living cave, breathing regret for years of secrets and solitude.

Then the elevator shuddered.

Hard.

A violent lurch rattled the cables overhead, sending a gust of stale air rushing down the shaft. Dust lifted off the floor in a startled cloud.

I took a step back on instinct.

The elevator groaned again—lower this time—as it began its descent. The metal gate rattled like it was clearing its throat.

Brandon stiffened, clipboard snapping shut in his hands.

"Well," he said quickly, upbeat in a way that felt rehearsed, "guess that's our cue. If anyone asks, we've been hard at work this whole time."

He pushed the goggles up again and left them there, forgotten, like most of the safety protocols he pretended to follow. "Be honest. Do the goggles scream '*I'm in charge*' or '*walk all over me*'?"

I smirked, tilting my head. "Guess we're about to find out."

The doors scraped open with a cough of old air.

And instead of the echoing clang I expected—

There was laughter.

Warm. Human. Completely out of place.

Six students stepped out of the elevator like they'd arrived at an off-campus adventure instead of the mouth of something ancient. The platform rattled beneath their feet as it settled, metal still creaking faintly from the descent.

Three guys.

Two girls.

And Jennifer Weiss.

The camera clicked the moment the doors opened.

A sharp flash burst through the cavern, white and sudden, catching dust midair and freezing the room in a split second of too-much light. Rock walls flared. Shadows jumped. For just a heartbeat, everything was visible—every crack, every hanging wire, every person standing there like they'd been dropped into place.

Then the dark rushed back in.

Jennifer lowered the disposable Kodak, blinking like she'd forgotten to breathe.

That was when she noticed us.

"Oh—" She glanced down at the camera, then up, suddenly aware of herself. "Sorry. I didn't even think—"

Her eyes flicked from Brandon to me, surprise blooming into something softer. Recognition. A quick, embarrassed smile tugged at her mouth.

"Hope you're not camera shy," she said, already half-apologizing, half-amused. "Habit."

She wasn't scared, exactly. Her eyes were wide, alert—but more like she was standing at the edge of something and hadn't decided yet whether to step forward or back.

She wasn't dressed for caves. None of them were, really. And I definitely wasn't about to win any awards for most prepared subterranean explorer. But Jennifer looked like she'd stepped in from an entirely different genre.

Dark brown polo tucked neatly into a denim skirt, clean sneakers already brushed with dust she hadn't noticed yet. She looked practical in a way that hadn't accounted for caves—like she'd dressed for a library, not the inside of the earth.

She held the camera delicately now, both hands wrapped around it like it was either precious or dangerous—or maybe both. The strap cut diagonally across her polo, grounding her in a way the rest of the cavern didn't.

Right beside her stood Stacy Trent.

Same girl from last year's lab. Same sharp posture. Same red hair flaring under the fluorescent lights like it had opinions. She'd dressed like the day planned to behave—fitted top, clean jeans, nothing that suggested she'd expected to crawl anywhere.

She leaned in and elbowed Jennifer lightly.

"Okay," Stacy murmured, low and quick. "Deep breaths. Worst case scenario, we fake a sprained ankle and sue the school."

Jennifer laughed—soft, breathy.

Stacy straightened, already scanning the cavern.

"I'm kidding," she added. "Mostly. But seriously—stick with me."

Jen always laughed like that.

Like someone raised in quiet rooms with invisible rules—don't be loud, don't be messy, don't draw attention unless invited.

Her gaze swept the cavern again—wide, curious, cataloging details even as she tried not to show it. Then it landed back on me.

Recognition flickered.

And then that same closed-lipped smile from the quad appeared—polite, practiced, careful. The kind of smile girls learn early. The one that says *I'm friendly*, but not an invitation.

"You again," she said.

Her voice echoed once.

Then vanished—like the cavern had decided it wasn't worth repeating.

"Guess so," I said, suddenly aware of the dust streaking my polo and the fact that she still looked like she belonged above ground. The fabric clung uncomfortably now, damp with sweat and limestone dust, like it had decided this wasn't what it signed up for.

She lifted the camera again—resting it against her chest.

"I'm documenting this for history," she said, softer now. "Or... at least trying to."

One of the guys snorted. "History. Damn. Didn't realize we were storming the beaches of Normandy."

Another groaned. "She's documenting this for her scrapbook."

I recognized that voice.

Matt.

Freshman year. Same dorm. Same floor, even. We'd shared exactly two conversations before he joined a fraternity and promptly vanished into a world of matching jackets and blacking out.

Stacy snapped toward him instantly. "And for memories, asshole. Some of us care about remembering things."

Matt lifted his hands, palms out, grin easy and unbothered. A fitted T-shirt clung to him under an open button-down, still crisp enough to suggest he hadn't expected the day to get messy.

"Whoa. Didn't say it was a *bad* scrapbook." He glanced at Jennifer's camera, then back at Stacy. "Just didn't realize we were going full *National Geographic*. Should I be doing something heroic in the background?" He winked at Jennifer. "Tell me when to look mysterious."

Matt ran a hand through his neatly styled brown hair as if the cave were a party he hadn't planned on staying at for long.

"Don't worry, I'm sure she'll capture the real you," I said.

One of the other guys adjusted his glasses, plain sweater pulled down neatly at the cuffs, like he preferred things uncomplicated and where he could see them.

"It is limestone," he said mildly, taking it all in, eyes roving across walls, ceiling, and floor, but not at the people in the room. Almost like he was talking to himself. "And it's structurally sound—though the acoustics are unusual. Sound absorption is inconsistent."

He said it like a conclusion, but he didn't sound convinced.

"It's silent, what are you talking about?" the third guy asked, tilting his head, blond hair falling into his eyes as he leaned past the lamps. His boots were planted easy, leather jacket creaking when he moved like it was used to speed. He didn't look lost—he looked curious. A thin scar cut through one eyebrow, pale against sun-darkened skin.

The one with the glasses frowned. "Exactly. And it shouldn't be."

Jennifer didn't react to any of it.

Didn't roll her eyes. Didn't snap back.

She just let the noise pass—like she'd been doing that her whole life. Commentary bouncing off before it could land anywhere tender. Unimportant in the world she was accustomed to.

Her gaze slid back to me, lingering a fraction longer this time.

Curiosity.

Recognition.

Or maybe relief—seeing someone familiar this far underground, where familiarity suddenly felt like currency.

Behind her, another girl hovered near the lamps, crouched slightly to examine the rock wall. She didn't say anything. Just traced a fracture line with her eyes, lips moving faintly like she was already cataloging it. Her oversized sweater brushed the wall, sleeves too long for her hands. Surprisingly though, she was a natural at moving through stone.

Marissa.

I didn't know her personally, but everyone in Geosciences did in that vague, orbiting way. She practically lived in the building. Slept there, probably. Breathed geology like oxygen. She had the posture of someone who knew exactly where she was—and the expression of someone still surprised anyone else noticed. Like it was normal. And somehow, she still ended up attached to Stacy and Jennifer, like gravity had pulled her sideways instead of straight down.

Maybe she saw them as a cover for her nerdiness.

Before I could say anything remotely intelligent, Brandon stepped forward and flipped his clipboard to the sign-in sheet.

"Alright," he said, voice shifting into tour-guide mode. "Let's make this official before anyone wanders off and becomes part of the scenery."

He scanned the page.

"Joshua Feldman?"

The wanderer lifted a hand. "It's Josh."

"Matthew Franklin?"

Matt didn't bother raising his hand. "Present and emotionally available."

Brandon blinked. "...Great. Marissa Klein?"

The girl by the wall startled—just a little—like she'd been pulled out of a thought mid-sentence. "Here!" She tucked a loose strand of hair behind her ear.

"Wait," I said, squinting. "You were in Sedimentary Systems last fall. Front row. Always color-coded your notes."

Marissa blinked. "—Oh. Yeah. Hi." She smiled, a little shy. "You were the one who asked if limestone could technically have a memory."

"Still standing by that," I said.

Her shoulders loosened immediately. "Thank God."

"Fun! We love a fellow sentient-rock enthusiast." Brandon smirked. "Alright, who's next... Stacy Trent?"

"Obviously," Stacy said, without looking up.

Brandon snorted. "I figured."

"Kevin O'Neill?"

The guy with the glasses adjusted them. Brandon squinted.

"I know that name—didn't we have a class together?"

Kevin shrugged. "Geo-Chem. Last semester. You TA'd."

"Right," Brandon said. "Total rock star." He tapped the page again. "And—Jennifer Weiss."

Jennifer nodded.

Brandon paused.

"Aren't you a history major?"

He gestured vaguely at the cave. The lamps. The rock walls. "This is geology. Caves. Mineral sampling. Literal rocks. Are you sure you didn't mean to sign up for, like... a museum tour? With lighting?"

Jennifer swallowed, then straightened.

"I filled out the forms," she said quietly. "They stamped them and everything."

Stacy stepped forward immediately, chin lifted, shoulders squared —ready for a fight she hadn't caused but was absolutely prepared to win.

"She did," Stacy said. "I was with her. Lady took her paperwork upstairs, stamped it, handed her a packet. So if there's a problem, it's not hers."

Brandon hesitated, then sighed.

"Okay. Fine." He checked a box. "But you stay close. No wandering. If something happens to a non-geo major, I lose funding and possibly my soul."

Jennifer nodded, visibly bracing herself.

Stacy squeezed her arm, leaned in, and whispered something I couldn't hear but could absolutely feel—low, fast, protective. Jennifer exhaled like she'd been holding her breath since the elevator stopped.

Brandon clapped his hands together. The sound cracked sharp through the cavern, loud enough to wake a sleeping beast if we weren't careful.

"Alright," he announced, confidence patched together with duct tape and optimism. "My name's Brandon, and some of you may know me as Mr. Pike. Welcome to your extra-credit adventure. Ground rules: stay close, do *not* touch the walls, and for the love of science, don't lick anything. I know how you undergrads get."

A ripple of laughter moved through the group—thin, tentative. Like no one was entirely convinced he was joking.

Josh grinned anyway. "You say that like you don't want us to lick things."

Another few chuckles from the crowd.

"I say that like I've *seen* what happens when people lick things," Brandon said. "And I don't get paid enough for mouth-related injuries."

Jennifer smiled.

This time it wasn't practiced. It was real. And something in my chest tightened—something closer to recognition.

Two people pretending they belonged somewhere they didn't.

Two people choosing curiosity over comfort.

Two people standing on unfamiliar ground, pretending not to feel the tremor under their feet.

Stacy nudged Jennifer again. "C'mon, history girl. Try not to trip over anything. Or anyone." Her eyes flicked toward me on the last word.

Jennifer flushed. "Stace, stop."

It was the first unguarded thing she'd said all day. And somehow, that felt important.

Matt leaned in. "Hey, if someone's gotta be the cautionary tale—"

Stacy cut him off without looking. "You already are."

Matt grinned, ducking slightly when the ceiling dipped, like it surprised him.

"Consistency is key."

I rubbed my jaw, distracted. The cave suddenly felt loud with all these people in it.

"Hey, can we chill?" I asked, before it could tip into something sharper. "It's 8 AM on a Saturday. Let's just follow Brandon's lead, and I'm sure we'll avoid bringing this whole place down—"

Kevin frowned. "I *told* you, everything here is stable. These caverns are older than all of us put together. Besides, bright flashes mess with depth perception underground. Best to avoid it."

Josh scoffed. "I don't know what you're all so worked up for." He said, stepping further past the lamp line. "It's a *cave*, not a haunted house."

Kevin didn't look at him. "Those two things aren't mutually exclusive."

"GUYS!" Brandon yelled, his voice echoing once. He hesitated, then smiled wider than necessary. "Josh, get back here."

Josh stopped — one foot still in shadow.

The noise dimmed. Like someone had reached for a dial without telling anyone.

"C'mon. Let's gear up." Brandon ordered. "Just give me a little bit more of your time, *then* we can start exploring." He looked at each of them individually. "And *do not* do anything on your own. Remember: Strength in numbers. That means *you*, Josh."

"Hell yeah, think we'll find some diamonds?" Josh flashed a look at Matt.

Matt shrugged, already stepping past the edge of the lamps. "Only one way to find out."

Kevin frowned. "That isn't how probability works." His brown hair cut short and practical, posture careful despite his height, like he'd learned early not to take up more space than necessary

Josh smirked and rocked back on his heels. "Works fine for me."

Matt glanced back over his shoulder. "Relax. Worst case, we find a cool story. Best case—" He tapped the rock wall with his knuckle. "—I retire early."

Brandon snorted. "If either of you finds diamonds in Vermont, I'll *personally* name the mine after you."

"Hold you to that," Josh said. "*Josh's Hole* has a ring to it."

"Absolutely not. That's how lawsuits happen," Brandon said, whipping around. "And I told you... No touching the walls. Not kidding people!"

More laughter followed, but fell a few feet from the speaker.

"Does it feel like the sound..." Marissa hesitated, then rushed, "—this is probably nothing—but like it curves?" She sounded curious. Careful. Like she didn't want to scare the idea away by naming it wrong.

I started to follow her gaze—then stopped when Jennifer shifted beside me. The hem of her skirt brushed the rock when she leaned in, close enough that she stiffened without realizing it.

Marissa's observation drifted through the group without catching.

Stacy glanced over, half-smiling. "She does this," she said. "Gives rocks feelings."

Then, softer, to Jennifer: "Don't worry. She's right ninety percent of the time. Just... early."

Marissa laughed softly. "Sorry. I get weird about acoustics." She smiled back, unfazed. "It's still geology," she said gently. "Just... trying to understand what we're working with."

Brandon knelt by the equipment crate and flipped the lid open.

Inside: a mess of university-issue helmets. Scratched. Dented. Stickered with faded logos and warnings from decades ago.

"Alright," Brandon said, hauling them out. "Gear up. If something falls on your head, I do *not* want to deal with the paperwork."

He handed them out with brisk efficiency.

"These smell like a bowling alley," Matt muttered. "Or—like a dirty locker room." He turned his helmet sideways, inspecting it. "Which is comforting, honestly. Means people survived long enough to sweat in them."

Brandon snorted. "That's... not the reassurance you think it is."

Stacy grimaced. "Oh my God. I knew I should've worn my old clothes. If I get tetanus, I'm haunting this place." She tugged at her sleeves like the dust offended her personally.

Kevin snorted. "That isn't how tetanus works."

Stacy shot him a look. "I'm not here for science."

"Right... Then why are you here?" Brandon asked.

"I—" She stammered, looking to Jen before placing her hands on her hips. "I'm here because I'm a good friend. Some would say the *best*."

Brandon shook his head and returned to the task at hand. When Brandon reached me, he hesitated—just a second—then leaned closer, lowering his voice. "They only gave me enough for everyone on the roster, but don't overthink it," he murmured.

"I won't—but is there a reason I wasn't on the list?"

"Technically we were at capacity, but I signed your name under group B. They come down around 1pm. Don't worry, though. You'll still get credit, *and* I got something better for you."

I let out a small laugh. "Can't wait," I said.

And realized, with a small jolt of excitement, that was true.

Josh slapped his helmet on crooked. "This thing even OSHA approved?"

"It was," Brandon said. "Once. Possibly during the Nixon administration."

Jennifer hesitated when one was handed to her. She slipped it on, adjusting the strap with careful fingers. She winced slightly when the band pressed against her scalp, then smoothed it away with a quiet laugh.

Marissa noticed immediately.

"Easy mistake," she said, stepping closer to Jennifer. "Those ones pinch right there." She tapped her own temple, miming it. "If you loosen it just a notch, it won't press on the nerve."

Marissa adjusted it with practiced ease, like someone who'd learned the rules by making mistakes.

Jennifer adjusted her hair. "Oh. That's—wow. Better."

Marissa smiled, small and pleased. "Yeah. Learned that the hard way."

Stacy took in the sight of Jennifer immediately. "Oh *no*."

Jennifer sighed. "Stacy."

"No, I'm serious," Stacy said. "This is *not* the look you want immortalized underground." She adjusted her helmet for her. It bumped against her shoulder, leaving a chalky smear on the collar of her polo. "There. Crisis managed. If we die, you're at least cute."

The joke didn't echo.

Next came the flashlights.

Brandon passed them out like he was dealing cards at the worst casino imaginable—heavy metal bodies, chipped paint, switches that clicked louder than felt necessary.

"This is your new best friend," Brandon said. "Treat it better than your GPA."

Josh flicked his on and aimed it straight up. "Whoa."

Kevin winced. "Don't do that. You're flattening the shadows." He held his own flashlight low and still, treating it like a measuring tool instead of a toy.

Josh lowered his, frowning. "You're really ruining my vibe, man."

"Good," Kevin said. "Might save your life."

Everyone held the lights the same way—tight grip, white knuckles. Like the weight alone might count as protection.

Jennifer tested hers differently, positioning herself closer to me.

She angled the beam across the rock instead of straight ahead, the way you do when you're checking for texture or moisture—anything that might bend the light.

It didn't refract.

It slid. Like there was a surface there that didn't want to be seen.

Like the light was avoiding something.

No one commented on the way it moved. No one wanted to name it. Or maybe I was the only one who found it strange.

Jennifer glanced at me like she was checking whether I'd seen it too.

"Here, Alex." Brandon reached deeper into the crate and pulled out a headlamp.

It had an elastic strap and cracked plastic, along with a bulb that looked like it had survived a small war.

He held it up once, then handed it straight to me.

"Hands-free is better. You'll be the *real* photographer," he said, then paused. "No offense, Jen."

"None taken," she called back. "Means I get to keep my pictures."

Josh snorted. "Congrats. You're officially in charge of proof."

"When was the last time you changed the batteries?" I asked, inspecting the headlamp.

Brandon waved it off. "It works. Test it."

I slipped it on.

The band hugged my forehead snugly—just a little too snug—like something molding itself into place. Everyone looked at me for half a second longer than felt reasonable. I adjusted the strap, suddenly aware of my own breathing. The beam flickered once, then stabilized, throwing light across the far wall. Dust swirled through it, drifting slow and deliberate, like ash refusing to fall.

Pressure built behind my eyes, a headache beginning to bloom. I told myself it was a focus issue.

And I liked the idea that something was finally clicking.

Jennifer glanced up at me, tracking the way the light moved when I turned my head.

"You look cool," she said. "Almost... official."

"I feel like I should start saying things in a documentary voice," I said. "*Here we observe the ancient idiot in his natural habitat.*"

Jen laughed—quiet, but real.

"*Another* photographer? Didn't realize I signed up for a photoshoot." Matt angled his helmet like it mattered. "Make sure you get the lighting right. I've got a brand." He tugged lightly at the open collar like it might make or break his image.

Kevin frowned. "This isn't about aesthetics."

Matt grinned. "*Everything's* about aesthetics."

Brandon reached into the crate again and produced a black camera case. Newer than everything else. Cleaner. Purpose-built.

"For your shots," he said. "Clips on. Don't drop it. I signed for that."

I fastened it to my belt. It bumped lightly against my hip when I shifted—solid, grounding. A role. A task. Something normal to focus on.

Marissa took a folded map from Brandon. She unfolded it carefully, like it might crumble or disappear if she moved too fast.

"I've only seen this in archives," she said, almost to herself. Then, realizing she'd spoken aloud, she flushed. "I mean—this is really cool."

Her eyes moved between the inked lines and the stone itself, checking one against the other. "Do you guys notice," she said softly, more to the space than the group, "how the branches narrow the deeper they go?"

Josh shrugged. "That's caves."

Kevin shook his head. He planted his feet before speaking, gaze steady, like he'd already mapped the space in his head. "That's stress fracturing. Different mechanism."

Marissa nodded, encouraged rather than corrected. "Right. I just mean—" She hesitated, choosing her words carefully. "—they're stable. But they're... compressed. Like everything's been asked to share space."

Jennifer frowned. "Share space with what?"

Marissa opened her mouth—then stopped. Her gaze drifted back to the wall. "I'm probably overthinking it," she said, apologetic but not embarrassed.

Stacy was already turning away, voice low. "Come on," she said to Jennifer. "Let's stick with the lights." Marissa didn't seem bothered. Just... quietly cataloging.

The space around us seemed to tighten, as if the cavern had leaned closer, curious who had noticed.

Finally, Brandon handed out the rest of the maps.

Thin paper. Simple lines. The tunnels sketched like branching veins —some thick, some spindly, all curling inward.

"No one gets lost," Brandon said. "Stick with me, follow the lights, and if you hear anything weird, assume it's pipes. Or raccoons. Or ghosts."

"Definitely ghosts," Josh said.

"Ghosts aren't real," Kevin muttered.

The laughter that followed was weaker now. Softer. Like everyone was aware they were laughing because silence would be worse. Still, the pressure behind my eyes faded when they laughed. I told myself that meant I was fine.

Brandon checked his digital watch. "Alright. Time to earn those credits."

He crossed to the tripod lamp and flipped the switch. The bulb buzzed—low and steady—then flared, casting long shadows across the cavern walls. Skeletal shapes stretched and bent, clinging to the rock like they wanted out.

"If anyone wants to turn back," Brandon began, "now's the ti—"

The elevator groaned behind us.

Metal strained. Chains rattled overhead, shaking more dust loose from the ceiling in soft gray flurries. The platform lurched upward, dragging itself back toward the surface.

It didn't feel like it was leaving us.

It felt like something had decided we didn't need it anymore.

We all watched it rise.

Josh whistled softly. "Well. That's dramatic."

Kevin didn't look away. "That's protocol. Said so on the waiver."

Matt watched the platform rise, grin fading just a notch. "...Huh." Dust had already dulled the edge of his shirt, the button-down hanging heavier than before. He shoved his hands into his pockets, forcing his bravado back into place. "Alright then. Guess we're officially underground people."

Jennifer glanced from the elevator to the darkness ahead, then back again—measuring something no one had asked her to measure.

Brandon glanced over his shoulder, then grinned.

"Well," he said, clapping his hands once—too bright, too loud— "looks like we're stuck with each other for now."

He gestured forward with his flashlight.

"But don't worry," he added. "We're here to have fun."

The darkness didn't argue. We kept watching the elevator until it disappeared.

Not because it was interesting.

Because it felt wrong to look away, like rubberneckers passing a fresh accident.

CHAPTER FOUR

THE ELEVATOR'S light shrank as it climbed — from a square glow to something coin-sized, then smaller still, thinning into a single bright pin lodged in the dark. And then it vanished entirely. Just a column of black where the exit used to be.

The shaft swallowed it whole.

When the last rattle of metal faded, the silence that followed didn't feel natural. It felt assembled. Like someone had carefully put it together piece by piece and left it standing there between us.

The earth seemed to hold its breath.

So did we.

We were officially alone down here now.

And yet, the longer I stood there, the more it felt like *"alone"* wasn't quite the right word.

"Okay—just checking," Marissa said softly, glancing around. "Everyone good?"

No one responded, but I gave her a small smile and nod. Marissa clicked her pen and leaned closer to the wall.

Brandon cleared his throat—a loud, deliberate sound—and swept his flashlight across the walls like he was drawing a line through the quiet. He stopped just short of the nearest standing lamp, positioning himself beside it without thinking, like muscle memory.

"Alright," he said, voice snapping back into tour-guide mode. "So. This whole cave system sits on an old limestone quarry. You can still see the tool marks if you look close enough."

He angled his beam toward the stone. Shallow grooves caught the light—neat, repetitive scars left by hands that had expected the earth to behave.

Marissa leaned back on her heels, peering at the grooves with open admiration. "They're so... neat," she said, then glanced back at us. "I get excited when people in history were... optimistic. Like they really believed the rock would cooperate if they were polite enough."

Jennifer smiled. "*Optimistic* feels generous."

Josh leaned in, peering at the grooves. "It's wild," he said, impressed in a way that had nothing to do with caution. "Imagine thinking you could just... carve through all this."

Matt snorted. "Yeah. Humanity's real good at restraint. That's basically our brand."

Kevin adjusted his glasses, squinting at the markings. "They're remarkably consistent," he said. "That suggests prolonged work, not panic. Whatever happened down here, it wasn't sudden."

Jennifer raised her disposable camera, hesitating for half a second before clicking the shutter. The flash popped—sharp and clean—and for a heartbeat the entire chamber froze in white once again.

When the light faded, the glow in the stone felt deeper somehow. Settled.

"What about those?" Josh asked, pointing upward.

"Yeah," Matt added, squinting up at it. "Why does the rock look like it's about to spit lava at us?"

Brandon tilted his light higher.

Thin veins of orange threaded through the limestone—dull at first, then brightening as the beam lingered. Almost as if it were... responsive.

"*That* is the reason we're down here. It's called Ghostglass," Brandon said. "Or Eurydium, if you want to be technical. Our very own Dr. Mercer coined the latter. Your mission, since you've chosen to accept it, is to document everywhere you see it and note how it behaves."

Matt huffed. "Sounds like the old man. Had him for Solid State Physics last semester. Guy likely couldn't name a sandwich without making it ominous."

Marissa lifted her pen halfway. "It's—um. It's kind of famous for being misunderstood," she said, then rushed, "not *famous*-famous, just —academically famous."

Kevin smirked. "Academically famous is my favorite kind of famous."

Stacy immediately looked away, angling her flashlight toward the ground like she'd dropped something. "Cool," she said briskly. "Very sparkly. Ten out of ten. Can we please keep moving before my helmet commits a hate crime against my hair?"

Josh grinned. "You're afraid of rocks, Stacy?"

"I'm afraid of *liking* them," she shot back. "That's how this whole nerd thing starts. And before you know it, I'm arguing about minerals and wearing cargo pants." She paused, looking me up and down. "No offense."

"None taken—they were clean..." I smirked.

Marissa paused her writing long enough to rub her jaw once— absently, distracted, like someone adjusting to altitude. "Does anyone else feel the pressure changing?" she asked.

Kevin frowned. "That would require a significant atmospheric shift."

Marissa shrugged, cheeks pinking. "Okay, wow, that sounded *way* more ominous than I meant. I just—science curiosity. Not *impending doom* curiosity."

Stacy waved a hand. "It's a cave. It's literally pressure and damp walls. That's the brand."

Marissa glanced at me. "You okay? You went quiet."

I didn't even realize I had. "I just think this place is kind of incredible," I said, before I'd fully decided to. "Like the space itself is... tuned."

Jennifer's eyes flicked to me, sharp and assessing.

"Folklore says miners used to talk about the Nine Layers," Brandon went on, clearly relieved to reclaim the floor. "Supposedly this stuff showed up more the deeper they went. And the story goes that once you hit the ninth—"

Jennifer's camera clicked again.

"—your echo stops coming back," Brandon finished. "They said that's where the earth starts listening instead of answering."

A laugh bubbled up somewhere behind us—too quick, too loud. Josh broke the tension. "That's metal."

Kevin didn't smile. "That's metaphor."

"They didn't mean it literally," Brandon said, waving it off. "It's just how miners talked. Long hours underground mixed with the silence down here... it messes with your head," he added lightly. "That's why they kept talking. Singing. Anything to keep sound moving. If you ask me, that sounds like my own personal version of Hell." He joked.

I nodded, though I wasn't sure why. The idea made sense in a way I couldn't explain.

"So that's why locals won't shut up about this place," Matt said. "Let me guess—someone went full cabin fever and started hearing God in the walls?"

"No," Kevin said quickly. "The quarry closed after a series of collapses. Structural instability. It's all documented."

He said documented like it ended the conversation.

Josh tilted his head, unconvinced. "Then what about the research section? Why'd that close in the sixties?" He glanced down the tunnel, grin tugging at his mouth. "I heard it was wild cats."

Stacy scoffed immediately. "Please tell me that's not a thing," she said. "Because I did *not* sign a waiver for feral cave cats."

"It is," Josh said easily. "People say the cats stopped coming around this side of the ridge. Happened when the noises started."

"Noises?" Brandon scoffed. "You mean construction?"

He turned slowly, arms spreading as he slipped fully into lecture mode—confidence settling over him like armor.

"Look. The university was built over an ancient cave system. Over a century ago, miners dug all through here and collapsed half of it. You mix that with unstable ground, mud season, and the occasional micro-quake and—yeah." He tapped his boot against the stone. "This place has opinions about staying upright. Both closures were safety calls. Nothing mysterious."

Kevin hesitated, then adjusted his glasses. "Technically," he said, careful, "the second closure wasn't listed as a safety failure. It was administrative."

Brandon glanced at him. Just a look. "Same difference," he said, already turning back toward the tunnel.

Matt hummed. "Yeah, well that's exactly what you'd say if something was *very* mysterious and *very* expensive to explain."

Marissa smiled faintly. "For what it's worth, every cave legend I've ever read started with someone saying, *'It's probably nothing.'*"

Brandon ignored her.

Marissa winced. "Which—sorry. Not comforting. I'm bad at timing."

Stacy wrinkled her nose. "Okay, so what about the cats?"

"Easy," Brandon said. "Cats and bats don't mix."

Jennifer blinked. "Bats?"

"Yes, bats," Brandon said, already tired. "They used to swarm these caves. Ever since construction started, their numbers tanked. That's all this is. Ecology being dramatic."

Kevin nodded. "I thought so. I'm nearly certain that rock back there had guano on it."

Stacy adjusted her helmet again, fingers fussing with the strap. "Great," Stacy said. "So rule one: don't touch anything. Rule two: burn our clothes when we get out." She tugged at her sleeves like she already felt contaminated.

"Too late," Brandon said, smirking. "You're standing in it. Most of us are."

"Oh," Marissa said faintly, lifting one boot an inch like that might help. "Okay. Good. Great. I was hoping today would challenge my relationship with my shoes."

"I'm going to throw up," Stacy muttered, shifting closer to Jennifer without realizing it.

Jennifer didn't comment. She just angled her flashlight down and took a careful step forward.

We moved deeper into the tunnel.

Our footsteps crunched through old sediment, the sound oddly muffled—too soft for how close the walls were getting. The ceiling dipped just enough to register. The air sharpened. Colder. Thinner.

And the hum I'd been pretending wasn't there pressed tighter against my ribs.

Against my teeth.

Dust drifted through our flashlight beams, glowing faintly like embers rising from something unseen.

I took another step.

Pain snapped through my jaw—sharp and hot, flaring beneath the gumline fast enough to steal my breath. I stopped short, heart jumping.

"What's up?" Jennifer whispered from behind me.

I looked up. "Hey. Sorry. Uh, nothing." The words came out wrong. Thinner. Like it had scraped something on the way up.

She hesitated. "You sure?"

"Yeah," I said too quickly. "Just—pressure shift, I think. Brandon said it happens."

Her brow furrowed, but she nodded. "Okay."

Jennifer watched me, focused. Like she'd noticed something she hadn't meant to—and was quietly filing it away.

Before anyone else noticed, I stepped forward. My headlamp shifted with me, sliding shadows across the rock.

Brandon reached the next tripod and flicked it on.

The tunnel opened.

The ceiling arched high overhead— layered limestone folded over itself in pale bands, scalloped and pocked from centuries of slow erosion. The rock looked wet even where it wasn't, catching the light in dull, pearly patches.

Standing lamps sputtered on one by one, casting overlapping halos across the stone. Their light wavered as dust drifted through the air in slow spirals, like snow suspended mid-fall.

No one spoke.

For a moment, the cave felt... finished.

Like it had been waiting.

Stalactites draped from the ceiling in slow, deliberate threads, thin as glass in some places, thick and columned in others, reaching down toward the floor where stalagmites waited in quiet reply. Some had finally met—stone fused to stone—pillars grown patiently over centuries, untouched, uninterrupted. The drip of water plinked softly through the chamber, each drop precise, a metronome of nature, like the cave was keeping time with itself.

The walls glowed faintly where Eurydium veins subtly threaded through the limestone. It was a soft warmth beneath the surface—not enough to illuminate anything on their own, but just enough to make the stone feel alive.

Every breath tasted faintly metallic, like copper pennies left too long in water.

"Jesus," Josh murmured.

Matt let out a short breath that almost passed for a laugh. "Alright," he muttered. "I hate that I like this."

Marissa followed their lead, emitting a small, breathless sound before she could stop herself. "I know this is probably the part where we're supposed to be cautious," she said softly, eyes shining, "but... I kind of want to live here?" She laughed at herself. "I mean—visit. Temporarily. With sunlight. I don't actually want to become a bat."

Even Brandon had stopped pretending to multitask. He stood near the center of the chamber, clipboard forgotten at his side, flashlight dangling from his wrist as the beam painted slow arcs across the floor.

"This," he said, softer than before, "is why people came down here."

Jennifer quickly raised her camera—almost afraid the moment would slip away if she didn't catch it.

The flash popped, sharp and brief, lighting the chamber in stark white before the lamps reclaimed it. The light was much too bright to have come just from that little disposable camera. The walls were reflecting back brighter than I imagined they could—or maybe that was just my eyes adjusting to the dark.

She stared at the camera afterward, blinking.

"I just wanted to make sure it was real," she said.

No one argued.

For half a second, I forgot we were underground. Forgot the noise. Forgot the rules about staying together, staying alert. The cave wasn't closing in—it was opening.

And the thought landed, quiet and dangerous:

If it keeps getting better than this... what else is down here?

Jennifer glanced at the veins again.

"Has anyone... ever gone all the way down? All nine layers?"

Brandon's pen paused mid-scratch.

"No one has," he said, laughing—quick and easy, the sound of someone who refused to let a question sit too long. "The Ninth Layer is just old miner folklore. Campfire stuff. Besides—" he grinned, tapping the clipboard, "—this is my first time down here too. Same as you guys."

Jennifer nodded. But she didn't smile.

"Still," she said softly. "Stories always start somewhere."

"They also end somewhere," Brandon said, shrugging. "People just don't like saying why."

Kevin cleared his throat. "There are records of collapses past a certain depth. Incomplete ones. That usually means lost equipment or unrecovered bodies."

"Kevin," Stacy said without looking at him, "you are *actively murdering* the vibe."

Marissa tucked her notebook closer to her chest. "I mean, Jen's right," she said carefully, then hesitated. "Legends don't usually come from nowhere. They're just... facts that lived too long without context."

Josh tilted his head. "Didn't the school buy this land dirt cheap in the thirties?"

Brandon considered that. "Yeah. After the quarry shut down. Officially? Insurance nightmare. Too expensive to reinforce past a certain depth. Easier to seal it and move on."

"Move on from what?" Jennifer asked.

Brandon's smile didn't quite stick. "It was listed as an *incident*," he said. "That's the word they used."

No one asked what that meant.

Stacy adjusted her helmet again, fingers tugging at the strap, forcing a grin that didn't reach her eyes. "Cool. Love a vague institutional cover-up. As long as this isn't where *our* story ends."

Brandon shot me a look screaming *back me up*.

"It's alright," I said, stepping in before the quiet could settle. "Every campus has a place like this. Doesn't mean it's haunted."

Matt snorted. "No, yeah. Completely fine. Ancient mine under a college. That's how nothing bad ever starts."

Josh laughed first—short, sharp. "Give it a decade and they'll be charging admission."

"*'The Haunted Bennington Experience,'*" Stacy added. "Free with tuition. Trauma sold separately."

"Don't forget the merch," Jen chimed in. "Glow-in-the-dark rocks. Branded helmets."

"Honestly?" Matt said. "If they don't turn this into a ghost tour, they're leaving money on the table."

The laughter came easier after that. The kind that smoothed over rough edges. The kind people used when they didn't want to sit with a thought too long.

Marissa fell into step beside Jennifer without thinking, their shoulders nearly brushing.

The Eurydium veins caught the light again. Thin, glassy streaks threaded through the rock — faint until the beams brushed over them, then brightening, bending the light in ways that felt... intentional.

Every time my jaw pulsed, the shimmer pulled at my attention.

Every time the hum deepened, the reflections flickered subtly, but consistent enough that my brain refused to let it go.

I shifted my weight, testing the ground.

Solid.

I pressed my tongue carefully against the sore tooth. The ache flared — sharp, electric — a quick white line of pain that made my eyes sting. And for one disorienting heartbeat—

—the shimmer on the wall brightened.

Just a fraction. Just long enough to notice.

I told myself it was coincidence. Light angles. Nerves. Adrenaline. A hundred rational explanations lining up to volunteer for duty.

But every good find I'd ever read about started with something feeling off.

And that didn't mean danger. It meant discovery.

So I pushed through it.

We all did.

CHAPTER FIVE

BRANDON STOPPED beneath the last standing lamp and turned, clipboard tucked under his arm like he'd finally decided this counted as official.

"Alright," he said, clapping once. The sound bounced weakly and came back thinner than it should've. "This is where we slow down. Everyone grab a worksheet, a clipboard, and let me know if you need a pencil."

A few people groaned as he unzipped his backpack. Josh exaggerated it.

"I'm serious," Brandon added, passing out the forms. "From here on out, we're documenting mineral distribution and structural integrity. That means no wandering, no shortcuts, no solo adventures."

Matt saluted lazily. "So... stay alive."

"Yes," Brandon said. "Exactly that."

Marissa had already crouched near the wall, fingers hovering just short of the stone like she was waiting for permission it didn't need to give. "Hey, Brandon?" she asked, not looking up. "The Eurydium concentration back there—it didn't just increase with depth. It shifted pattern. Like it was following stress lines instead of sediment layers."

Brandon blinked, interest cutting through his rehearsed authority.

He stepped closer, peering where she pointed. "That's... actually a good catch."

Josh leaned in, squinting. "So if you follow the stress lines..." He tilted his head, glancing at the dark. Curiosity flickered brighter than caution. "...you find the good stuff."

Matt's grin sharpened immediately. "Diamonds?"

"Diamonds." Josh smirked, already backing toward the darkened path.

"Nobody leaves the room 'til I say—". Brandon's hand lifted, palm out, like a school crossing guard flagging someone exceeding the speed limit.

Josh didn't wait to hear the rest. He took off. Boots slipping, flashlight slicing into darkness, laughter trailing behind him like a dare.

Brandon stared at the dark a fraction too long.

"Son of a—," Brandon swore under his breath.

"You can't just say diamonds and expect me not to follow—." Matt took off after him.

"Matt—!"

"Guys—!" I called, stepping forward without thinking.

Josh's flashlight vanished around the bend.

Brandon looked at me, a wordless exchange that said: *If we don't go now, we lose them.*

"Stay here," he said to the group—then immediately broke his own rule. "Alex. With me."

We ran.

The narrow path dropped and twisted, limestone slick beneath our boots, the ground tilting just enough to steal traction without warning. The darkness didn't swallow sound so much as bend it—footsteps too loud one second, then gone entirely the next, like the cave was editing us in real time.

Left. Right. Down again.

Josh's flashlight cut hard angles into the dark, bouncing off walls that looked the same no matter how fast we passed them. Every turn felt shallow, almost gentle—nothing dramatic enough to register as a choice until it was already behind us.

"Josh!" Brandon shouted.

The sound hit once.

Then scattered.

My jaw buzzed with each step, a low vibration that synced with my heartbeat. I clenched my teeth and kept moving.

The path narrowed, widened, then narrowed again. A dip. A rise. Another bend that shouldn't have been there. The slope evened out so gradually I didn't notice until my boots stopped slipping.

And then—

Josh stopped.

His light swung once, twice, then froze.

Matt nearly ran into him. "What—"

Josh lifted a hand. "Hang on."

The chamber opened around us—not all at once, but enough to feel it. The ceiling lifted beyond the reach of the beam. The air dropped several degrees, cold blooming across my skin like a held breath finally released.

"Did we just loop?" Matt said, quieter now.

Brandon slowed behind us, breathing hard. "That's not possible."

Josh turned slowly, sweeping his flashlight in a slow arc.

Nothing familiar came back.

The tunnel behind us didn't look like a tunnel anymore—just another smooth fold of limestone, identical to the walls on either side. No markers. No lamps. No obvious incline to follow.

Josh exhaled a short laugh that didn't land. "...Okay," he said. "That's different."

Matt straightened, trying for swagger and missing by an inch. "So. Either this is the diamond room, or we just sprinted into a screensaver."

Brandon stepped forward, voice tight now. "No one move."

Josh looked at him. "We moved already."

That's when I felt it. Orientation slipping. Like the cave had gently turned us around while we weren't paying attention—and was waiting for a reaction.

Matt doubled over, hands on his knees. "You should see your face, Pike."

"That's not my name," Brandon snapped. "And you don't run off in caves. We stick to the lamps, remember? Lamps good. Darkness bad."

Josh shrugged, like the rules were a suggestion he'd already outgrown. "It's just rock. It's not mad at us."

Matt spread his arms and leaned in, confrontational. "Yet."

Brandon planted himself there, hands on his hips, breath fogging faintly in the cooling air. "This section isn't part of the research path," he said, forcing calm into his voice. "No lamps means no ground survey. No survey means no structural check. Which means you are—" he stopped, jaw tightening. "—one mistake away from getting someone killed."

Matt clicked his tongue. "See? He *does* care."

Then—

Movement behind us.

Footsteps. Too many.

Flashlights spilled into the chamber one by one, beams overlapping, colliding, filling the dark with jittery light.

Jennifer. Stacy. Marissa. Kevin. Everyone.

Brandon turned slowly. "I said stay put."

Stacy folded her arms. "You said that right before you sprinted off. What happened to strength in numbers?"

Josh glanced back at the group, then at the chamber, then shrugged. "Guess they followed the noise."

Marissa hadn't said anything yet. She was turning in a slow circle, notebook forgotten at her side, eyes wide and shining like she'd just walked into a cathedral instead of a geological error.

"Oh," she breathed. "Wow."

Jennifer raised her flashlight, sweeping it across the walls with care. "Are we... supposed to be here?"

I knew the answer was no.

I also knew I didn't want to turn around.

I didn't want to admit it, but this could be it: Our King Tut moment.

Brandon answered without looking at her, already flipping back into authority mode like muscle memory. "We're still within the system. Distortions happen. Old quarries collapse, shift. We log it and move on."

Jennifer hesitated. Just a beat. Long enough to say she didn't buy it.

Then she nodded anyway.

The walls curved inward, smooth and pale. The limestone folded tight like it had been pressed and reheated. The air felt different here —cooler, heavier.

I became aware, all at once, that the standing lamps were gone. All of them.

It was like we'd crossed something, an invisible line between university field trip and illegal trespass into something Biblical; random, historical, and frightening in its beauty.

The only light left came from my headlamp and the flashlights — jittery, nervous beams that barely pushed back the dark before it swallowed them whole.

Brandon cleared his throat, pulling his authority back on like a jacket that didn't quite fit. "Okay. Everyone stay close. We'll retrace our—"

He stopped, frowned, then started again.

"We'll retrace our steps."

That's when we saw it.

It appeared ahead of us in the darkness, low against the stone — a pale smear at first, soft and cool, like dawn leaking through a crack in storm clouds. A thin wash of blue-white glow spread across the cavern wall, clean and even, illuminating nothing beyond itself.

People talk about darkness underground — how it presses in on your lungs, messes with distance, makes you feel watched. But no one ever warns you about light.

We all stopped. Every one of us. Even Brandon froze mid-sentence, mouth half-open.

Jennifer lifted her flashlight slowly, breath catching. "Is that... daylight?"

Her voice echoed once.

Then vanished.

No second return.

The glow didn't pulse. Didn't shimmer. Didn't flicker.

It just... existed.

Steady. Calm. Impossible in the Stygian pitch.

Yet there it was.

My skin prickled.

"No," Brandon said too fast. Too thin. "Can't be daylight. Underground like this? No way. It's—bioluminescence. Happens when mineral decay mixes with moisture. Totally natural."

He didn't step closer.

Neither did anyone else.

Josh tilted his head, studying the light. "That's a lot of *'totally'* for something you're not walking toward."

Matt snorted. "Yeah. Usually when people say that, it's right before something jumps out of the shadows and takes a limb."

I noticed something then—small, but wrong enough to lodge behind my eyes.

Every time a flashlight beam swung toward the glow, it didn't land. The light thinned at the edges. Softened. Lost definition. Like it was being diluted by the air itself—fading out a few feet before touching the wall. Like the glow wasn't *reflecting* light.

It was *refusing* it.

Jennifer glanced at me, alert.

My headlamp did the same thing. The beam bobbed with my breathing, slicing cleanly through the dark ahead of me—steady, reliable—right up until it angled toward the glow. Then it softened. Scattered. Like the distance between us and that light was far greater than our eyes were being told. We weren't as close as we thought.

Depth didn't mean anything down here.

"Why won't the lights reach it?" Stacy whispered, voice pitched lower than usual, like she didn't want the cave overhearing.

"They *are* reaching it," Brandon said immediately.

Kevin pushed his glasses up, short brown hair already damp with sweat. "That's not how light works."

The glow was beautiful. Calm. Inviting in a way that made it hard to remember why we'd stopped.

My feet moved before I consciously decided to let them. Just a step. Then another. The headlamp bobbed with me—left, right, forward—its beam trembling slightly with each breath. The glow tugged at my eyes, bottomless and quiet, like it wasn't emitting light so much as holding it. My hand brushed the camera clipped at my belt. I didn't think. I lifted it.

Click.

The flash went off like a small explosion. White. Clean. Surgical.

For one impossible heartbeat, the cave peeled itself open.

And we all saw it.

Jennifer gasped—sharp, involuntary. Matt swore. Flashlights jerked toward the wall, frantic and useless, like they could force the image to stay.

Because the glow wasn't coming from the wall.

It was coming *through* it.

A fracture split the stone—jagged, forced—and beyond it the flash revealed something no one had been prepared for:

A mining station.

Old timber beams bowed under centuries of pressure. Rail tracks half-buried in rock dust, their metal gleaming faintly. A rusted electrical box hung crookedly from a frayed wire like a dead limb. And bolted to the stone, half swallowed by rubble, a metal sign caught the flash dead-on:

NO. 9 –– SUBLEVEL

When the flash died, darkness slammed back into place. But it didn't matter. We'd all seen it.

"Oh my god," Stacy whispered, the words brittle, like she didn't trust the air to hold them.

"The old tunnel system," Jennifer said quietly.

"You said it was closed off," Josh said, realization sharpening their voice.

Brandon swallowed. Tried to pull himself together. "It was," he said, but the confidence was gone now. "Blast walls. Collapse barriers. Cement fills. This whole shaft system was reportedly shut down decades ago." He stared at the sign in the darkness. "I—I don't know how this opened."

"You sure it wasn't always like that?" I asked.

Brandon shook his head fast. "No. No chance. This wasn't here during the last survey. Someone would've flagged it. Someone would've—"

He stopped himself.

Behind him, Marissa's flashlight drifted.

Not to the sign.

To the Eurydium vein running along the stone beside it—thin, branching, brighter near the fracture. The beam lingered there, tracing the glow, following it instinctively.

She stepped closer to the breach without realizing she'd moved.

Then she spoke.

"This... this explains it," she said, breath quick with excitement rather than fear. "The pattern shift. The way the Eurydium clusters changed back there—it wasn't random. It was responding to stress lines." She glanced at Brandon, eyes bright. "From what people said about the miners—and from what we've logged so far—we weren't approaching the Ninth Layer."

A beat.

"We were already on top of it."

"Cool," Stacy cut in immediately, voice sharp with nerves. "So when do we turn around before we end up on *Dateline*?"

I took another step closer. The edges of the breach were warped—stone torn outward in jagged pieces, like something inside had pushed. Or pried. Or broken free. The metal supports framing the opening were scored with long, parallel gouges. Deep ones.

Jennifer raised her flashlight slowly, tracing the marks. Her breath hitched—but she didn't step back. "Those look like..." She stopped herself.

No one finished the thought.

Stacy edged away, glancing toward the tunnel behind us. "Should we —should we go get someone? Campus safety, a professor, literally *any* adult with a helmet?"

No one answered.

Kevin frowned, stepping closer despite himself. "Those striations aren't consistent with collapse damage. They're too uniform."

Matt snorted. "Great. So it's not falling apart. That's almost comforting."

A flashlight beam caught on scattered flecks near the breach—tiny points of orange glimmering in the stone. Marissa pointed. "Is that Eurydium too?"

Brandon grabbed onto the question like a rope thrown from above.

"Yes. Eurydium," he said quickly. "Log that. Everyone—log it. Temperature, luminosity variance, proximity to fracture points."

Authority snapped back into his voice, forced and brittle.

"Do not enter the breach. Shafts like that are unstable. A collapse could kill you instantly."

His light caught a vein of the mineral near the crack. It shimmered, just once.

"Once finished, we keep moving," Brandon said, too loudly. "Good work, everyone."

No one moved.

"I don't have my worksheet," Stacy said flatly.

"Neither do I," Jennifer added.

Kevin sighed. "Am I seriously the only one who brought mine?"

We all nodded.

Even Marissa.

Matt glanced at the breach again, then at Brandon. A crooked smile tugged at his mouth. "So just to recap," he said lightly, "we've discovered a secret death tunnel, no one's insured for it, and the plan is... homework."

Josh huffed a breath through his nose. "Bold strategy."

Matt tilted his head, eyes still on the dark. "I admire the optimism."

Josh added, almost to himself, "Feels like the part where the band keeps playing."

No one responded but they all knew what he meant.

Marissa didn't even look up.

Behind us, the cracked wall seemed to throb—the way a bruise pulses when you touch it wrong. A glimmer crept along a Eurydium vein, catching the beam of my headlamp and refracting it in a brief flare of orange.

And that's when the itch came back.

It was like a strange, insistent awareness, a sensation that didn't belong to pain or adrenaline, like a limb falling asleep and forgetting how to wake back up.

At first, it was nothing—just that same faint tingle under my gums, like the static you feel before lightning. But it sharpened, fast, like someone dragging a hot needle through the root of my tooth.

I pressed my tongue against the molar to ground myself.

It wobbled.

A nauseating, impossible wobble.

My heart sprinted. I clenched my jaw; thought pressure might steady it. Might fix it. Instead—

Snap.

A tiny, wet crack.

A metallic taste rushed across my tongue — blood mixed with something sour, chemical.

My breath stuttered. I pressed my tongue to the sore spot and felt my molar detach completely. It rocked once, falling against my cheek and landing on my tongue. I spat it out, landing wet in my palm.

It was warm. Whole. Bone and memory, like it had never really been attached.

I curled my fingers around it and shoved it into my pocket, heart hammering. Something embarrassing. Something explainable. Something I could deal with later.

A laugh cut through the quiet.

Too loud. Too thin.

"Wow," Matt said, tilting his head. "That's one way to get out of midterms."

I opened my mouth to answer. Before I could, Josh leaned in, eyes unfocused, voice light in that wrong, floaty way as he held something in his hand.

"Yeah," he said slowly. "It—uh. It just... popped out."

A pause.

"Didn't even hurt. I was just at the dentist too—"

Brandon stepped in fast, irritation snapping through his voice. "Okay. That's enough. What did you do, bite down on a rock?"

Josh opened his mouth, then closed it. "No, my tooth, it—"

"Josh," Brandon cut in, sharper now, "I don't have time for this."

The cave answered for him.

Not with silence.

With weight.

A low vibration rolled through the stone, subtle but unmistakable — the kind you felt before you heard. It pressed against my ears like pressure underwater. The Eurydium veins along the wall shimmered faintly, responding, and the vibration slid straight up through my boots, into my legs, into my spine.

Into the raw space in my gum.

My breath stuttered.

Jennifer stepped closer, her flashlight shaking just enough to notice. "We all hear that," she whispered. "Right?"

I prayed it was just that familiar vibration that had followed us since the elevator.

But this time, it was something else entirely.

Something none of us were prepared for.

CHAPTER SIX

THE VIBRATION KEPT CLIMBING.

It crept—patient, invasive—the way cold seeps through a window-pane you forgot to insulate. First, your fingers ache. Then your palms. Then suddenly the whole room is winter, and you can't remember what "comfortable" ever meant.

The limestone hummed under my boots. A low, ugly note. My teeth buzzed in response, and the raw gap in my gum—where the tooth used to be—lit up like a live wire. Every tremor turned it into a tuning fork pressed straight into my skull.

This cave had a frequency.

And it was finding me.

Jennifer stood close, closer than she had to. Her flashlight beam cut across my hands, lingering there like she was checking they were still real. She kept her eyes on the floor, watching it the way you watch ice when you're not sure it's thick enough to hold your weight.

Brandon did what Brandon always did when the world got weird: he tried to name it. Tried to shrink it down to something academic. Something that could be filed away.

"Microquake," he said. His voice was tight, stretched thin like plastic wrap. "Everybody relax. We should all be used to them by—"

The cave took his sentence and snapped it clean in half.

A sharp crack rolled through the chamber, loud and close, like something massive just shifted its weight. My stomach dropped, sudden and sickening, the same way it had in the elevator—like gravity itself had reconsidered our arrangement.

Dust rained down in a soft, glittering sheet. It caught in our beams and made the air look like a shaken snow globe full of bone powder.

The lamps we'd left behind—those neat rows of artificial daylight—felt imaginary now. Like something we'd dreamed, before things got serious. All our light came from our bodies. From our hands. From my head.

We looked like a little constellation of idiots.

Stacy grabbed Jennifer's sleeve so hard Jennifer actually rocked back a step.

"Oh my God," Stacy said. "No. No. This is not—"

Kevin cut in before she could finish, his voice clipped and professional, like he'd been waiting years for Stacy to panic so he could finally step into his role. "Watch the ceiling. Limestone can shed. Everyone keep your heads down."

"Great," I said, tapping the casing of my headlamp. "Perfect time for me to be stuck without a helmet."

I looked at Brandon. He didn't look back.

Matt laughed. Just once. It sounded intentional. Practiced. The kind of laugh you use when things have already gone wrong and pretending otherwise feels embarrassing.

"Awesome," he said. "We're going to die under a bunch of wet rocks in a state nobody can find on a map."

Josh stood apart from us, head tilted, listening. He held his flashlight low, beam trained on his boots like he didn't trust the ceiling either. He looked calm in a way that made my skin itch. Josh had that thing where his face stayed neutral but his eyes stayed busy, like they were seeing something the rest of us couldn't.

"Feels like the cave's clearing its throat," he said.

Stacy stared at him. "Who says that."

Josh shrugged, loose and easy, like the answer lived somewhere above ground and he didn't feel like hiking all the way up to retrieve it.

Marissa finally looked up from her notes, eyes quick and sharp. "Hey," she said. "Everyone still standing?"

We were. Technically.

Brandon's clipboard was gone. I hadn't seen it drop, but without it, something about him sagged. His authority looked thinner, like a costume missing key pieces. He swallowed, eyes darting between the breach—toward the faint glow we'd seen earlier, toward the dark mouth that had been waiting for us to notice—and the tunnel behind us.

"Back," he said. "We go back. We find the lamps. We get out."

He turned to me for back-up.

"Okay," I nodded. "One step at a time. Nobody rushes."

Jennifer turned her flashlight toward the corridor we'd come through. The beam hit rock. The rock curved. The tunnel swallowed the light and bent it, shortened it, made distance feel dishonest.

"We came from there," she said carefully, the way you talk to a skittish dog you're not sure won't bolt. "Right?"

Brandon didn't answer right away. His eyes stayed locked on the tunnel like it owed him something. Like it was withholding.

"We did," he said finally. The words came out thin. "We'll retrace it."

Matt leaned closer to Josh, making a little show of it, like they were two guys at a party watching someone bomb onstage.

"Retrace," he murmured. "In a cave. That's cute."

Josh's mouth twitched. "We're going to be a legend."

"Shut up," Stacy snapped.

And then the second hit came.

Not louder—

Closer.

The cave didn't crack this time. It answered.

The floor kicked up under my boots and my knees bent on instinct, like the cave had reached up and shoved me.

I didn't decide to drop. My body just did it. Muscles folding, spine bowing, hands flaring out for balance as gravity lurched sideways. Somewhere deep in the rock, something moved. A low, hollow sound rolled through the limestone—not sharp, not violent. Old. Like something enormous shifting in its sleep after being disturbed.

The wall to our right groaned.

It wasn't a clean sound. It was tired. Timber somewhere beyond the breach answered it with a splintering complaint, wood fibers stretching too far, too long, finally remembering they could still break.

Marissa's pencil flew out of her hand, a yellow blur vanishing into the dust.

Someone screamed.

Stacy.

It tore out of her fast and ugly, like her body pulled the fire alarm before her pride could argue it down. The sound hit my back teeth and stayed there.

Then something cut through the shaking—sharp and brittle.

Not a collapse.

A snap.

Several stalactites fractured at once, stress finally outrunning patience. They broke with a dry, cracking sound, like glass rods struck together. Fragments rained down, clattering against helmets and shoulders, while larger pieces tore free from the ceiling they'd been clinging to for centuries.

The cave shed a fistful of rock.

It hit Matt.

A chunk the size of a microwave—sharp-edged, wet with condensation—dropped straight down and clipped him hard across the shoulder as he turned. He staggered, momentum carrying him half a step forward before the rock slid down his arm, caught his hip, and then smashed into his shin.

The sound it made—thick, final—was like someone snapping a branch over their knee.

Matt went down.

His flashlight spun free and threw light across the chamber in wild, useless arcs. For half a second, Eurydium veins flared warm orange along the walls—beautiful and wrong—then vanished back into shadow.

Matt's mouth opened.

Nothing came out.

Then air did. Thick. Strangled. Like his lungs were trying to remember how this was supposed to work.

Brandon was on him instantly. I didn't think. I dropped too, hands in the dust, palms stinging as I crawled into the spill of Matt's light. My tooth screamed in my skull, the vibration finding it again, tuning it.

Jennifer hit the ground beside me, knees smacking stone, breath sharp and fast.

"Matt," she said. Her voice stayed low, steady in a way that felt deliberate. Her hands hovered over him, open, waiting for permission. "Hey. Look at me."

Matt's face had gone pale beneath the grime. Sweat cut clean lines through the dirt on his temples. He tried to grin anyway—like humor was a lever he could still pull to stay in control.

"Yeah," he panted. "This is... so... rock and roll."

Kevin shoved in close, urgency burning through his usual stiffness. "Move your leg," he said. "Can you move it?"

Matt tried.

His jaw clenched. His whole body shook, a full-body flinch he couldn't hide. His boot twitched—barely—a fraction of an inch.

A wet sound came from somewhere deep under the denim.

I felt it in my stomach before I registered it with my ears.

Brandon lifted the edge of Matt's jeans carefully, like he was unwrapping something he already knew he didn't want to see.

The fabric was darkening.

Stacy stood frozen a few feet away, hands clamped over her mouth. Her helmet had slid back crooked in her hair, the strap biting into her chin. She looked furious about the helmet. Terrified about everything else.

"Oh my God," she whispered. "Oh my God—Matt, you're bleeding—"

Matt's eyes flicked to her. Even now—even like this—he found the energy to be himself.

"Thanks," he breathed. "Hadn't noticed."

Josh crouched on Matt's other side, silent now. His eyes kept moving—ceiling, tunnel, breach—tracking the cave the way someone tracks weather when they know it can turn without warning.

Jennifer fumbled open her bag, fingers shaking, then stopped. Her gaze snagged on Matt's open button-down, hanging crooked off one shoulder.

Brandon didn't wait.

He grabbed the shirt and yanked.

The fabric tore free with a sharp, ugly sound, louder than it had any right to be. Matt cried out—more surprise than pain—then bit it back hard enough that I saw his jaw tremble.

Brandon wrapped the torn cloth around Matt's shin, pulling it tight. Tighter. The way you do when you're afraid of what happens if you don't. The pale fabric soaked through almost immediately, dark blooming fast and unstoppable.

"We can't stay here," Kevin said. "Aftershocks—"

As if the cave had been listening and wanted to weigh in, the vibration rolled through again. Smaller this time. Not angry. Just present.

Grit rained down. Pebbles skittered. The Eurydium flickered faintly in the walls, a low, warm glow—like the cave clearing its throat again, reminding us it wasn't done.

And neither were we.

Marissa stared at the shimmering veins in the rock with a kind of fierce concentration, like if she looked long enough they'd rearrange themselves into something helpful. Our lights washed her face pale and flat, the color leeched out of her skin. She blinked slowly, deliberately, then forced her gaze away from the glow and back to Matt.

"I—I have duct tape," she said. Her voice pitched too bright, like she was trying to sell us on it. "I don't know if it helps, but I have it."

Stacy snapped her head around. "Why do you have duct tape."

Marissa swallowed. "I panic-pack," she said. "It's a thing."

That tracked. If the world ever ended, it would be because someone forgot duct tape—or because they brought it and thought that meant they were prepared.

Brandon took the tape without comment. His hands didn't look like his anymore. The joke layer was gone. The calm layer too. These were hands that moved straight from thought to action, skipping over doubt entirely. He tightened the makeshift bandage, the tape rasping softly as it wrapped.

Matt sucked air through his teeth.

His eyes squeezed shut, then opened again, glassy and unfocused, like he was looking at us through water.

"You're gonna have to carry me," he said, casual as an order at a bar.

Josh opened his mouth like he was about to say something.

He didn't.

His jaw worked once, like he was chewing on something bitter he didn't want to swallow. Then he nodded and shifted closer to Matt's injured side, already adjusting his stance.

Brandon swallowed. "We're gonna get you out."

Matt's laugh came out broken, jagged around the edges. "Yeah? Which *out*?"

That hung there.

Brandon exhaled sharply and dug into his jacket pocket, fingers fumbling like he'd forgotten what lived there. "Maps," he said, sudden and relieved, like he'd just remembered a word in another language. "We all have maps."

Paper rustled as we dug through pockets and packs with clumsy, shaking fingers. It felt stupidly hopeful. Like pulling out receipts after a car crash and thinking that might help.

Marissa had hers out first. She smoothed it against her thigh, hands pressing down on the creases like muscle memory could still save her. Under her flashlight, the tunnel lines looked neat and obedient—clean curves, labeled junctions, careful handwriting. The work of someone who believed the cave could be understood if you were patient enough.

"This section—" she started, then stopped.

She flipped the page. Then flipped it back. Her finger hovered, uncertain, like it was waiting for the map to confess.

"We should be... here," she said, quieter now. "Or—no. Maybe here."

Brandon leaned in, jaw tight. "That doesn't make sense. We didn't take that turn."

Marissa shook her head, already apologizing before anyone asked her to. "I know. I just—nothing's lining up the way it should."

Kevin pulled his own map free and held it up beside hers. Our flashlights overlapped, washing the paper in uneven light.

"They're identical," he said. "Which means one of two things."

Stacy's voice cut sharp through the space. "Don't say it."

Kevin swallowed. "Either we're reading them wrong," he said carefully, "or we're not where we think we are."

Marissa let out a small, helpless laugh. It didn't have any humor in it. "I promise I'm better at this when the ground isn't trying to kill me."

Brandon's gaze flicked to Jennifer, then to me. I felt it land and slide off, like he was checking inventory and realizing he didn't have enough hands. Then his eyes went back to the tunnel behind us.

"We go back," he said again. Slower this time. Like repetition could anchor the idea in place. "We find the lamps. We get to the elevator."

Kevin's eyes narrowed behind his glasses. "The elevator isn't down here," he said. "It belongs to the research staff. We were allowed down because of paperwork. It won't come back until the next group—"

"Kevin," Stacy hissed. "I swear to God, I will shove your glasses into the cave wall."

Kevin didn't flinch. "If someone is injured, we need a plan that is based on reality."

Josh stood. His flashlight beam stayed level, steady as a horizon line. "Reality says the cave is moving."

Brandon snapped his head up. "Don't."

Josh's mouth twitched. "I'm serious."

As if to underline the point, another vibration rolled through the stone. Smaller than before. Not violent. Intentional. A warning tapped out through limestone.

Matt winced hard, his body jerking despite himself. Jennifer reached out without thinking, steadying his shoulder, her hand staying there like she was afraid if she moved it something worse would happen.

Brandon looked at all of us—really looked—then made a decision the way someone chooses between two bad doors.

"Okay," he said. "We get him somewhere stable. We wait for the elevator. No more running."

Stacy laughed, sharp and too small. "Love that for us. Stability. *Underground*. For the record, I was having a perfectly okay time before someone decided to play Indiana Jones."

Marissa scooped up her pencil and clutched her notebook to her chest like it mattered more now that it had been dropped.

I stared at the maps in our hands—clean lines, confident labels—and felt something settle in my gut.

The cave didn't care what we thought "out" looked like.

Jennifer's eyes found mine for half a second.

It wasn't a long look. It didn't need to be. It carried too many questions to risk saying out loud: *Are you okay? Are you in pain? Are you about to come apart right now, right here, where everyone can see?*

I nodded.

I nodded even though my jaw throbbed with every step, a dull, pulsing ache that synced up too neatly with the hum in the rock. I nodded even though my pocket felt heavy with the tooth, like I was carrying proof of something I didn't want to name. I nodded even though the vibration pressed on the inside of my ribs like an extra heartbeat, one that didn't belong to me.

I didn't want to scare her.

I didn't want to scare *me*.

Brandon turned to Josh. "Stay with the group."

Josh lifted his hands in a loose, almost amused surrender. "I'm with the group."

Matt made a sound that might've been a laugh and might've been a sob. It fell apart halfway through.

"I knew college would kill me," he muttered. "Just assumed it'd be alcohol poisoning."

Josh looked at him. Then away. Whatever he might've said stayed in his mouth.

They tilted Matt up.

It took Brandon on one side and Kevin on the other to get him upright. The moment his weight shifted, he screamed—raw and unfiltered—and my stomach flipped like I'd missed a step on a staircase.

Marissa was there immediately.

"Hey," she said, crouching low so Matt could see her, so her face filled his vision instead of the ceiling. "You're doing really well. You're breathing. That's the job right now. Just that."

Her voice had found a register that felt older than the rest of us.

They lifted him, Matt sagging into them, his weight angry and uncooperative. His boot dragged along the stone. The fabric of his button-down kept darkening fast, spreading around the edges of the duct tape in a way that made me want to look anywhere else.

Jennifer stayed close to his injured side, flashlight aimed low and steady so no one tripped. Her body moved with purpose now. The hesitation she'd been carrying earlier had burned off, leaving something leaner behind.

Stacy hovered near Jennifer's shoulder, talking louder than necessary, words tumbling out like she could build a wall with them.

"I cannot believe this is happening," she said. "I'm going to sue the university. I'm going to sue the cave. I'm going to sue whatever dead miner put up that stupid sign."

Marissa walked behind them, eyes flicking to the walls whenever the light caught Eurydium. Her hands shook around her notebook. She noticed—and tightened her grip anyway, like she could will the tremor into stopping.

Josh took the rear, flashlight sweeping in slow, deliberate arcs. He kept glancing back toward the breach like it had a gravitational pull.

I walked at Brandon's pace because Brandon set the pace. He leaned into the carry as if it were penance. His breath came hard and shallow. Every other word died in his throat before it made it out.

We started back the way we'd come.

And the tunnel did a strange thing.

It folded.

I don't have a better word for it. One moment the corridor ahead of us looked familiar—smooth limestone, a gentle slope, the curve we'd sprinted around earlier—and the next moment it felt... longer. Not wider. Not narrower.

Longer in the way hallways stretch in bad dreams.

And the formations changed.

The stalactites here weren't graceful. They crowded low, thick and uneven, like teeth grown without a plan. Some leaned at odd angles, stress fractures spiderwebbing through them, calcite dulled by age and vibration. Below, the stalagmites rose sharp and mismatched, snapped in places and half-regrown, as if this tunnel had tried to heal itself too many times and finally given up on symmetry.

This was a place the cave had never finished stabilizing.

The beam of my headlamp reached out and the dark swallowed it early, like it had places to be.

Stacy noticed. Her fear had sharpened her senses into knives.

"Why does it look different?" she said.

Brandon's voice came out strained. "It's the same."

Kevin answered anyway. "Caves distort perception. Without fixed light sources—"

"Kevin," Stacy snapped. "Let the tour guide speak."

"I don't like it either," I said. "But stopping here won't make it better."

Josh's voice drifted from behind us, calm and unpleasant. "We've been going the wrong way."

Brandon snapped a glance back. "No, we haven't."

Marissa turned toward Josh, already trying to smooth the moment before it broke something. "And even if we are—that doesn't mean we can't fix it. Okay?"

Josh didn't argue. He just kept scanning, light gliding over stone as if he were reading weather patterns.

The air shifted as we moved. It cooled. It thickened. It carried that familiar copper taste, like pennies soaking in water.

My headache bloomed behind my eyes. It softened the edges of the flashlight beams, making everything look slightly out of focus, as if the world were pulling away from me by degrees.

Matt groaned suddenly, his weight dipping.

Brandon stumbled, caught himself, then swore under his breath. The sound snagged halfway out, like his mouth forgot how to shape it.

Stacy's eyes went wide. "Are you okay?"

Brandon blinked hard. "I'm fine."

Kevin shot him a look. He didn't say anything. His jaw tightened.

And we kept moving.

Because stopping felt worse.

The tunnel stopped behaving like a path.

It took us down, then up, then sideways, the floor tilting underfoot like it couldn't decide what it wanted from gravity. A fork appeared where I didn't remember one being—two mouths where there should've been one.

Brandon took the left without thinking.

Then hesitated, just for a fraction of a second, like the choice had surprised him after the fact.

I didn't question it. I just followed.

Jennifer's flashlight swept ahead and caught on something wrong.

A wall—too close, too abrupt—its surface scraped raw. Long grooves ran through the limestone. Parallel. Deliberate. Deep enough that shadow pooled inside them instead of light.

She stopped so fast her breath hitched.

"Brandon," she said quietly. Not panicked. Worse than that. "Look."

Brandon couldn't stop. He was holding Matt, Matt's weight dragging him forward whether he wanted to go or not. He turned his head anyway, eyes catching the marks.

Whatever humor he'd been holding onto finally let go.

"That wasn't there," he said.

Marissa leaned in, curiosity warring with fear—then immediately recoiled, heart hammering like it had hit a wall of its own. "I don't like that," she said softly, like the cave might hear her and take it personally.

Stacy grabbed her sleeve and yanked her back. "No. No touching. No reading the serial killer wall."

Josh's voice came from behind us, calm and flat. "Something came through here."

Matt let out a dry, shredded laugh. "Great."

Josh didn't say anything after that.

I noticed because usually he did.

Brandon's hands tightened on Matt's waist, fingers digging in like he was afraid Matt might slip out of reality if he loosened his grip.

"We keep moving," Brandon said.

He said it like denial was a structural support. Like if he didn't acknowledge the cave changing, it would politely stop.

We rounded another bend.

A standing lamp should've been there.

I knew it should've been there. The memory of it sat heavy and solid in my head—metal post, warm artificial light, the feeling of being seen by something that didn't breathe.

There was nothing.

Just rock. A low ceiling. And a stretch of darkness that felt deeper than it had any right to be, like the tunnel had exhaled and taken something with it.

Stacy's voice came out thin. "Where are the lamps?"

Brandon's throat worked. "They're—" He swallowed hard. "They're around here."

Kevin's flashlight swung in a tight, precise circle, trying to impose order. "This system may have multiple access corridors," he said. "If we veered into a service tunnel—"

Matt lifted his head with visible effort and stared at Kevin like he wanted to bite him.

"Service tunnel," Matt rasped. "You make it sound like we're in a mall."

Jennifer didn't raise her voice. She didn't need to.

"We're lost."

Brandon's eyes flicked to her. His face tightened like she'd struck something fragile.

He didn't deny it.

He opened his mouth to speak.

The cave answered first.

A crack tore through the limestone behind us—sharp, violent—and a gust of cold air punched down the corridor, slamming into the back of my neck like a hand. Dust erupted into our lights, thick and frantic, turning the air into a blizzard of stone.

Something heavy moved deep in the rock.

Not falling.

Shifting.

The ceiling groaned.

"Move!" Brandon shouted.

They lurched forward with Matt sagging between them. Stacy squealed and bolted ahead, boots slipping on damp stone, hands scraping walls she didn't want to touch. Jennifer stayed tight to Marissa's shoulder, flashlight angled down and forward, guiding them like she'd done this before in another life.

I ran too.

Josh ran last.

The space narrowed without warning, forcing us into single file. Rock pressed in close enough that my shoulder scraped hard, pain flaring bright and sharp. My headlamp beam shook with every breath, jittering across walls that felt too close, too interested.

Matt cursed through clenched teeth. His injured leg dragged uselessly. The torn shirt slipped on the wet pants despite the duct tape, blood darkening everything it touched. Brandon's grip tightened, knuckles white, his mouth making a sound of effort that didn't sound like him at all.

A jolt slammed through the floor.

Stacy screamed again.

And the tunnel collapsed behind us.

The sound was enormous. Final. A roar of stone and dust and history coming down all at once. The ground shuddered. Air punched forward like the cave was slamming a door.

Then—

Silence.

The kind that presses in.

The kind that means the cave has decided something.

And we weren't part of that decision.

CHAPTER SEVEN

Rock, dust, and old timber slammed down behind us, sealing off the corridor we'd just come through. The impact shoved a wave of grit through the air, thick enough to turn our lights into hazy cones, like we were all standing inside our own private fog banks.

The sound didn't end when it should have.

It didn't echo cleanly, didn't bounce and fade the way sound is supposed to underground. It smeared. It clung to the walls and dragged itself forward, following us like a ghost with bad manners that didn't understand the concept of personal space.

We stopped because we had to.

The air was too thick to breathe right. Dust coated my tongue, dry and chalky. Matt wheezed, every inhale rattling like it had to fight its way in. Kevin hacked into his sleeve, glasses fogging instantly. Stacy pressed both hands to her helmet, fingers splayed like she could physically hold her head together if she tried hard enough.

I realized we hadn't come prepared for any of this; no trail markers, no nitrile gloves, no water... Just a bunch of kids playing at something they shouldn't.

As the dust thinned, the space around us sharpened.

And my stomach sank.

The ceiling here rose higher than the tunnel we'd been running through. The walls curved inward, smooth and pale, limestone folded tight like a sloppy layer cake that had slumped under its own weight.

I knew the shape before my brain agreed to it.

We were back in the chamber.

The one with the glow.

My first thought was, "*This is good.*"

But that recognition didn't come with relief. It came with the cold certainty that the cave had decided to put us here on purpose.

Brandon bent forward, hands braced on his knees, still holding Matt upright like he didn't trust the ground with him. His breath came in rough pulls. He didn't look up.

Jennifer crouched and aimed her flashlight back toward the collapse. Rock filled the corridor completely. No gaps. No slivers. Just packed stone and timber, crushed together like they'd always belonged that way.

She looked up at Brandon, eyes wide and shining.

"That was our way back."

"That can't be the only way," Stacy said, sudden and sharp. But there was something else under it—memory, not hysteria. "This place isn't sealed like a tomb. It's sealed like... liability."

Everyone turned to look at her.

"What? I came down here freshman year," she went on, more defensive now, like she'd realized how it sounded. "Not this far. We weren't idiots. There was an entrance above ground—way above. Off a service road. Half-hidden. You could just walk in."

Kevin frowned. "That entrance was closed years ago."

"Closed doesn't mean erased," Stacy shot back. "It was fenced. Locked. Posted. Not collapsed."

Brandon finally straightened. His jaw tightened. "And you didn't mention this earlier because...?"

"Because we weren't lost earlier," she snapped. Then, quieter, the edge cracking. "And because we didn't go anywhere near this deep."

Brandon's face went blank for a second, like his mind refused to take the information in. Like it hit a wall and bounced.

Then he nodded once. Stiff. Mechanical.

"Okay," he said. "Okay. We find another way."

Kevin opened his mouth immediately. "Another way doesn't guarantee—"

"Stop," Stacy snapped.

Marissa wiped dust from her notebook with shaking hands, smearing it across the page instead of clearing it. Her eyes kept darting —to the walls, to the ceiling, to the Eurydium veins that glimmered faintly through the haze like something breathing under skin.

"It's okay," she said, too bright, like she was narrating a documentary she wanted to believe in. "Mining systems have multiple shafts. Safety corridors. Emergency exits."

Matt let out a weak laugh that fell apart halfway through. "Sure," he rasped. "Emergency exits. The cave's got fire doors."

Josh didn't join the conversation.

He moved past us instead, toward the far side of the chamber— toward the place where the wall had already failed once. Toward the old mining layer. A narrow slit yawned there, edges warped and scored, rock torn open instead of cleanly cut.

His flashlight slid into it.

And angled up at the beam light.

It wasn't yellow. Wasn't warm. It was a faint blue-white wash, thin and steady, streaming in just beyond the mining sign.

"Josh," Brandon said.

Josh kept walking, footsteps measured. He moved like someone following a thread he trusted, even if he couldn't explain why.

"Josh!" Brandon said again, louder.

Josh glanced back, calm as ever. "There's light."

"Maybe we don't go into the creepy light," Stacy said.

Josh's mouth twitched. "What, like you see other options? It's the most useful thing down here."

Kevin stepped forward, fear sharpening his voice into edges. "That could be mineral fluorescence. Gas ignition. Structural stress."

Josh nodded, like he'd heard the speech already somewhere else. Then he turned back toward the slit and stepped inside.

Brandon swore under his breath.

He looked at the collapse behind us. Then at Matt, still sagging between him and Kevin. Then at the narrow passage, where Josh's light was already thinning, already being swallowed.

"No," Brandon said. Firm. Final. "We do not split up."

Josh's voice floated back, echoing slightly now. "I'm not splitting. I'm checking."

Brandon took one step forward—

Then stopped.

The decision showed on his face. The math of it. The inventory. Who could move. Who couldn't. Who would be left holding consequences.

Someone had to stay.

Someone had to keep track of everyone left breathing.

"I'll go," I said.

The words came out before I weighed them.

Before I asked myself *why* my chest felt tight in a way that had nothing to do with dust.

Brandon turned to me.

"Alex—"

"I'll keep him in sight," I said, before he could finish whatever warning he was building. "I won't let him do anything stupid."

Josh's laugh drifted out of the passage, soft and almost pleased. "Appreciate the confidence."

Brandon hesitated. I watched it happen. The delay between instinct and permission. The part of him that wanted control arguing with the part that knew he'd already lost it.

Jennifer stepped forward.

"Then I'm going too."

"No," Brandon said immediately, the word snapping out of him like reflex.

"Yes," she replied. Calm. Certain. The kind of certainty that didn't ask to be debated. "You need eyes. And if something goes wrong, you need someone who won't freeze."

That landed harder than an argument would've.

Brandon looked at her. Then at me. Then back at the group behind us—Matt slumped and pale, Kevin supporting him like a human brace, Stacy hovering too close to be helpful, Marissa watching us with her notebook hugged tight to her chest like it was the only thing still behaving predictably.

Brandon exhaled.

"Fine," he said. "You three. No further than the light. You keep each other in arm's reach."

Then—

"Wait."

He adjusted Matt's weight carefully, murmuring something low I couldn't hear, then reached one-handed into his backpack. His fingers closed around something small.

He pulled out a short cardboard book of matchsticks. Plain. Old-fashioned. The kind you'd find in a diner that still smelled like coffee even when it was empty.

Kevin noticed immediately. "Checking air?"

Brandon nodded. "Just pockets. Dead zones. If there's bad gas, the flame'll tell us before our lungs do."

Stacy stared at the matches like they'd grown teeth. "That is not comforting."

"It's not supposed to be," Brandon said.

He struck one.

The flame flared—small, steady. It didn't gutter. Didn't dim. Didn't panic.

Brandon watched it like it might blink first.

Then he let out a slow breath. "We're okay. For now."

Josh's flashlight bobbed once in the passage, like a nod.

Brandon pointed at me. "You watch him."

I nodded.

Jennifer squeezed my arm once—quick, grounding. A physical reminder that I was still here, still in my body, still more than the ache in my jaw and the hum pressing behind my ribs.

Josh waited at the other side of the slit, flashlight aimed down the passage like a guide rope. He didn't look impatient.

He looked settled.

We went in.

The fracture widened just enough to breathe.

Stone gave way to timber. Timber to iron. The remains of a place that had once had rules revealed themselves in pieces—support beams bowed inward like tired backs, rails half-buried under silt, a mining cart tipped sideways across the tracks like it had been abandoned mid-thought.

Not destroyed.

Just... finished.

Everything felt settled. Old. As if it had stopped waiting to be discovered a long time ago.

Our lights skimmed the space in slow arcs. Nothing wanted to hold them. Shadows slid away instead of breaking.

High above us, a narrow column of light spilled down through a break in the ceiling.

It didn't spread. Didn't brighten the room. It simply fell—thin and pale—cutting through the dust like a finger tracing a line no one else could see.

The beam touched the rails, glanced off the cart's rusted frame, then vanished into shadow again, like the room absorbed it on purpose.

I couldn't tell where it came from. Daylight. Mineral glow. Something deeper in the rock. From down here, it all looked the same.

Josh tilted his head, tracked it once, then looked back to the tracks.

Jennifer reached into her jacket pocket.

The soft plastic rasp cut through the silence.

She pulled out her disposable camera.

The sight of it hit me harder than it should've. Something small. Normal. Human. A relic of before, when going somewhere strange didn't automatically mean documenting it for evidence.

"You don't have to—" I started.

"I know," she said quietly.

She raised it anyway.

The click was loud. Sharp. Final.

The flash popped, briefly bleaching the space white—the rails, the cart, the beam of light falling like it had been caught doing something it wasn't supposed to.

Then the darkness rushed back in, more offended than offensive.

"For reference," she said. "In case we need to explain what we saw. Or remember it."

I nodded, even though the idea of remembering this place made my stomach twist.

Josh moved first.

Careful. Flashlight low. The beam traced the rails, skimmed the cart's rusted edge, then followed the tracks forward until they vanished into shadow.

Jennifer leaned closer to me. "Is that blocking the only way through?"

Josh nudged the cart with his boot.

It didn't budge. "Anyone bring the WD-40?"

He leaned over it, peering underneath. "It's jammed on the axle," he said. "You can't shove it from up here."

I followed his light.

Alongside and below the tracks, a shallow bench had been carved into the wall—not a path. A worker's footing. Just wide enough for boots. Worn smooth where weight had pressed into it again and again, hundreds of times, by people who'd known exactly where to put their feet.

Josh saw it too.

His mouth tilted, thoughtful.

"Probably how they moved carts past jams," he said. "Someone walks the ledge, gets to the other side, shoves."

"What," Jennifer said, flat, "do you do this kind of thing often?"

Josh glanced back, a flicker of something almost nostalgic crossing his face. "Urban exploring? Yeah. Places like this were kind of my speed in high school. Abandoned hospitals. Abandoned churches—"

Jennifer's shoulders tightened. "Abandoned mines—"

"No," Josh said, smirking. "This would actually be my first. But I've done some research. And this is more in my field."

He gestured at the ledge, the cart, the light.

"Look. It'll be a short trip. I push, you pull, cart moves, we all live."

"And if the ledge collapses?" Jennifer asked.

Josh glanced down into the drop. Then back at us.

"Then I make a strong case against doing this twice," he said. "Besides—it's my fault we're down here."

My jaw pulsed, sharp and insistent.

"Josh," Jennifer said carefully, the way you talk to someone standing too close to an edge, "you don't have to—"

"I do," he said, already lowering himself. "Because I'm lighter than Alex, stronger than you—no offense—and statistically harder to miss."

"That is not comforting," she said.

Josh grinned at me, bright and easy, like this was still a story he'd tell later. "You're pulling, yeah?"

I nodded. I hadn't realized my hands were already on the cart's edge until my knuckles ached.

Josh swung one leg down, boot searching for the bench below.

He landed with a soft thud, knees bending to take the impact. Stone dust puffed up around his boots like a held breath finally released. The rock held. He shifted his weight once, testing it, flashlight swinging as he leaned out to look down.

The beam slipped past the edge.

It vanished.

Swallowed by open space before it touched anything.

Josh let out a short breath—half laugh, half surprise. "Okay," he said. "That's a longer way down than I thought."

He moved sideways, one careful step at a time, flashlight tucked close to his chest. He reached the far side of the cart and braced himself, feet planted wide.

"On three," he said. "One—"

Then he shoved.

The cart groaned. Rust screamed. The sound ripped through the chamber like a complaint that had waited decades to be voiced. I pulled hard, boots skidding in the dust, muscles burning.

The cart rolled.

Not cleanly. Not gracefully. But it moved—just enough to clear the tracks.

Josh laughed, breathless. "See? Functional danger."

Jennifer exhaled sharply, relief snapping tight around her words. "Josh. Come back. Now."

He nodded and hopped down onto the carved path. He inched back toward us, my hand reaching to pull him back.

Then the ledge made a sound.

Soft.

Like damp chalk under pressure.

Josh froze.

My body moved before my brain did.

My hand closed around his sleeve—wrist, skin—then caught on the flashlight cord wrapped tight around his arm as he pitched forward. The impact sent a sharp vibration through my teeth, through the hollow in my gum, straight into my skull.

"I've got you," I said. "Gimme your hand."

It came out strained. Too thin. Like the words themselves didn't believe me.

Josh's breath hitched once.

Then steadied.

"Yeah," he said. "Okay. That's... wow. Bad idea in hindsight."

The cord bit into my palm. The hum surged—louder now, closer, like the cave had leaned in to watch.

Josh shifted his weight again.

Just a little.

The ledge crumbled.

Not all at once. Just a handful of limestone. Enough.

The cord snapped.

The sound was small. Sharp.

Like a wire cutting skin.

Josh's eyes caught mine.

Then he dropped out of the light.

There was no scream.

Just the sound of impact below.

Wet.

Final.

Silence rushed in behind it, fast and suffocating. I stayed frozen, arm still extended, fingers curled around air.

Jennifer grabbed my collar and yanked me back hard enough to snap me into myself. I stumbled, headlamp jittering wildly, breath tearing loose from my chest like it had been trapped there.

My headlamp found him.

Josh lay on a lower shelf, half-lit. His helmet was split clean along the side. His neck bent at an angle no part of me wanted to understand. One arm twisted beneath him, wrong.

His eyes were open.

He didn't move.

Jennifer's hands stayed firm on my shoulders, anchoring me to my body, to the moment, to the fact that I was still standing.

"We can't—" Jennifer swallowed, eyes flicking once toward the drop. Her hand clenched at my collar. "Back. Now."

I nodded.

My feet didn't move.

Beside us, the mining cart sat where Josh had pushed it.

Ready.

We turned in the narrow corridor, shoulders scraping rock, breaths too loud, too human.

Behind us, the blue-white glow stayed steady at the seam in the stone.

Like an eye that didn't blink.

When we reached the others, Stacy took one look at our faces and went pale.

"Where's Josh?" She demanded.

Brandon's mouth opened.

Jennifer answered before he could speak.

"He fell," her voice cracked, sharp and sudden. "He—he's gone."

Stacy stared at her like Jennifer had started speaking another language. Something foreign. Impossible. Then her face twisted into fury, bright and sharp enough to hurt.

"Oh my God," Stacy said. "Oh my God, he *fell*? How do you fall—"

"Stop!" Brandon snapped, louder than I'd heard him all day. It echoed. It stuck.

Stacy turned on him. "Don't tell me to stop."

He ignored her. "What do you mean, gone. Gone like missing or gone like dead?"

Kevin's eyes flashed behind his glasses. He looked at Brandon. Then Jennifer. Then me. He took in the dust on our shoulders, the way my hands still trembled like they hadn't received the update yet.

Kevin swallowed hard.

"We need to move," he said. His voice dropped into something colder. Sharper. "The cave is collapsing in sections. We have one injured person. We have one dead. We have no route back."

"There's a tunnel," I said.

My voice sounded far away. Like it had traveled to me from somewhere else.

"It keeps going," I added. "Josh—he—he cleared the way."

The words landed between us.

Heavy.

Irreversible.

Matt made a wet, ugly sound.

His head lolled against the wall, helmet scraping stone. His face had gone a color I didn't like—gray, slack, like blood had decided it had better places to be.

"Awesome," he rasped. "So we're all gonna fall to our deaths like he did. Any other updates from the committee?"

Kevin didn't rise to it. He braced a hand on his knee instead, like he was holding himself together by force.

"Tracks mean load-bearing routes," he said. "They didn't haul ore up ladders. These tunnels were built to move weight. They have a chance of supporting us."

A *chance*.

That was the best word we had left.

Marissa stood very still, notebook pressed flat against her chest like a second ribcage. Her eyes weren't on us. They'd drifted past, toward the corridor we'd come from—toward the deep. Her flashlight beam slid onto a Eurydium vein and stayed there, the glow catching and holding like it wanted her attention.

Jennifer noticed.

She reached out and touched Marissa's wrist gently, guiding the light down and away, back to stone.

Marissa blinked, startled, like she'd been pulled out of a dream she hadn't realized she was having. When she spoke, her voice stayed quiet. Steady. It didn't match the tremor in her hands.

"Josh didn't fall because the path was wrong," she said. "He fell because it wasn't finished."

Everyone turned toward her.

"Mining stations don't just end," she went on, words precise, careful, like she was assembling something fragile. "They branch. They connect to processing rooms, storage levels, service corridors. If the tracks are still intact, then the station ahead is more stable than anything we've already crossed."

She hesitated.

Then, softer—almost apologetic— "Staying here won't make what happened undo itself. But going forward might keep it from happening again."

The sentence landed heavy.

Brandon finally lowered himself to a crouch beside Matt. He pressed his forehead into his fist, knuckles white. His shoulders shook once—just once—then stilled.

When he lifted his head, his eyes were different. Stripped of something.

"THEN THAT'S WHERE WE GO," he said. His voice came out rough, scraped thin. "We'll try to find a map. Mining stations have routes. Service tunnels. We keep going forward until we hit something we can use."

Kevin nodded, jaw tight. "Forward," he said, like agreement hurt.

Stacy let out a sharp, watery laugh. "Forward into *what?*"

Brandon looked into the darkness ahead.

Not at us.

Not at Matt.

Not back the way we'd come.

Something hardened in his face. A line set.

"Into whatever this place is," he said. "Because up is gone. We can't carry Matt back through a collapse. We don't have any other option."

No one argued.

Because there wasn't an argument left to make.

So we moved.

We carried Matt.

We followed the tracks deeper, because the cave had already made the decision for us and was patiently waiting for us to catch up.

The hum stayed tight against my bones, no longer probing—settled. And as we crossed the threshold into the mining tunnels, the sign surfaced again in the light, its uninvited welcome invading my thoughts.

Now entering Sub-Level 9.

CHAPTER EIGHT

MATT HAD to hold onto Brandon's shoulders from behind, hopping, agony ripping through him as we piled into the mining shaft single file. Once we got to the cart, he was lifted into it.

No one said who went where. The order assembled itself the way crowds do after accidents—instinct sorting bodies faster than language. The cart rolled ahead of us on its own tired momentum, metal wheels whispering over rusted rails as we guided it by hand. The sound felt intimate in the narrow passage. Too loud for something so careful. Like the cave could hear every inch we gave up to it.

Matt lay curled inside the cart, one arm braced across his ribs, jaw locked like he was holding himself together through force of will alone. His breath came shallow and uneven, each inhale negotiated instead of taken. He didn't look down into the shaft.

He didn't look at anything.

Brandon walked beside the cart, shoulders hunched, both hands gripping the frame now. He didn't hover. He didn't offer encouragement. He just pushed—steady, silent—like if he kept moving, the cave wouldn't stop him and ask what he thought he was doing.

We all avoided where Josh had fallen.

Not deliberately. Not ceremoniously. Our bodies just... adjusted.

Steps shortened. Eyes lifted. Space was given to a place that didn't deserve it anymore.

Jennifer stayed close to me. Close enough that when the cart jolted over a bent section of rail, her hand found my shoulder without thinking. She didn't apologize.

Neither did I.

Behind us, the breach darkened.

Ahead, the tunnel widened.

Stone peeled back in slow increments, the way rooms reveal themselves in dreams. The ceiling lifted a few feet at a time. The air changed first—cooler, looser—then the sound followed. Footsteps stretched longer. The wheel noise thinned as the walls pulled away, losing their urgency.

Dust clung to us now in layers, dampened by sweat. It turned every movement into a soft scrape, like the cave was filing us down gently, patiently.

The rails carried us into a chamber that felt built for decisions.

Tracks split outward across the floor, branching in multiple directions like veins cut into the rock. Some lines vanished straight into darkness. Others bent sharply and slipped behind stone pillars reinforced with timber and iron braces. Several abandoned carts stood where they'd been left decades ago, frozen mid-task—some piled high with limestone, others holding faint, glassy seams of Eurydium that caught our lights and refused to let go.

Kevin's voice dropped instinctively. "It's a transfer hall."

The room answered him with its shape.

This was where carts had been redirected. Where weight changed hands. Where one decision backed up a hundred others behind it. The kind of place where mistakes didn't disappear—they accumulated.

We stopped without meaning to.

Stacy planted her boots and turned in a slow circle. "Great," she said. "A geological choose-your-own-adventure. I hate those."

Her voice didn't fade.

It stretched instead. Thinned. Clung to the ceiling like it had found something interesting up there before drifting back down toward us.

She noticed.

Her smile faltered. "Okay," she said. "Why did that sound... sticky?"

"We'll figure it out," Brandon said quickly, like speed alone could keep the space from paying attention.

Kevin adjusted his glasses, scanning the tracks. "They likely lead to different extraction zones. Storage areas. Depth access."

"Super reassuring," Stacy said. "Because nothing says safety like *options*."

My headlamp tilted upward, seemingly on its own.

I hadn't decided to look.

That's when I saw them.

The lights hung from long chains bolted into the ceiling—industrial housings, evenly spaced, deliberate. The same silhouettes as the fixtures near the research chamber entrance. Enough illumination to guide movement.

Never enough to feel held.

My jaw throbbed, sharp and insistent, like my body recognized the pattern before I did.

"Brandon," I said. "Those lights."

He followed my beam, squinting up into the dark.

"If they're part of the same system," I went on, the words lining themselves up carefully, "they might trace back toward the research access. Or close to it."

Kevin exhaled slowly, thinking it through. "Mining operations didn't wire lights independently. If they're connected, they lead somewhere central."

Brandon seized the idea like it might slip away. "A generator. A control junction. Somewhere with a map."

Matt shifted in the cart, a sharp sound escaping him before he could stop it. "So," he rasped, "light equals not dying?"

"Light equals direction," Brandon said. "I'll take direction."

Stacy crossed her arms. "Or it equals deeper. Which I feel like we're skipping past."

"Everything's deeper," Brandon shot back. "At least this gives us a plan."

Hope hovered. Uncertain.

Like it was waiting to see if we'd earned the right to keep moving forward—or if the cave was about to correct us again.

Brandon kept talking. Just enough sound to keep the room from closing in on us completely.

"We can't stay here," he said. "Another collapse and this place becomes a coffin." His eyes flicked toward the tunnel behind us, the way it narrowed and disappeared. "We move. Slow. Together. No stopping."

Marissa nodded, already working. Her gaze darted between the tracks and the ceiling, rearranging the room in her head like it was a puzzle she refused to leave unfinished. She crouched beside the nearest rail and traced it with her fingers, breath uneven.

"Okay," she said quietly. "Okay. These split for a reason. They wouldn't bottleneck carts here."

Her hand trembled.

She noticed. Curled it into a fist. Kept going anyway.

"They'd need visibility at junctions," she continued, voice careful. "If carts were moving fast, I mean." She glanced up at Brandon. "Do you know what the research access used to be before the shutdown?"

Brandon shook his head. "No. But—"

He stopped.

Something shifted at the far end of the hall.

Not a shape at first—just absence rearranging itself. A tall, narrow shadow slipped between the pillars where the tracks vanished. It moved too smoothly for a person walking, too deliberately for a rock settling. By the time my light chased it, there was nothing to catch—just darkness resuming its place, unbothered.

Brandon sucked in a breath through his teeth.

"Okay," he said. "That's new."

"Did anyone else—" I started.

Metal whispered overhead.

One of the hanging lights adjusted. The chain slid against stone in a slow, testing drag, like fingers finding purchase.

Then the sound came.

Thin. Drawn tight.

Like crystal against stone.

Clink.

The sound fractured on impact—splintered into skittering noises that came back wrong, angled, layered. It returned from places the chamber shouldn't have allowed, bending around pillars, slipping behind us, threading through the rails at our feet.

Behind it, a guttural cry rose slowly, raising in pitch, before falling off.

Marissa's voice came out small. "That sounds like echolocation. Or —something close."

Stacy's fingers tightened in Jennifer's sleeve. "Sound doesn't do that. Is it bats?"

"No," Jennifer said. Slow. Certain. "It's bigger."

Thmp.

A light overhead shifted suddenly, another chain whispering above it.

Closer now.

The cry came again. Cleaner. Corrected. Like it had adjusted its angle after the first pass.

"Cats?" Stacy flinched.

"Mountain lions don't place sound," Marissa said. Her voice thinned as the thought finished forming. "This isn't yelling." She swallowed. "It's... shaping."

"It's mapping," Kevin said.

The sound came again.

This time it rang through the stone like struck glass.

Perfectly.

The resonance carried too well—too precisely—like the chamber itself had been tuned for it. I felt it in my teeth. In the hollow where bone was missing. In my ribs, where the hum was claiming space.

"It's not trying to scare us," Marissa said—

Jennifer turned toward her. "What do you mean?"

"I don't know," Marissa said honestly. "I just—whatever it is, it's listening. But not the way we do."

Jennifer tracked the darkness with her flashlight.

Every time the beam swept wide, the shadow shifted. Adjusted its posture. It stayed where illumination thinned, where certainty dropped off. It never crossed into full light. It never needed to.

It felt like it was mirroring us.

Our stillness.

Our angles.

Without looking at anyone—without thinking—

Jennifer raised her camera.

The flash detonated white.

The chamber rang back.

A shriek tore from one of the side corridors—directional, focused —followed immediately by another, higher up, harmonized. The sounds aligned. Layered. Multiplied.

They rang through the cavern like cracking crystal.

Kevin stopped moving.

His eyes squinted, listening. His eyes followed the sound the way someone follows a pattern revealing itself too late. The noise clung to the chamber, folding around stone where it should have shattered and died.

Kevin swallowed.

"It's reacting to us," he said quietly. "Every sharp sound gives it definition."

Something slid along the far tunnel mouth.

The movement was wrong—too vertical, too segmented.

Another shadow caught briefly where the wall met the ceiling, then vanished the instant Jennifer's beam held steady on it.

It froze when it knew it'd been seen.

Matt shifted in the cart, pain flashing as he tried to lift himself.

"You're joking," he said, breath hitching. "You're messing with me because I can't see."

Kevin raised his hand.

The gesture was small. Exact.

"Everyone," he said. "Be still. No talking. No shouting."

He pressed his finger to his mouth—firm, deliberate.

Matt's breathing went ragged, hands locking around the cart's rim like it might keep him anchored to the living.

Marissa drew in a breath—

Then cut it off halfway, like she'd realized the intake itself was information.

Stacy moved without looking.

Her hand came up and covered Jennifer's mouth, palm braced along her jaw, dust smearing across skin.

Not panic.

Protection.

A decision already made.

Jennifer went quiet.

But her body didn't relax.

Her shoulders stayed lifted, coiled—like she was bracing for an impact that hadn't arrived yet.

And in that unnatural stillness, with the chamber holding our last noise like a memory it refused to release, I understood something cold and final:

The cave wasn't hunting us.

It was *learning us.*

The change was immediate.

All sound vanished.

No echo. No drip. No distant grind of stone. Even the cart seemed to lose its weight, like friction itself had been edited out of the world.

My own breath felt like a violation.

The silence pressed inward—against my ears, my chest, my thoughts. My pulse thudded loud and ugly inside me, obscene in its insistence, something warm and alive that didn't belong here.

Marissa froze mid-breath. Her shoulders locked, spine rigid. A dark smear appeared along her lower lip before my brain caught up enough to name it.

Blood.

She noticed it too—eyes flicking down, registering—and pressed her lips together harder, like the blood was just another sound she couldn't afford to make. Her fingers came up and flattened over her mouth, firm, deliberate, as if even thinking too loudly might give us away.

Stacy didn't move.

She stood perfectly still, eyes locked on Kevin, like she'd decided panic would make more noise than screaming ever could.

Brandon swallowed. Shifted his weight. His mouth opened—then closed again. His jaw tightened hard enough that I saw the muscle jump, like he was physically holding words inside him.

I took half a step closer to Jennifer without thinking.

Close enough to react.

Kevin lowered his hand.

Then he stepped forward.

One careful step. Slow. Testing. Like he was waiting for the cavern to respond—to acknowledge him, to push back.

Jennifer inhaled sharply, breaking free of Stacy's grip.

"Kevin—"

His flashlight flickered.

Once.

The beam thinned. Died.

Marissa's hand lifted halfway, fingers twitching toward him—then stopped, like she'd hit an invisible wall of restraint.

The flashlight struck stone with a hollow clatter and rolled, spinning until it came to rest beside the rail. It blinked back on—steady, unwavering—flooding the exact spot where Kevin had been standing seconds ago with clean, unforgiving light.

There was nothing there.

No Kevin.

The silence held.

Brandon took half a step forward before anyone could stop him.

"Kevin?"

The name barely made it out.

The chamber answered.

Kevin's body fell out of the dark.

It dropped straight down between the tracks. Sudden mass meeting stone. The impact punched the air from my lungs like I'd been hit. Bone cracked with a sound too clean for what it was. Something wet followed, splattering where the light caught it. His helmet bounced once, spun uselessly, and rolled to a stop against the rail.

His glasses skittered away like ice across rock.

The sound detonated.

Marissa's knees buckled. She caught herself on the rail, breath stuttering once before she crushed it flat again, jaw clenched tight.

Then every scream came back at once.

From the walls.

From the ceiling.

From places our lights couldn't touch, couldn't reach, couldn't map.

Shrieks multiplied and bent inward, folding over themselves until the chamber vibrated with them. The air shook. The stone beneath our feet felt alive, resonant, thrilled.

The quiet hadn't been safety.

It had been a pause.

A breath drawn in.

Stacy's hands dropped slowly to her sides, fingers curling with careful precision—like something inside her had locked instead of shattered. Her face emptied, all expression drained clean away.

None of us dared to make even the smallest sound. Not a whisper between us. But the panic in everyone's eyes was evident.

Above us, the hanging lights swayed.

Patiently.

Chains creaked as they settled into new arcs, shadows stretching and retracting across the ceiling like something adjusting its posture.

Waiting.

Not for us to run.

Not for us to speak.

For us to understand.

That it wasn't listening anymore.

It already knew us.

CHAPTER NINE

"RUN!" Brandon screamed.

The word didn't echo.

It clicked.

We didn't have time to analyze it.

Or grieve.

Jennifer moved first.

No hesitation. No checking behind her. Whatever part of her still negotiated outcomes burned off in an instant. She grabbed Stacy's arm and yanked hard, voice cutting through the chaos like a blade.

"STACY, C'MON!"

Stacy stumbled, boots skidding on loose stone. She caught herself with a sharp, disbelieving breath, eyes flashing once—*this can't be real*—and then something in her hardened. She ducked and ran.

Marissa was already in motion. Her steps were quick, controlled, breath shallow and fast. Her head kept turning as she ran, tracking angles, distances, timing—like if she stayed ahead of the variables, this could still be solved.

"Which way?!" Jennifer cried out.

Brandon pointed. "There! Far left! Go! Go!"

We ran for the far end of the chamber. Toward the lights that didn't sway. Toward the narrow cut in the rock that promised out, or at least not here.

Brandon and I hit the cart together.

Steel screamed.

The rails shrieked under the sudden weight as we shoved. Matt jolted inside, teeth bared, hands white-knuckled around the rim. Every breath he took sounded forced, compressed—like the air was being rationed.

"Almost there," Brandon gasped. "Almost—keep it moving—"

The tunnel mouth rose ahead of us, jagged and low. A rough slit carved into the stone.

Jennifer reached it first.

Stacy ducked inside without slowing.

Marissa slid after her, already twisting back, eyes flicking to us, calculating distance like she could still beat the math.

None of them stopped.

Behind us, the sound shifted.

Closer.

Not louder—denser.

Like the space itself had compressed.

Thmp.

Thmp.

Thmp.

Marissa stumbled, caught herself, then looked back over her shoulder. "It's not speeding up," she said, breathless. "It's—matching us."

The hanging lights whipped violently. Metal ground against metal. Chains smashed into rock. Shadows tore free from the walls and snapped back again like elastic.

The screams changed.

They lost their echo.

Sharpened. Narrowed. Focused.

Not louder.

Clearer.

"They're not reacting to noise!" Marissa shouted. "They're reacting to patterns! I mean—rhythm! Like... beats!"

They weren't searching anymore.

They were tracking.

We shoved harder.

Then something hit me.

Not a body.

Hooks.

Claws punched through my backpack straps and into my back—sharp, sudden, scraping the skin through my shirt—and I was yanked off my feet. My pack tore free with a ripping shriek and I slammed down hard, breath detonating out of me in a white-hot flash.

Stone rushed up.

I watched the pack being dragged away—saw my father's textbook split open as claws punched through paper and binding like it wasn't there at all.

Pain lit my back everywhere at once. Hot. Scattered. Directionless.

"Alex!"

Jennifer's voice cut through everything.

Hands locked onto my arm—strong, certain—and she hauled me upright with brute force, dragging me back into motion before my body could argue.

I staggered.

Nearly went down again.

Didn't.

The pain didn't stop.

It just... stopped mattering.

Jennifer didn't ask if I was hurt. Didn't look at me. She stayed close, shoulder brushing mine, ready to grab me again if I faltered.

We dove into the access tunnel.

Behind us—

Metal slammed with a concussive *crack*.

I turned.

Brandon had stopped pushing.

The cart had slammed into a buffer stop like it had reached the edge of existence. The impact jolted Matt forward with a strangled cry, pain ripping a sound out of him that he couldn't hold back. He tried to brace himself.

Failed.

Slumped against the rim of the cart, gasping wetly.

The wheels spun uselessly, screaming against the rails.

The tracks ended.

The tunnel narrowed immediately beyond them—no rails, no clearance. Just rough stone and a low clearance meant for bodies, not weight.

Hope died instantly.

We chose wrong.

"No," Brandon said, breath tearing loose. "No—no, no—"

"Okay," Brandon said too fast, already moving. "Okay—okay, that's fine. That's fine. We get him out! We carry him!"

He didn't wait for agreement.

He grabbed Matt under the arms and hauled.

I was already moving back toward them. I ducked under Matt's other side, shoulder driving up into his ribs, hands locking automatically where they could take weight.

Matt screamed as his ruined leg dragged free of the cart.

The sound tore out of him—sharp, unfiltered, helpless.

And the cavern answered immediately.

Not with volume.

With precision.

Like we'd just given it exactly what it needed.

"Sorry," Brandon gasped. "I've got you. We've got you."

Matt's breath fractured into pieces that didn't fit together anymore. His hands clawed at Brandon's jacket, fingers slipping on sweat and limestone dust, grabbing at fabric like it might anchor him to the world.

"I can't—" he tried. The words broke apart in his mouth. "I can't walk—I—"

His foot slipped on the blood-slicked bottom of the cart.

The scream that tore out of him wasn't anger or pain anymore.

It was naked. Raw. Like a wild beast in agony.

It burst into the chamber and came back multiplied, shattered into perfect, ringing echoes that laced themselves through the stone like wires pulled tight.

"If it's tracking sound," Marissa said suddenly, eyes flicking every-where at once, "then dragging him like this is—"

She stopped. Swallowed.

"It's the loudest thing we could be doing."

Something answered.

A hanging light tore loose overhead and slammed into the stone beside us, exploding into glass and metal. Shards skittered across the floor like ice. Chains hissed—not clanging now, not random—cutting violent arcs through the air, sweeping lower, closer, deliberate.

"It's right above us," I said under my breath. "Whatever *it* is."

Brandon didn't hear me.

He pulled harder.

Matt screamed again. Whatever composure he'd been clinging to finally tore free. There was no bravado left. No sarcasm. Just terror spilling out unchecked.

Jennifer had already turned.

Her eyes tracked the ceiling, the chains, the moving shadows—then snapped to me.

She saw it.

"We have seconds," she said. Her voice didn't rise. It didn't need to. "Not minutes."

Marissa nodded once, sharp. "Every sound is narrowing the space," she said. "It's not guessing anymore."

Brandon shook his head violently, like he could physically shake the truth loose. "No. No—no, we can do this—"

"If we stay," I said—and this time he heard me— "we die. All of us."

He refused anyway.

He hauled again, muscles trembling, teeth bared. Matt sobbed now, no edge left to his voice, no anger—just fear.

I tried again, pulling with him.

"Please," he said. "Please, man—don't—don't leave me—"

The words hit harder than the screams.

At the tunnel mouth, Stacy stood frozen, hands clenched at her sides, face emptied of everything but shock. Marissa stared upward, eyes dart-ing, lips moving soundlessly as the equation finished itself in her head.

I knew it immediately.

We're out of time.

Jennifer looked at me.

Nodded.

I reached for Brandon.

I wrapped my arms around his chest and yanked.

"Alex—!" Brandon fought me for half a second. Pure instinct. Pure refusal.

Jennifer grabbed his other arm and pulled—hard.

Brandon stumbled backward into us, losing his grip on Matt.

Matt screamed as he slammed down on the end of the cart.

"WAIT—WAIT—NO—!"

The tunnel shuddered.

Jennifer and I frantically dragged Brandon away, boots scraping stone, her grip iron-locked on his arm. He fought us, twisting toward the sound of Matt's voice like it was a rope he could still grab.

Above us, the final hanging light at the tunnel exit slammed low, swinging on its chain in a wide, violent arc that was suddenly much too close. Dust sifted down in a steady stream, coating our shoulders, our hair, our mouths, turning every breath into grit.

We piled into the tunnel. Marissa ushered us in as screeches burst forward from the darkness, the cries ricocheting off the stone walls. Her eyes flicked wickedly around the space, before her gaze snagged on the timber beside the tunnel mouth.

"The beam!" she shouted.

I saw it then.

The support timber wasn't straight anymore.

It bowed inward, fibers splitting along its length, dark rot exposed where fresh wood should have been. Each jolt from above sent a tremor through it—small, cumulative.

A metronome.

Jennifer saw it too.

The sound pressed closer, thick and immediate, filling the space like breath drawn deep into a lung.

She didn't hesitate.

She drove her heel into the beam's weakest point—right where the split had already started, where rot met strain.

The wood gave with a dull, final crack.

Not dramatic.

Decisive.

The ceiling answered immediately.

Dirt spilled first, choking and blinding. Then the beam snapped fully, folding inward as stone followed—heavy, brutal, unstoppable. Timber broke like bone under a weight it was never meant to hold.

Brandon screamed Matt's name as the world collapsed between them.

The wall came down.

Earth. Wood. Stone.

Matt's scream didn't stop right away.

It went on—bouncing, breaking, turning wet and wrong—until it wasn't a voice anymore.

Then—

Nothing.

Silence slammed into place like a sealed door.

And I understood something I would never be able to unlearn:

Sometimes survival isn't running faster.

It's choosing who the cave takes when it finally decides to close its mouth.

CHAPTER TEN

WE STOOD THERE, gasping, lights shaking in our hands like they didn't trust us anymore.

"Matt?" Brandon cried.

The name hit the wall and fell apart.

No answer.

Marissa stared at the collapse, hands trembling like they didn't belong to her. "I'm sorry," she said, voice cracking under the weight of it. "He was still—" She stopped herself. Pressed her lips together hard. Shook her head once, sharp. "I'm sorry."

Stacy had both hands locked around her helmet, fingers digging in, breathing fast but controlled—like she'd forced herself into a manual override. Her eyes didn't leave the wall. "I didn't even try," she whispered. "I didn't even try. Why did I freeze?" she paused. "What was that thing?"

Jennifer turned away. Swallowed hard. Her jaw clenched so tight it trembled.

I looked down at my hands.

They were empty.

Brandon dropped to his knees like the floor had reached up and taken him. "I could have saved him," he said hoarsely. "I was so close."

No one argued.

Behind us, the cavern shifted.

Listening.

Only five of us remained.

And the silence wasn't empty.

It was full.

"Is it going to hold?" Stacy asked.

No one answered right away.

We stood a few feet back from the cave-in, lights trained on the wall of dirt and timber and stone that had sealed Matt away. It didn't look solid so much as decided. Packed tight. Wedged at bad angles. A mess that had found equilibrium and wasn't interested in renegotiating.

Brandon pressed his palm to the rock, then leaned into it carefully, like he was testing an animal that might bite.

"It's holding," he said. "For now."

"*For now* is not comforting," Stacy said. She didn't lower her light. Didn't blink. "Is it *holding* holding?"

Brandon nodded. "It won't come down on its own."

"Great," she said flatly. "Thank God for whoever installed that crappy beam."

"It probably used to be stronger," Marissa threw in. "That or the man was fired shortly after."

"Happy to have you back in the land of the living," Jennifer said, managing a small, crooked smile in Stacy's direction.

Brandon turned away from the collapse—

—and doubled over, coughing hard into his sleeve.

The sound echoed wrong.

Wet.

He spat.

Something clicked against the rock.

Everyone froze.

Brandon stared down at it, then crouched and picked it up between two fingers.

A tooth.

"Right," he said after a moment. Too calm. Too measured. "I wondered if that would happen."

Jennifer stepped closer. "Wondered if *what* would happen?"

"Lose a tooth," he said. He rolled it between his fingers like it was data instead of bone. "Like Josh. It didn't make sense at the time, but the longer we've been in here..."

"It wasn't just Josh," I said. I stepped toward him before I realized I was doing it. "I did too. Around the same time."

Stacy swore. "So you all have terrible hygiene. What does that have to do with us?"

"Maybe nothing," Brandon said automatically. He rubbed his jaw. Winced. "People grind. Stress fractures happen. Especially under—" He stopped. Pressed his knuckles against his mouth. "Okay. Yeah. That hurts."

Jennifer's voice dropped. "Brandon."

"I'm fine," he said, smiling too fast. "I mean, not thriving, but—"

"Don't," Stacy cut in. "Don't make it a joke. What's going on?"

He sighed.

Rolled the tooth between his fingers again.

Thoughtful. Distracted. Like he was trying to keep his hands busy so his brain didn't wander somewhere worse.

"It's possible Eurydium isn't inert," he said. "Early readings were weird. Low-level. Constant. Not uranium, but not nothing either."

He spoke without touching anything now—hands tight to his sides, like the walls might answer back if he brushed them.

Marissa's attention sharpened immediately. Our flashlight beams washed her face pale—more than the cave justified—like the color had been leeched out instead of shadowed.

"That's comforting," Stacy said. "In a 'we're definitely dying' kind of way."

"I'm saying it explains things," Brandon said. "Headaches. Fatigue. Jaw pain. Tooth sensitivity." He pressed his knuckles to his mouth again, gentler this time. "All textbook exposure symptoms."

"To what?" Jennifer asked.

For a second, I forgot she didn't study this. That she was only a tourist in our world. That she hadn't signed up to learn new vocabularies underground.

Brandon glanced at me, surprised—like he hadn't realized he was narrating out loud until someone tuned in. Then his eyes locked back on her.

"Radiation," he said. "Or something close to it."

The word dropped heavy.

"It would explain a lot," he continued. "Even those things back there. You see mutations in fish near runoff sites. Bugs near reactors. Stuff adapts."

Marissa's hand tightened around her backpack strap. "Okay," she said softly. "That's... not great. But it's also not immediate, right?"

Jennifer frowned. "Those things didn't look adapted. I only saw them through my viewfinder, but—"

"They looked... off," Brandon said. He hesitated. "If something lived down here long enough, in the dark, it wouldn't just adjust."

He swallowed.

"It would change."

The word stayed with us.

"So, what," Stacy said, "we're just in a very angry petting zoo? Did you not see what it did to Kevin?"

"I *saw* what it did to Kevin," Brandon snapped—and then immediately pulled back, like the volume itself startled him. He dragged a hand down his face, breath hitching once. "Listen. I'm not discounting those things. I'm just saying this could be an environmental hazard." He gestured vaguely at the walls, the ceiling, the dark. "Not intentional. Just... under-inspected. The school might not even know. There are short-term side effects, sure, but as long as we get out soon, we shouldn't see long-term damage."

I watched him talk.

Not because I believed him.

Because he needed to hear himself say it.

"And the noises?" I asked. "The way those things shrieked, then stopped. Like they were listening."

Brandon hesitated. His fingers went to his jaw again, rubbing at it like he could grind the thought down into something manageable.

"All I know is caves have bats," he said. "Radiation messes with echolocation. Maybe they're just... wrong. Disoriented." He shrugged weakly. "Could explain our echoes too."

Marissa turned her head away, sleeve brushing her nose. When she faced us again, she kept it tucked close, like she didn't want the air touching her skin.

"Great," Stacy said. "Radioactive bats. The second we make it out of here, my lawyer's going to have a field day."

Brandon slipped the tooth into his pocket and clenched his fist around it like he needed proof it was real. His breathing still hadn't slowed. Even standing still, his chest rose too fast, too shallow—like the cave had minimized the air itself.

I stepped closer and put a hand on his shoulder. Kept my voice low. "You sure you're okay?"

"I'm fine," he said again.

Quieter.

Less convincing.

His hands shook. Just enough to notice if you were looking for it.

"I—" Brandon started. Stopped. Took a breath that didn't quite go anywhere. "Alex," he said instead. "Can you—"

He didn't finish.

I stepped in anyway. "I'll take point for a bit," I said. "Throw on your headphones or something. We might be walking a while."

His eyes were glassy. He nodded once, small.

Marissa stepped closer, careful not to touch him. "You did the right thing," she said. "No one doubts that. That matters."

Jennifer shifted beside me. "We should start moving."

Not a suggestion.

I agreed.

Because beneath all of it, I felt the hum again.

Low. Steady. A pressure behind my eyes that didn't hurt anymore.

Brandon's explanation fit too neatly.

That was the problem.

Not the tooth—Josh had lost one too—but the timing. The alignment. Same depth. Same exposure window. Same moment everything else started behaving wrong.

Dad would've clocked that immediately.

Not coincidence.

Variable.

Then—

Clink.

A sound from the collapse.

Small.

Metallic.

Another followed.

Clink. Clink.

Stacy's breath hitched. "Please tell me that was a rock settling."

Brandon lifted his light again, pulling the headphones down to his neck.

My headlamp slid over the packed dirt. The splintered timber. The wall that had decided where Matt ended.

Another sound answered.

Not a strike.

A tap.

Measured.

Intentional.

Something on the other side of the wall was testing it.

"Alright," I said immediately. Final. "Pick up the pace. We move. Now."

As if in agreement, the tapping came again—faster this time. Not harder. Just... curious.

Marissa swallowed. "That's not pressure," she said. "That's contact." She paused. "Which means we're not crazy for being scared."

Brandon took a step back from the collapse.

Then another.

"Okay," he said. "Okay. We go."

And none of us looked back.

Because whatever was behind that wall wasn't finished with us yet.

And in some small recess of my mind, I couldn't help wondering if it was Matt.

We walked fast.

Lights forward. Backs prickling with the sense of being measured as we went—not followed exactly, not chased, just noted. The tapping behind us thinned with distance. It didn't stop. It just became irrelevant, like a thought you choose not to finish.

The tunnel curved upward, then widened. The air shifted again—cooler, drier, less rot. Like the cave had decided to change subjects.

Marissa fell in behind Stacy without saying anything, then adjusted her pace just enough that Stacy didn't have to notice. It was subtle. Intentional. The kind of care that doesn't announce itself.

Brandon took the rear.

His light kept drifting—not to the tunnel behind us, but to us. Counting. Checking. Like he wasn't sure what would fail first: the rock, the air, or the people still breathing.

After a while—long enough that my breathing evened out, long enough that the hum inside me smoothed instead of spiked—I realized Jennifer was matching my pace.

"You okay?" she asked quietly.

I nodded.

Then shook my head. "I don't know."

She accepted that. No follow-up. No correction. Like not knowing was a valid answer instead of a failure.

A few more steps passed. Footfalls. Breath. The cave settling around us like it was recalculating our combined weight.

"You didn't hesitate back there," she said.

"With Brandon?"

"With Matt."

My heart pulsed once. Subtle. Insistent. Thumping like a weight in my chest.

"I did," I said. "I just—hid it better. I keep thinking if I'd moved a second faster, if I'd grabbed him harder, if I'd yelled instead of thinking —maybe he'd still be here."

Jennifer exhaled through her nose. Not impatient. Not dismissive. Just... honest.

"Yeah. That part never feels great."

"You sound like you've been there."

She shrugged, eyes still forward, light steady. "I have."

That surprised me. Not because I didn't believe her—but because she didn't advertise it.

"I lost someone," she continued. "Not like this. Not... cave-and-monsters dramatic. But sudden. Unfair. The kind where everyone tells you what you should've done differently, even though they weren't there."

I nodded. I knew that flavor.

"Who were they?" I asked before my mind had time to think better of it.

She didn't answer right away.

"My brother," she said finally. "His name was Aaron."

I looked at her. Really looked.

"Older," she added. "By four years. Loud. Annoying. Thought he was invincible because nothing bad had happened to him yet."

I stepped around a fallen rock, careful to tread lightly as she spoke.

"One night in high school," she went on, eyes still forward, "he was going out with friends. Party. Nothing dramatic. I told him not to drive. He laughed. Said he was fine. I followed him all the way to the driveway."

She swallowed.

"I almost grabbed his keys."

My chest tightened.

"Almost?"

She nodded. "I didn't want to be the nagging little sister. Didn't want to be dramatic. Didn't want to be wrong."

She let out a breath that sounded like it had been waiting years to leave.

"He died on the way back."

The words landed clean. No embellishment. No shield.

"I used to replay that moment," she said. "Over and over. The door. The keys. The space between us. I kept thinking if I'd been louder. Meaner. Faster. If I'd just done something instead of calculating how I'd look."

I felt something settle into place between us. Not comfort. Recognition.

"I used to think," she said after a beat, "that if I moved fast enough after that—stayed sharp enough, stayed useful—I could outrun the bad endings."

"And?" I asked.

"And turns out," she said, dry but tired, "they're very committed to keeping up."

That almost got a smile out of me.

"I keep seeing their faces," I said. "Josh. Kevin. Matt." My throat tightened. "Not like ghosts. Just... empty space. Like the cave keeps recalculating around what it took."

Jennifer slowed half a step. Just enough to be with me.

"That's grief," she said. "It's annoying like that."

"That's one word for it."

She glanced at me. Really glanced. "I'm not great at it either, you know."

I frowned. "You seem... steady."

She gave a short, humorless huff. "Yeah. That's the outside version."

"What's the inside version?"

She thought about it. "The part where I don't sleep much. Where I keep lists in my head of everything I could lose next. Where I move because standing still feels dangerous."

That mirrored me so cleanly it almost hurt.

"I don't wait around to understand things," she said. "If something feels wrong, I move. That's how I survived losing him. That's how I survive most days."

"And if you stop?"

Her jaw tightened. "Then the math catches up."

I felt it again. The hum. Gentle. Persistent.

"You don't have to carry all of them alone," she said. "Josh. Kevin. Matt."

"I kind of do," I said. "I'm someone who remembers the details. The timing. The choices. Brandon can try to solve it. Stacy can try outrunning it. Marissa can attempt to measure it. But I—" I hesitated. "I know I'll carry it."

Jen considered that. Then shook her head, gentle but firm.

"No. You *witnessed* it. That's different."

I frowned. "Is it?"

"Yeah," she said. "Because carrying implies responsibility. Witnessing just means you were there and you cared. Big difference."

"I don't feel like I'll get to stop," I said. "Thinking about it. Replaying it."

"You won't," she said simply. "Not right away."

"That's not comforting."

She smiled, small and sideways. "I know. But here's the part people skip: you don't ever forget. It's just...remembering doesn't hurt so much. It gets... lighter. Not better. Just lighter. Enough that you can move again."

I looked at her. The way she stood—steady, unflinching, but not hardened.

"And if it doesn't?" I asked.

"Then you don't do it alone," she said. "You let someone walk next to you until it does."

That landed harder than the cave ever had.

"Is that what you're doing?" I asked. "Walking next to me?"

She didn't dodge it.

"Yeah," she said. "I am."

We walked for a few seconds like that. Shoulder to shoulder. Lights steady. Silence no longer sharp.

"I'm glad you didn't hesitate," she added.

"I did."

She smirked. "Yeah. But you moved anyway. That counts."

"For what?"

"For surviving without losing who you are."

Behind us, Marissa slowed just enough for Brandon to catch up beside her.

The hum pressed again—firmer this time.

"Hey, do you feel that?" I finally asked.

She glanced at me. "Feel what?"

"The—" I hesitated. There was no clean word for it. "The vibration. Like something's... listening to us in the dark."

Jennifer paused—not with fear, but focus. Then she shook her head. "No," she said. "I don't stop to take inventory of that kind of thing."

"Inventory?"

She adjusted her grip on her light. "Yeah. The second you start naming it, you give it time to decide what it wants. I don't do that."

I studied her as we walked. The way she didn't tune in. Didn't linger. Just acted.

The hum didn't bother her.

It wasn't calling to her.

"Good instincts," I said.

She huffed softly. "It's kept me alive so far."

We walked on. Shoulder to shoulder.

Then the tunnel widened without warning—not into a cavern, but into a decision.

The rock walls cut cleaner here, reinforced with old beams bolted deep into stone. The ceiling lifted just enough to breathe without thinking about it.

Marissa slowed. Her light swept across the space once, then stopped.

She opened her mouth.

Closed it.

Swallowed.

"This is—"

She didn't finish.

Ahead of us, a rusted metal sign hung crooked from a support beam, its lettering eaten thin by time but still legible:

LOWER OPERATIONS
AUTHORIZED PERSONNEL ONLY

Beneath it, the floor dipped into shallow grooves—steel tracks sunk into the rock, half-buried in dust.

A mining cart sat abandoned near the wall, its wheels locked, frame collapsed inward like it had been left in a hurry. Old tools lay scattered nearby—pick heads without handles, coils of cable, a lantern cracked but not shattered.

Work paused.

Not finished.

The air felt different here.

Not safer.

Older.

Like the cave remembered hands.

"It's the official station," Brandon said quietly. "We found it."

He sounded steadier saying it. Naming things helped. Facts were easier than choices.

I looked at the tracks again. At the sign. At the way the past pressed close, heavy with purpose.

Guess this was where the stories began.

And where we'd have to decide which ones we were still allowed to finish.

CHAPTER ELEVEN

WE DIDN'T SPEAK at first.

The tunnel sloped downward, widening as it went, and the air changed in layers—less damp, more dust; less rot, more old iron. The station didn't announce itself so much as accept us. Cut stone replaced collapse. Squared corners replaced panic. Beams and bolts replaced the cave's improvisation. The place had rules once. That was the difference. That was the lure.

Behind us, the access tunnel narrowed into shadow, and with it the last thin illusion that we could turn around and undo anything.

The place where Matt was no longer existed.

It wasn't a dramatic thought. It wasn't even a cruel one. It was just the kind of fact your brain produces when it runs out of other fuel.

Stacy broke first.

"This isn't what I agreed to."

No one answered her.

"I mean it," she pressed, louder now like volume could make the world cooperate. "We said we'd keep going until we found a way out. This is—" she gestured at the squared walls, the beams, the rusted conduit strung like veins along the ceiling, "—something else."

Brandon stopped walking without straightening all the way. Like standing up fully would require him to become a person again, and he wasn't ready for that.

He turned slowly, the movement costing him. "You want to go back?"

The silence that followed wasn't empty. It was crowded with everything none of us wanted to say, stacked shoulder to shoulder behind our teeth.

Stacy opened her mouth. "Considering that's where we just killed Matt—no."

"What, like you tried to help?" Brandon's voice rose. "You didn't even try. None of us did!"

He wasn't accusing. Worse. Part of that was true.

Jennifer's head snapped toward him. "We did try."

Brandon's jaw worked. He swallowed. I saw the flash of red at the corner of his mouth before he wiped it away with the side of his thumb, like it offended him to be bleeding.

"We didn't try hard enough," he said. His voice didn't rise. It didn't need to. "I had him. I had him under my arm. If I'd chosen another path, if I'd just—"

"If you'd stayed," Jennifer said, controlled but firm, "we'd be talking about you in the past tense too."

Brandon didn't argue.

That was new.

He looked like he wanted to. Like the fight was right there in his throat. But he didn't take it. He just stared at the floor like it was a map he couldn't read anymore.

I stepped forward before the silence could harden into something else—something mean, something that would make us split in ways the cave didn't even have to work for.

"Matt's gone," I said.

Every head turned to me.

Not because it was cruel.

Because it was final.

"There's no path back," I continued. "And even if there were—" my voice snagged, just for a second, on the memory of chains and screaming and the way sound got *used* down here, "—we know what's waiting for us. We don't have the strength, the light, or the time."

Brandon's eyes stayed on the ground.

"So, we just keep walking until something else kills us?" Stacy said sharply.

"No," I said, surprising myself with how steady it came out.

I scanned the station: the beams bolted into the stone, the equipment tucked into alcoves, the scars in the wall where work had been done on purpose. This place wasn't natural. It had been carved. Designed. Wired. Labeled. Someone had tried to control it once.

"We stop drifting," I said. "We find control."

That did something.

Jennifer looked at me—not surprised. Measuring. Like she'd been waiting for someone to say the word that matched her heartbeat.

"Options," she said.

"Exactly."

My feet carried me toward a pile of abandoned equipment without asking anyone's permission. The metal smelled like pennies and old rain. A tarp half-covered the heap, caught on broken bolts, stiff with age.

A pickaxe lay half-buried beneath the rusted mess.

The handle was worn smooth by hands that had trusted it. The head was heavy in a way that didn't pretend to be anything else.

I lifted it, and the scratches across my back lit up in protest—hot and scattered where the creatures hooked into me. For a moment, I saw my pack tearing away, my father's textbook splayed open like a wound, pages punched through by claws, like paper meant nothing.

I blinked hard.

The pickaxe settled into my grip and somehow steadied me. Like weight was a kind of honesty.

"If this place was built," I said, "then it has power. Access points. Exits. We don't guess our way out—we use what's already here."

Brandon nodded, slow and distracted, like agreement took effort. He wiped his mouth again and didn't comment on the blood. Like if he acknowledged it, it would become a problem he had to solve.

Instead, he crouched near the pile and dug through it with one hand. Metal scraped. He flinched. Kept going anyway.

He came up with a length of steel drill rod—three feet long, thick as a baton. One end blunted from use, the other fractured jagged where it had snapped. He tested the weight, grimaced, then nodded to himself and kept it. He switched hands once, then again, like neither one wanted the job.

"Better than nothing," he muttered, mostly to the floor.

Jennifer was already moving. Of course she was. She sifted through the tools quick and efficient, like she'd done this before. Her hand found a short shovel: worn, useful, the kind you could dig with or swing with if you had to.

She tested the weight once.

"I guess this'll do," she said.

Stacy crossed her arms.

"Great, very medieval," she said. "So I don't get anything?"

"Do you want to carry the heavy rod?" Brandon turned. "No? Then live with it."

Marissa drifted closer to the wall, fingers hovering near a thin vein of orange mineral—caught herself at the last second and folded her hands into her sleeves, as if she could hide her curiosity from the cave by hiding her skin.

Within seconds, Jen's flashlight flickered.

Once.

Twice.

Then it went dark.

She stopped walking—but only long enough to register it. No panic. No curse. She shook it once, listened to the batteries rattle like loose teeth, then set it down on a nearby bench with care, like it had reached the end of its shift and deserved rest.

Stacy scoffed, tightening her grip on a pry bar. "Cool. So what's the plan when all of our batteries decide to unionize?"

I tilted my head up, following the angle of the ceiling.

Above us, the hanging fixtures waited. Their housings were dark, glass dulled with dust, but intact—lined up with intention, spaced the way people do when they expect to come back.

"If they're afraid of light," I said, "then we don't rely on what we carried in."

Everyone looked at me.

"We use what the miners built."

Brandon shifted the drill rod in his hands, adjusting the balance like he was weighing an argument as much as the metal. "Alex... the power down here's been off for decades. The school's generator is back in the research section."

"We won't know until we try," I said. I nodded toward the corridor ahead, toward a rusted sign bolted crooked into the stone like a forgotten promise.

LAMP CONTROL

"All we need is a chance."

Jennifer followed my gaze. I could see the thought click into place behind her eyes. "We'll give it a shot," she said. "Worst case, we learn something."

That was enough.

As we moved deeper into the chamber, more structures came into view.

Support beams rose out of the rock like ribs. Conduit lines ran in deliberate paths, bolted cleanly into the walls. Panels. Benches. A place shaped by decisions instead of damage.

Jennifer slowed—and without a word, lifted her camera.

The flash cracked sharp and white against the stone.

For a split second, the station existed all at once: every beam, every bolt, every scar made by hands that had trusted this place to hold. Then the light collapsed back into shadow, leaving the afterimage burned behind my eyes.

Jen lowered the camera, checked the winding mechanism by feel, and didn't explain herself.

She never did.

Thin calcite had begun creeping along the edges of the station—

clinging to beams, stitching itself over bolts and conduit seams in pale, chalky threads. Not enough to hide the machinery. Just enough to suggest the cave hadn't stopped working just because the miners had.

The air changed again.

Dry. Mineral. Like chalk ground between fingers.

My molars flared—sharp and localized—as if the cave had reached up through my jaw and pressed a finger there. The pain wasn't spreading. It was precise. Deliberate.

I tightened my grip on the pickaxe.

"Anyone else feeling that?" Stacy muttered. "Or is this just my personal dental hell?"

Brandon swallowed before answering. "You'll get used to it," he said. "Probably."

Probably didn't help.

The ache faded as suddenly as it had come, leaving something behind that unsettled me more than the pain had.

Quiet.

My thoughts felt... aligned. Like static had been dialed down. Less overlap. Less noise. Everything lining up too neatly.

That scared me.

It reminded me of being twelve years old, standing in my father's office when I wasn't supposed to be there.

I remembered how that room always looked like it was in the middle of losing a fight with paper. Charts everywhere. Coffee-stained journals. Piles of research he swore he'd organize someday.

But that day, it had something else.

A wrinkled poster on his desk. Torn from somewhere. Folded and unfolded too many times.

A missing girl.

One I'd never heard of.

One no one talked about.

He hadn't noticed me at first.

He was staring at the poster like it was delivering bad news in a language he almost understood. One hand pressed to his mouth. The other shaking as he tried—and failed—to light a cigarette.

I'd never even seen him smoke.

For a second, my dad looked small.

Afraid.

Then he heard me.

He straightened instantly, fear snapping into place like it had never existed at all.

"Alex," he'd said, voice too calm. "You know you shouldn't be in here."

He stepped in front of something on his desk—a metal box I hadn't noticed before.

I remembered the way his hand lingered on it.

Protective.

Possessive.

I hadn't understood what he meant then.

I hadn't understood why the box glowed faintly at the seams.

Down here, in the station, I understood it too well.

It was all around me now.

I blinked and forced my focus back to the tunnel ahead, to the steady overlap of our remaining lights.

"Stay close," Jennifer said quietly. Not afraid. Intentional. "Last thing I need is to trip in the dark."

No one questioned it.

The station began to open itself to us.

We pushed open the door to the control room, dust billowing as the hinges protested. It was the first room on the left—small, tight, lined with panels and old rotary switches. The switches were fat and black, built for gloved hands. Rows of long industrial housings ran overhead, most of their tubes blown out, others intact but filmed with decades of dust.

A metal placard was bolted crooked to the wall beside the door, its edges curled with rust.

BENNINGTON SUBSURFACE STATION, 1933
AUTHORIZED PERSONNEL ONLY

The lettering was still crisp beneath the corrosion.

Like it had mattered once.

Like it still did.

Stacy hovered instead of stopping, shifting her weight from foot to foot like standing still was worse than whatever waited ahead. The room felt calibrated for motion—for hands, for purpose—and we were violating it just by hesitating.

Brandon tilted his light upward, tracking the rows of housings. "These aren't emergency fixtures," he said. "They ran this place full-time."

I took in the space slowly. The panels. The dials. The careful spacing. The way nothing was smashed or torn out. It felt less like abandonment and more like interruption—like everyone had stepped away expecting to come back after lunch.

A mausoleum with instructions.

A sheet of yellowed paper was taped across one of the dials, the handwriting sharp enough to cut through the dust.

DO NOT TURN ALL ON

Another note clung beside it, half-torn, edges curled inward like it had tried to escape the wall and failed.

One bank at a time.
Wait for the hum to settle.

The feeling in the air tightened, subtle but unmistakable.

Like it had heard its name.

Marissa tilted her head—not to read, but to listen past the words. Her gaze unfocused, tracking something beneath the surface.

"I don't think it likes being rushed," she said.

Not fear. Not warning.

Just observation.

Brandon glanced at her. "You good?"

"Yeah," she said.

Too fast. Like she'd already practiced the answer.

Stacy laughed once, sharp and hollow. "Light switches with person-alities. This place is unreal."

Jennifer didn't look at her. She was studying the switches, commit-ting them to memory. "Real enough to have rules," she said. "How do we know which ones to turn on?"

"We don't." I stepped closer—and that's when I saw it.

The lever.

It jutted from the far panel, thicker than the others, wrapped in cracked rubber that had once been soft under work gloves. The metal plate beneath it was cleaner than the rest, less corroded, like it had been touched more often.

MAIN LINE
ON / OFF

It was set firmly to OFF.

Stacy stared at it. "Nope."

Brandon rubbed his jaw. "That's our light switch."

Jennifer glanced between the lever and the warnings. "If there's still current—"

"—then whoever flips it becomes the test subject," Stacy finished flatly.

"I don't think it's angry," Marissa said quietly. "Just... waiting."

Stacy shot her a look. "I don't care what its mood is."

The hum pressed closer—not louder, just more attentive. Like something leaning in.

Brandon flinched. Not toward the sound, but away from it.

No one moved.

Finally, Brandon exhaled and reached into his pocket. He pulled out the matchbook. The cardboard was bent, the cover softened by sweat and worry. He flipped it open.

Five matches left.

He held it out between us. "We can't just... volunteer someone," he said. "That's not fair."

Stacy squinted at the matchbook. "You're suggesting what, exactly?"

He snapped off four matches in quick succession. The sound cracked sharp in the quiet room. The broken stems dropped into his palm like spent bones.

"We draw," he said. "Shortest one flips it."

Jennifer hesitated. "Brandon—"

"We're already gambling," he said. "At least this way it's honest."

He kept the final match intact and shuffled it into the stack, then offered them out.

No one argued.

We each took one.

Marissa's fingers brushed mine as she picked hers up. Cold. Steady. Not shaking.

Stacy glanced at her match and scoffed. "Of course."

Jennifer turned hers once between her fingers, then tucked it away like the result didn't matter.

I looked down.

Mine was longer than Stacy's.

Brandon compared his. Longer.

Marissa looked at hers.

The shortest.

The room held its breath.

"I'm fine," she said immediately. Too fast. "It's just a switch."

Jennifer stepped toward her. "We don't know that."

Marissa shook her head. "We know less if we don't try."

"I can do it," she said. Calm. Flat. Certain. "If it's nothing, then it's nothing. If it's not... we'll know."

Stacy opened her mouth. Closed it again. Her jaw tightened like she'd bitten down on something bitter.

Brandon looked sick.

I should have stopped her.

I didn't.

Marissa stepped up to the panel.

The lever looked too big for her hand, but she wrapped her fingers around it anyway. For a moment, she paused—not listening outward, but inward. Like she was syncing her breathing to something old and patient.

Then she pulled.

The lever shifted with a dull, mechanical thunk.

And—

Nothing.

No spark. No surge. No answering glow.

The lights stayed dead.

The panel stayed dark.

Marissa didn't flinch.

She waited a beat. Another.

Then she let go and stepped back.

Stacy exhaled hard. "Okay. So. We did the dangerous thing and lived."

Brandon swallowed. "That means the line's dead."

"Or," Jennifer said quietly, "the power's somewhere else."

Marissa glanced at the wall again, fingers brushing the stone. She hummed once, low and unconscious.

"It's not here," she said. "But it has to be close."

I looked at the broken match still resting in my palm.

"Then we find what feeds it," I said.

Jennifer nodded once.

Decision made.

WE PASSED another room marked SURVEY OFFICE, its door hanging half-open like it had been interrupted mid-sentence. Papers lay scattered across the floor, yellowed and curled at the edges, maps and notes overlapping in no particular order—as if someone had stood up too fast and never sat back down. Someone in a big hurry. Or someone—or some *thing*—ransacking without a plan.

Beyond it, a wider area opened up. Lockers lined the walls in neat rows, dented but intact. Benches ran down the center, their surfaces worn smooth by bodies that had once rested there, eaten there, complained there.

We didn't stop.

Jennifer glanced in once, catalogued it, then kept moving. "Later," she said.

Not a promise.

A decision.

The tunnel narrowed again, forcing us into single file. Overhead, the ceiling buckled where the rock had folded in on itself, swollen and uneven, like a kneecap that never healed right. We ducked without being told, shoulders brushing stone, the air cooling as we passed beneath it.

Then the passage widened.

And there, tucked into the fractured belly of the shaft, was something that shouldn't have been there.

A chapel.

Not a church chapel. Nothing holy in the way surface people meant it. No altar. No cross. Just a shallow pocket carved into the rock, smoothed by hands that had stayed too long, worked too carefully.

Candles had melted directly into the stone. Their wax fused to the floor until it looked like the cave itself had wept. Old offerings clustered together where someone had tried to impose order: a union pin dulled by mineral bloom, a photograph sealed beneath calcite, faces blurred into suggestion, a child's marble clouded orange, a rosary whose beads had gone the same faint, unhealthy hue as the veins in the walls.

Brandon swallowed. "That's... kind of sad."

"It's..." Marissa drifted closer without realizing it, her head tilting, listening past the space. Her sleeve brushed her mouth. "The cave-in victims. All the ones who didn't leave."

Names were carved into the wall.

Dozens.

Some were scratched deep. Some shallow. Some careful, almost reverent.

And some were crossed out.

Not gouged away.

Not vandalized.

Crossed out cleanly—two deliberate lines through each name, like items completed on a list.

The hum pressed harder here, dense and approving. Like it recognized the inventory.

My fingers tightened around the pickaxe handle until the wood creaked softly in protest.

"Okay—no," Stacy said suddenly. "We don't do this. We don't stand here staring at it."

She grabbed Jennifer's sleeve and tugged once. "Move. Please."

Jennifer's shovel bumped her hip as she passed through the space. She didn't stop. Didn't stare. She moved like movement itself was a kind of prayer.

"Don't linger," she said quietly.

No one argued.

Further in, the station opened up again. The ceiling rose and disappeared into shadow. Thick wires ran along the walls in bundled veins, converging upward through conduits that vanished into the dark.

"Follow those," Brandon said.

Not confident.

Hopeful.

He didn't move first.

I did.

The wires led us to a door.

The sign above it hung crooked, one bolt torn free, the lettering barely legible beneath rust and dust.

GENERATOR

The door was nothing like the others.

No soft edges. No rot. No panic scars.

Heavy steel, reinforced, built to endure. The keyhole sat dark and hollow, like a jaw left open too long. The wires feeding into it were thicker than my wrist, bundled tight, disappearing into the ceiling like arteries feeding a heart.

Stacy saw it and broke into a run.

She slammed her shoulder into the door and yanked the handle hard.

Nothing.

"Dammit, dammit, dammit!" she snapped, kicking the base once before stepping back, breath sharp and uneven.

I stepped closer.

And then I felt it.

Air.

A faint draft brushed my cheek—cool, unmistakable.

"Hold on," I said.

I followed it a few steps left.

The corridor ended abruptly in black.

An elevator shaft.

What might once have been a platform lay crumpled at the bottom like discarded skin. Rails ran straight up into darkness, vanishing beyond where our lights could reach. If you squinted, you could almost convince yourself there was daylight far above us—a suggestion of escape, cruel in its distance.

We were still several stories down.

A ladder clung to the wall beside the shaft, twisted and incomplete. Bolts were missing. Rust bloomed thick along the rungs. It stretched upward into darkness, as if trying to remember a shape it once had.

Something violent had happened here.

Too fast to understand.

Brandon tilted his light up, tracking the rails, the ladder. "Guess the ladder's not a—"

"Don't," Stacy said immediately. "Don't say it."

Jennifer stepped closer to the shaft, careful with her footing. She didn't look up at first, as if doing so would shatter something she was still holding onto.

We clustered together without meaning to, our lights overlapping, shadows slipping and tangling across the walls like they were trying to decide where to settle. Every beam felt thinner than it had an hour ago. Brandon's light juddered whenever his grip loosened, the beam wobbling like it was second-guessing itself. Stacy's cut sharp but didn't reach as far as it used to. Marissa's blinked—on, off, on again—like it couldn't quite commit to staying awake.

Even mine felt wrong. Fuzzier. Dimmer at the edges. Like the dark was pushing back now.

And beneath it all, the vibration in the air didn't just continue.

It amplified.

Not louder exactly—denser. More present. As if the cave liked the idea of us standing still, weighing our options. Like it was challenging us. A game of chess, waiting for the next move.

That generator felt like...

Hope.

And hope, I was learning, was just another kind of lever.

"Is this it?" Stacy said finally, quieter now, her arms still locked tight against herself. She looked from the elevator shaft to us, then back again. "The generator's our way out?"

Jennifer didn't answer immediately.

She crossed back toward the generator door, shovel still hooked at her hip, and studied it like a locked puzzle box—eyes tracing the seams, the hinges, the way the steel met stone. She didn't touch it. Didn't test it yet.

"Maybe," she said.

Brandon scrubbed a hand down his face, leaving a streak of dust across his cheek. "If the things down here really are scared of light..." He trailed off, swallowed, then tried again. "Then lights buy us time."

Time.

Not safety.

Stacy let out a breath that shook despite her effort to keep it steady. She turned fully toward the generator room now, like facing it head-on might make it easier to accept. "Okay," she said. "So step one: lights."

Brandon followed her gaze. "Which means power."

"And power means getting through that door," Stacy said, gesturing sharply at the generator. "So not today," she added, voice flat. "Great. Fantastic. Love that for us."

No one laughed.

I looked at the generator door again. At the wires feeding into it. The way the hum pressed closer every time I thought about it, like the cave itself was leaning in, curious to see what we'd do next.

Hope sat there between us, heavy and unresolved.

Not a way out.

Just another decision waiting to be made.

CHAPTER TWELVE

I TURNED BACK to the generator room door.

It wasn't like the others.

The steel was thicker. Darker. Layered with overlapping plates riveted together like armor, each seam deliberate, each joint reinforced twice over. The hinges were massive, bolted deep into the rock—so deep it felt less like they'd been installed and more like the mountain itself had been conscripted into keeping this thing shut.

This wasn't neglect.

This was intention.

Old warning placards clung to the surface, their paint blistered and peeling, words half-erased by time but still sharp enough to feel like commands.

NOT AUTHORIZED
HIGH VOLTAGE
RESTRICTED ACCESS

The language was bureaucratic, but the tone underneath it was unmistakable.

Stay out.

The door didn't just block entry. It refused it.

Something about it radiated finality, the way sealed rooms do in old buildings—places no one ever talks about because the talking already failed.

"There's something here," I said.

My voice sounded smaller than I meant it to.

Mounted beside the frame was a recessed glass case, the pane cracked and fogged from the inside like it had breathed once and never again. A clipboard rested within it, clipped neatly in place, edges squared, as if someone had left it expecting to return before the dust settled.

At the top, typewritten in faded black ink:

BENNINGTON SUBSURFACE STATION
GENERATOR ACCESS — KEY LOG
(All entries required)

Below it, columns ruled clean and patient:

DATE | NAME | TIME OUT | TIME RETURNED

3-17-33 | E. Parse | 09:40 | – | 10:20

3-17-33 | K. Miller | 11:15 | – | 11:43

3-18-33 | J. Caldwell | 08:02 | – |

No return time.

No signature.

Nothing after that.

The page didn't look unfinished.

It looked abandoned mid-breath.

Stacy shifted beside me. Her breath caught—small, sharp. Her eyes widened just enough that I noticed before she smoothed them out.

She leaned closer to the glass, like proximity alone might change what she was reading.

"Stacy?" Jennifer asked, glancing back.

Stacy swallowed. "I... used to know someone with that last name."

Brandon frowned. "What do you mean?"

She didn't look at him. Her eyes stayed fixed on the ink.

"Her name was Nicki," she said. Quieter now. "Nicole. Only Parse I ever knew."

No one filled the silence that followed.

Finally, Stacy straightened too fast, like standing upright might knock the thought loose. "So," she said, forcing air into her voice. "That's comforting."

Marissa stepped forward—and stopped.

Not hesitated. Not slowed.

Stopped, like she'd crossed an invisible boundary the rest of us couldn't feel.

Her gaze lingered on the last entry longer than the others. Her fingers lifted an inch toward the glass, then curled back into her sleeve, pressing the fabric hard into her palm like she was grounding herself against something that wanted her attention.

Brandon leaned in, squinting. His jaw tightened. "If the key's not here," he said slowly, "then someone took it with them."

"And?" Stacy snapped. "That's not exactly helpful."

"More helpful than your friend's last name," he said. "Because it means the key didn't just vanish. It went somewhere."

"And not randomly," Marissa added. Her voice was level. Observational. "They logged returns. That means the key stayed close to work. Not exits."

The vibration shifted.

Sharper.

Jennifer crouched, scanning the base of the door, the hinges, the floor for scuff marks that time hadn't fully erased. "You don't log something like that unless the key matters."

"Great," Stacy said. "So now we're hunting ghosts with a clipboard."

Marissa didn't rise to it. "He didn't run," she said instead.

We all looked at her.

"The last one," she continued. "Caldwell. He signed it out early. He expected to come back."

A beat.

"The place probably changed after."

No one argued.

Jennifer turned her head—and I felt it when she did. The dark behind us pressed closer, like the space itself had decided to listen in.

Marissa shifted again, and this time she reached back, steadying herself against the rock wall. The contact looked deliberate. Necessary.

Brandon caught it immediately.

"You okay?" he asked.

"Yes," she said at once.

"You don't sound okay."

Jennifer clocked it too. The way Marissa hadn't moved her jaw once since she stopped. The way her breathing had gone shallow, measured —like she was rationing air... or attention.

Marissa didn't answer.

Her face looked washed out in the beam of my headlamp, the color leeched clean away. Not pale from fear.

Pale from focus.

The silence thickened until Stacy broke it with a sharp, echoless clap. "Okay. We're not standing here letting the cave think for us. We split up. Cover ground."

Jennifer straightened immediately. "No."

Brandon blinked. "No?"

"We don't scatter," she said. Flat. Certain. "That's how horror movies happen."

"This isn't a movie," Stacy snapped. "And we don't have time to hold hands."

Brandon rubbed his mouth again, slower now. "We can do pairs. That's not scattering. Two and two," Brandon continued, forcing steadiness into his voice. "Stay in sight. Call if you find anything. I can go off on my own."

Marissa shook her head before anyone could point at her.

"I can't."

The words weren't panicked. They weren't apologetic. They landed with the finality of a diagnosis.

Brandon frowned. "Are you hurt?"

"No."

"Then—"

"I can't do it," she repeated.

Same tone. Same stillness. Like she was stating a law of physics.

Brandon hesitated, then stepped closer. "Okay. Then I'll carry you."

It wasn't gallant. It wasn't dramatic. It was just instinct—the kind you default to when your brain runs out of better plans.

Marissa looked at him then. Really looked.

Something softened in her expression. Recognition. Gratitude, maybe. Or the understanding that he meant it.

"No," she said gently. "That won't help."

Jennifer moved immediately, closing the space before the moment could harden into something else. "We'll stay here with her," she said. "Alex and I can check the rooms we passed. You and Stacy take the other offshoots."

Brandon nodded, sweat beginning to bead along his hairline. He didn't argue. Arguing took energy he didn't have anymore.

Marissa didn't resist. She let her shoulder rest against the stone one second longer before pushing off. When she moved, it was slower now. Measured. Like she was budgeting herself.

And so we split.

Brandon and Stacy took the right-hand corridor, their lights angling away into the dark. Stacy was already talking—sharp, fast, filling the space with noise like she could outrun the quiet if she kept moving.

Jennifer turned left, toward the survey office. I followed.

Marissa came last. Not lagging—separate. Just far enough back that her light didn't overlap with mine.

The room we entered was smaller than the others.

Smarter.

This wasn't where work happened. This was where danger had been translated into numbers.

The air smelled faintly of paper rot, kerosene, and lard oil. The scent was rancid, like something that had been handled too much and then left alone to decay. Maps covered the walls—hand-drawn routes pinned to corkboard, their edges curled and brittle. Shafts, drifts, and crosscuts spidered across the paper in careful ink. Some were neat. Some frantic.

Several locations had been circled in red grease pencil.

X after X after X.

On one map, someone had written in block letters along the margin:

RESONANCE — LAYER 9 — DO NOT IGNORE

An arrow pointed inward, toward a narrow chamber marked with a single note:

HUM STRONGEST HERE

Below it, a date had been circled so hard the paper had torn.

3-18-1933

Something in my chest locked into place.

It matched the final entry on the generator log.

The cave-in.

Here, it didn't look like an accident.

It looked like an appointment.

Jennifer moved through the room with intent—drawers, desks, shelves. She opened filing cabinets just enough to glance inside, not committing to anything yet.

"Keys would've been hung," she said. "Visible. Accountable."

My headlamp swept over a row of cabinets. One drawer sat half-open, like it had been abandoned mid-thought.

Inside, the folders weren't labeled with names.

They were labeled with layers.

Marissa stayed near the doorway. Not searching. Not scanning.

Listening.

A clipboard lay face down on a desk, its pages curled with age. I left it there at first. It felt like the kind of thing you didn't touch unless you were ready for it to touch back.

Then the vibration shifted.

Not louder.

More precise.

I picked it up.

The paper looked like it had once been folded into quarters and pinned to a board, its edges browned and brittle, corners eaten soft by decades of bad air. Mineral bloom spidered along the margins like frost.

At the top, a triangular emblem was still faintly visible.

Embossed.

Not printed.

I knew it instantly.

The same symbol from the research flyer.

Only this time, there were letters beneath it.

O.S.R.D.

The typeface was old—struck hard enough to leave dents you could feel if you dragged your thumb across the page. The kind of machine that didn't ask if you were sure.

I leaned closer, squinting past water stains and time.

Whatever this was—

It was meant to *not* disappear.

And it definitely hadn't been meant for us to find it this way.

OFFICE OF
STRATEGIC RESEARCH & DEVELOPMENT
Subsurface Division — Preliminary Authorization
Bennington Site
March 14, 1933

My chest tightened.

The following site has been approved for initial extraction testing following confirmation of a high-density anomalous mineral deposit located beneath the ninth stratigraphic layer.

Early samples demonstrate unusual resonance properties when exposed to mechanical vibration and electrical current.

Further analysis is recommended in coordination with Project HELIOS, pending final approval.

Comparable material signatures have been tentatively identified in recovered artifacts from a recent archaeological excavation near [ILLEGIBLE], Iraq, though full provenance remains unverified.

Due to the instability of the surrounding limestone and the material's apparent interaction with human sensory perception, all personnel are advised to limit exposure time until containment protocols are finalized.

That was where the ink gave up.

The rest of the page had been eaten away by moisture and time, the words dissolving into nothing but fibers and dust.

In the margin—barely legible now, but pressed hard enough that the grooves still caught my light—someone had written by hand:

Auditory effects reported. Teeth.

The words sat there like a diagnosis that never made it into a report.

I stared at the date again.

1933.

Project HELIOS.

My mouth went dry.

Whatever this was, it wasn't mining. And it wasn't meant to be buried and forgotten. It had been placed here—studied, measured, pushed until it pushed back.

Behind me, Jennifer shifted. "Alex?"

Marissa didn't move from the doorway.

"I told you," she said quietly. "They knew."

I didn't look at her when I answered.

"I think they were trying to figure out how much they could touch it," I said. "Before it touched back."

The hum smoothed. Like something had been waiting for us to catch up.

My light drifted back to the wall—to the map with the torn date, the red grease-pencil circle scarred into the paper like a wound that never healed. Without really deciding to, I reached up and tore it free.

The sound was small. Dry. Final.

The cork resisted for a second, then gave way. I folded the map quickly, once, then again, creasing it along lines that had already been bent by other hands, other decisions. I slid it into my pocket and felt the weight settle there—thin, but deliberate.

Proof.

Or a warning.

Marissa's gaze followed the empty space where the map had been.

"They knew," she said again—not accusing. Not afraid. Just... stating a fact that no longer needed proof.

We moved on.

The next room was the locker room.

Human scale. Human mess.

I slowed without meaning to.

The locker room was warmer than the corridor, the air thicker, holding onto old heat the way bodies do after they're gone. As I stepped through the doorway, the fabric of my shirt dragged against my back—and pain flared sharp enough to steal half a breath from me.

I reached back, fingers sliding under the torn cotton.

The scratches were still there.

Not deep enough to bleed through anymore, but raised—angry lines crossing my shoulder blade and spine, scabbed in places, raw in others. Those things hadn't just ripped the pack free. They'd taken skin with it. Left me marked.

When the frequency shifted closer, the scratches burned. Not unbearable—just present. Insistent. Like the cave was reminding me it had power; it knew where I'd been touched and could do it again.

I let my hand fall away.

This wasn't the moment to say anything. We'd seen worse injuries. There were still worse things waiting.

I rolled my shoulders once, testing the pull, and kept moving.

Rows of rusted lockers stood in crooked lines, their paint blistered and peeling, doors dented outward in places—as if something had pushed from the inside and failed. Nameplates were still bolted to the fronts. Some bent. Some clean.

Benches ran down the center, scarred and gouged by decades of boots, boredom, jokes told too many times. The kind of room built for bodies that expected to leave at the end of a shift.

Actual steel-toed boots lay scattered near the far wall.

One pair stood upright on its own, toes angled forward like they'd been mid-step when the rest of the body decided not to follow. The leather had hardened into something almost reflective, thin seams threaded with dusted orange mineral—as if it had grown there instead of settled.

Jennifer stepped inside carefully. Her shovel tapped once against a bench as she leaned forward to look underneath.

A lunch pail sat nearby, its metal buckled inward like it had been squeezed by a hand that didn't know restraint. The latch had fused shut, rust webbing across it in delicate, deliberate patterns.

"Can I get some light?" she called.

I moved closer, sweeping my headlamp along the lockers.

Most were shut. Some were cracked open just enough to suggest interruption. One hung wider than the rest.

The nameplate was still intact.

CALDWELL, J.

"Bingo," I said, nudging the door.

A small screech tore free from it.

Inside, the space was orderly.

A helmet hung from the top hook, its lamp cracked but not shattered. A jacket was folded beneath it, the sleeves neatly tucked in. A ration tin sat unopened on the lower shelf.

Someone who expected to come back.

Pinned to the inside of the locker door was a piece of yellowed paper.

Handwritten. Careful. I read it aloud.

Sorry, James. Had to borrow the generator key.
Lights have been acting up again.

Don't wait up.
—Ed

That was it.

No urgency. No warning. Just the assumption of time.

"So the key's with Ed," Jennifer said.

Marissa hovered in the doorway.

She didn't step fully into the room. Instead, she leaned back against the stone, eyes closing—not like she was tired, but like she'd finally found a place where she was allowed to stop.

Her palm flattened against the wall.

She adjusted her hand—slow, careful—like touching something hot that hadn't crossed the line into pain yet.

The hum shifted immediately. Steadier. Focused.

Marissa exhaled.

Then she leaned her head, cheek and ear pressed to the stone. She listened the way you listen to a body when it stops hurting—not to enjoy it, but to make sure it doesn't start again.

Her sleeve stayed tucked beneath her nose. Her breathing went shallow, even. She didn't comment on the smell, or the air, or the way the vibration thickened here like recognition.

"Marissa?" Jennifer said.

"I'm alright," she replied gently. "It's just—pressure."

Jennifer didn't move.

Neither did I.

Maybe we should have said something.

Down the hall, Stacy's voice cut through the space—loud, sharp, alive.

"Guys! Guys—I found something!"

"Guess it's our lucky break," I said, already turning toward Jennifer.

That's when Marissa slid down the wall.

Her back met the stone fully this time.

Her palm never left the Eurydium vein threading through it.

"Marissa," Jennifer said, already crouching beside her. "Hey. Look at me. What is it—are you alright? Here, take off your bag."

Jennifer helped shrug her out of it, and Marissa winced like the effort itself hurt. Her lips pressed together, skin cracked now, split at the corners. She swallowed hard before speaking.

"I just..." Her breath stuttered. "I can't. Please. Just—let me stay here. Just a little longer."

Jennifer's voice sharpened instantly. "You're not staying here alone—"

"GUYS!" Stacy shouted from somewhere down the corridor. "Where are you?! Don't act like you can't hear me!"

Jennifer froze, torn, then looked at me.

"You go," I said. The words came out steadier than I felt. "I'll stay with her."

She hesitated—just a fraction of a second—then nodded. "Marissa —can I borrow your flashlight? I'll be right back. I promise."

Marissa lifted the light with hands that shook more than they should have.

Her nails were wrong.

Clouded. Brittle. The edges caught the beam strangely, throwing off little prismatic flares beneath the dirt—like glass that hadn't decided what shape it wanted yet.

I told myself it was dust. Stress. The cave messing with my eyes.

She pressed the flashlight into Jennifer's palm.

"Go," I said.

Jennifer ran.

Her light receded fast, swallowed by the corridor, and the dark folded in behind it like it had been waiting its turn.

For a moment, neither Marissa nor I moved.

Then she spoke.

"You should've gone with her."

"She's faster," I said.

"Yes," Marissa agreed softly. "She is."

The humming picked up.

"Marissa," I said. "Talk to me. What's happening?"

She smiled at me.

Clear. Almost relieved.

But her lip pulled wrong when she did it.

There was a small gap where a tooth should have been.

A thin line of blood slid from her nose. She didn't wipe it away. It traced her lip slowly before dripping onto her sleeve. Where it touched fabric, the fibers dulled—edges stiffening, crystallizing faintly, like frost deciding to become ice.

Her nails caught the light again.

Sharper now.

Promising.

She didn't notice any of it.

"It makes sense," she said quietly. "When you stop fighting it."

She lifted her hand fully and rested her fingers against the Eurydium vein running through the wall.

The mineral almost brightened.

Responded.

Her shoulders dropped.

Whatever tension she'd been carrying drained out of her like breath finally released.

"It doesn't hurt anymore," she said, almost surprised by the fact of it.

Her head tilted, listening past me. Past the room. Past the walls. Like the cave had leaned close and whispered something meant only for her, and she was being polite enough to hear it out.

Then—without ceremony—she stood.

No rush. No urgency. Just the quiet confidence of someone who knew exactly where they were going.

"Alex!" Jennifer screamed, her voice tearing through the dark as her flashlight bobbed back into view, light slicing across the stone.

My eyes flicked toward her for one second.

One.

When I looked back—

Marissa wasn't there.

No sound of footsteps. No scrape of boots. No shadow retreating.

Just absence.

"Marissa?" I said, the name coming out wrong, like I'd mispronounced it.

I stepped forward, light sweeping the wall, the floor, the space where she'd been leaning not even a breath ago.

"Marissa?!" I shouted.

The cave didn't answer.

It didn't echo her name back. It didn't mock me with sound.

It simply held the space where she should've been.

Empty.

And somehow... complete.

CHAPTER THIRTEEN

JENNIFER CAME BACK SECONDS LATER—WITH Brandon and Stacy hard on her heels.

Stacy's eyes were wide, too bright, like they were reflecting something that wasn't there anymore. Brandon's face had gone gray, his breathing uneven. Blood glistened at the corner of his mouth before he wiped it away with the back of his hand, distracted, like he hadn't noticed it happen.

Jennifer stopped short when she saw me standing alone.

"Where's Marissa?"

"I don't—" I tried.

Nothing came out. The word stalled somewhere between my chest and my throat and refused to finish the trip.

"Marissa! Get out here!" Stacy called. "We think we found something!"

For a moment, no one moved.

Stacy's beam swept past me, then the doorway, then down the corridor where we'd lost Matt. She didn't step closer. She didn't look at my face.

"She's not here—" I finally said.

"What do you mean, *not here*," she said, already shaking her head. "She wandered off?"

"Stacy—" Jennifer started.

"She does that," Stacy cut in too fast. "She zones out. She listens to stuff no one else does. She probably followed a sound or—whatever. She'll come back. She always comes back."

She stared down the corridor like if she held it in place long enough, it would obey her. Like the dark could be bullied into giving something back.

Brandon swallowed. His mouth worked like he wanted to say something and didn't trust himself to choose the words.

Jennifer looked at me again.

"Alex?"

I opened my mouth.

"It took her," I said. "One moment she was standing beside me, and the next... she wasn't."

I swallowed. "She didn't fight it. She just—went."

The words landed final. Heavy.

I argued with myself the way you argue with a bad memory—like if you turn it over enough times, the edges will soften, and the thing will stop cutting you.

But Marissa didn't soften.

She wasn't dragged away. Not screaming. Not taken the way Kevin had been taken, as if the cave had reached up and claimed him.

Marissa had waited until her name was called.

Like she'd had an appointment.

"You're telling me there's another one of those—those *things*—in here?" Stacy said, stepping closer. "That it just... happened again?"

"It's not that simple," I said. "If there were another one, we'd know. The tapping. The cries. The warning signs."

I shook my head. "This was different. Something took her—and she chose to follow it."

"No," Stacy said immediately, voice tight. She pressed her palms to her temples like she could physically force the idea back inside. "No. That wasn't real. That wasn't—she didn't get taken. She didn't *leave*. People don't just... opt out of reality like that."

Jennifer stood a few feet away, shovel braced against the ground, knuckles white around the handle. She didn't look toward the corridor. She kept her eyes on Stacy the way you keep your eyes on someone stepping too close to a ledge.

"Stace," Jennifer said. Steady, but not soft. "Hey. Look at me."

"She was right there," Stacy said. "How does someone just *vanish* when you're standing there pretending you're paying attention?"

My head dropped. In the back of my mind, I told myself there was some truth to her words. That there was more I could've done.

"Regardless," Brandon said, exhausted, "she went."

"That does not mean it makes sense," Stacy snapped. "It doesn't mean we just—accept it like a scheduling error."

"It doesn't," I said.

My voice surprised me—how even it sounded. Not calm. Something flatter. Like the cave had sanded off the top layer of panic and left the rest behind.

"But it happened. Something... got her."

Stacy rounded on me. "Wow. Okay. Cool. So that's it? We just... log her under *unexpected losses* along with Matt, Kevin, and the other guy and move on?"

"His name was Josh," I said, staring at the floor.

Stacy flinched—just for a second. Then she looked away.

"I know that," she said too quickly. "I just—this is not the moment for trivia."

Jennifer stepped closer—not blocking Stacy, not crowding her. Just there.

"No one's moving on," she said. "But we don't fall apart here. Maybe we can—"

"I am *not* falling apart," Stacy said immediately.

Her breath hitched on the next inhale.

Jennifer didn't call her on it. "Breathe anyway."

She swept the room with her light again—slower this time.

"Her bag's still here," she said.

It sat where Marissa had left it, slumped against the stone near the locker room doorway. The straps were loose, the zipper half-open like she'd meant to come back for it.

I crouched and pulled the bag toward me. It felt heavier than it should have. Inside: a pencil case. Her roll of duct tape. A pair of gloves she didn't wear. And her notebook.

I pulled it out.

"What are you doing?" Stacy asked, before turning her attention back to the darkness like she heard something.

"The way she talked," I started, flipping it open. "It was like she knew something. Like she understood something we didn't yet."

I scanned the pages.

The first few looked normal enough—observations, rough sketches of Eurydium, margin notes written in her precise, careful handwriting.

"She wrote down practically every word Brandon said." I looked up for a moment.

"Glad someone was listening," Brandon said, but there was no humor in his face.

The farther I read, however, the less her words behaved.

Sentences shortened. Then vanished.

Diagrams repeated. The same curve, over and over again. Arrows pointing inward with nothing labeled at the center. Notes layered on top of themselves until the page looked worn thin.

One page was nothing but lines.

Not random. Measured. Slight variations between each one, like she'd been tuning them. Listening for something the rest of us couldn't hear.

Jennifer leaned in. Her breath caught.

"This isn't—" she started, then stopped. "This isn't gibberish."

"No," I said.

Stacy shook her head. "She was stressed. We all are. That doesn't mean—"

"She was figuring something out," Jennifer said quietly.

I turned another page.

Toward the end, the writing almost disappeared entirely. No words. Just shapes. Patterns. The same mark drawn again and again, tighter each time, like she'd been closing in on the right version.

On the very last page, one line had been pressed so hard into the paper it tore.

Not a note.

Just a sentence.

Help them.

I closed the notebook.

Brandon scrubbed a hand through his hair and started pacing. Took three steps. Stopped. Forced himself still.

"I need everyone to listen to me," he said too fast. He winced, then tried again. "Okay. I need you to actually listen, because I think I was wrong."

Stacy let out a short, brittle laugh. "Fantastic. This day just keeps giving."

"Not wrong-wrong," Brandon said quickly. "Just... incomplete. The radiation thing doesn't fully explain this. What we're seeing—it's too clean. Too reactive."

"Reactive," I said. The word felt wrong in my mouth—too scientific for something that felt personal.

Brandon nodded. "Like it's responding to us."

"Stop," Stacy said. "Stop saying it like it's aware. Like it's making decisions. Because if it is, then this isn't an accident—and I don't know how to live in a world like that."

"It doesn't have to be aware," Brandon said quietly. "That's the problem."

The silence pressed in around us, thickening, like the cave had leaned closer to hear what we'd decide next.

Jennifer tightened her grip on the shovel. The metal squeaked faintly where her hand shifted—too loud in the quiet. "Okay," she said. "Then we work with what we know. We keep moving. We stay together."

"And if together isn't safe?" Stacy shot back.

Jennifer hesitated.

Just for a second.

And Stacy saw it.

Jennifer's gaze flicked to me, then back to Brandon. "You said something earlier," she said. "About the miners. About how they didn't... lose it down here."

Brandon blinked. "What?"

"What they did," Jennifer said. "To keep themselves together. Say it again."

Brandon swallowed. His eyes tracked upward, unfocused, like he was reading something that wasn't there anymore. "Long hours underground, mixed with the silence..." He tried for casual and failed. "It messes with your head. That's why they kept talking. Singing. Anything to keep sound moving."

Stacy let out a sound that wasn't quite a laugh. "So what, we're doing show tunes now?"

Her voice cracked halfway through the sentence.

"Because Marissa is—"

Her flashlight strobed—hard white flashes snapping the room into broken pieces—walls, faces, shadows jumping out of sequence—

And then it died.

Dark slammed closer.

Stacy froze, breath hitching sharp. "No—no, no—"

Jennifer moved instantly.

She didn't hesitate. She shoved her flashlight into Stacy's hands. Marissa's.

"Here," she said. "Take mine. You'll need it more than I will."

Stacy stared at it like it might disappear too. Her fingers closed around it anyway.

And that was when Stacy folded.

Her knees buckled. She dropped, hands clamped over her face like she could hold herself together by force.

Jennifer dropped with her without setting the shovel down, resting it against her shoulder, one hand still gripping the handle, the other locking onto Stacy's arm—firm, grounding, undeniable.

"I'm sorry," Jennifer said.

No explanations. No reassurances.

Just truth.

Stacy shook her head hard. "No. No, this isn't—this isn't how this goes."

I crouched too, forcing myself into her line of sight. Her pupils were blown wide, headlamp glare caught in them like panic had turned her into a mirror.

"What did you want?" I asked.

She stared at me like I'd slapped her.

"What kind of question is that?" she hissed.

"What did you want," I repeated, quieter. "Before this. Before the cave. Before Matt and Kevin and Josh. Before it all went sideways."

For a second, I thought she might swing at me.

Then something shifted—less defensive, more exposed.

"I didn't want this," she said. "I wanted to stay home."

Jennifer stilled. Brandon stopped pacing.

"Then why come?" I asked.

"I asked her to," Jennifer said before Stacy could stop her. "I wanted to meet you. To see what it was like down here. I wanted to... be brave about something for once." She huffed, the corner of her mouth twitching despite everything. "And yeah, okay—turns out this was not the low-stress bonding opportunity I envisioned."

I snorted despite myself. The sound felt wrong and necessary at the same time. "High marks for understatement."

"We have to leave," Stacy said suddenly, pulling away, forcing herself upright. "We have to get out of here. Try that corridor again—"

"What is she talking about?" I asked, turning to Jen and Brandon.

"We thought we saw something," Brandon said. "But it didn't make sense."

Stacy sucked in a breath and pointed her flashlight down the corridor she and Brandon had taken. Her hand shook so badly the beam jittered across the walls.

"We saw it," she said. "Down there. At the end. A light."

Jennifer's jaw tightened.

"It was blue," Stacy said. "Not glowing. Not shaking. Just... there. Like daylight. Like a sky. I swear I heard birds."

Brandon winced. "It could've been a reflection. Mineral deposits can—"

"It was not a rock trick," Stacy snapped. "It was real. And I'm not ending up like Marissa."

Jennifer exhaled through her nose, slow and controlled. "We can't chase it," she said—not just to Stacy, but to the room. "We split up, we die faster."

"We can't stay here," Stacy shot back. "We don't even know if that stupid generator thing works. And even if it does, it's not an exit. It's a stall."

She looked between us, daring someone to contradict her.

"I'm not dying in a cave because you people want to play electrician."

And like the cave had been waiting for her to say it—

—we heard it.

Clink.

The sound slid down the access tunnel.

Then something smaller.

Tighter.

A series of them, thin, glassy taps, like teeth tapping together in a mouth too full of hunger.

My skin prickled. Not fear. Recognition.

Brandon went pale. "It's here," he whispered.

Jennifer rose in one clean motion. The shovel came up with her like a promise she fully intended to keep.

The tapping multiplied.

Not louder—closer. A chorus syncing to itself, overlapping and adjusting, the way something approaches when it isn't worried about time. When it knows you'll still be there when it arrives.

"They—it—made it through," I said, and my voice didn't shake.

I hated what that steadiness cost.

Hated how tempting it was to let go and stop paying.

Brandon's gaze snapped to the generator room door—rusted steel, thick as guilt, the kind of door built to outlast men. "We need that door open—*NOW!*"

"We don't have the key," Stacy said, and it came out like a wail she hadn't meant to make.

"We don't need it!" Jennifer said.

Then she sprinted.

We followed.

.   .   .

THE CORRIDOR to the generator room felt longer than it had any right to be, as if distance itself had become another variable the Eurydium could tune. The sounds behind us sharpened as we ran, clarifying into pattern, the clicking resolving into a rhythm that made my molars throb.

My headlamp flickered.

For half a second, the dark felt organized. Like it knew where I was.

A metallic taste bloomed at the back of my tongue—sharp, sudden, like I'd bitten down on a coin. I swallowed hard and forced it down. Pain was a distraction. Distractions were how people lost control.

Jennifer slammed her shoulder into the generator door.

Metal rang through the chamber.

The sound wasn't just loud—it announced us. She didn't care.

"Jen—" I started.

The creatures shrieked in answer.

"Stacy—your light!" Jennifer snapped, already jamming the shovel blade into the rusted seam, wedging it like a lever. "Now! I need it now!"

Stacy skidded to a stop behind her, breath ragged. For half a second the beam wavered—wild, unfocused—then she forced it steady with both hands and locked it onto the seam where Jennifer was prying.

"I'm here," Stacy said, voice tight. Not encouragement. Instruction. To herself. To the light. To the universe.

Brandon and I turned just as a shape entered the edge of our beams.

Not fully.

Not cleanly.

Just a shape where the corridor should've been empty.

It clung to the wall, half outside the beam, half inside it, like it was testing how much of itself it needed to exist. The light caught movement before it caught form—something pulling itself forward in short, violent increments. Stop. Jerk. Stop again. As if walking had been an inefficient suggestion it had abandoned.

My headlamp flickered.

"No, no, no, no! Not now!" I barked at it.

For half a second, the dark felt organized. Like it knew where I was. Then it flashed back on.

The thing shifted closer, and my beam skimmed across it—not enough to explain it, just enough to make my stomach drop. Limbs bent where they shouldn't. Joints locked, then flowed, then locked again. Claws dug into the stone and stayed there, nails scraping as it hauled itself forward.

Its mouth opened.

It screamed.

Not loud.

Directional.

The sound punched through the chamber in a narrow arc, sharp enough that my vision stuttered, like the world had skipped a frame.

Stacy flinched—but she didn't drop the light.

"Oh God," she whispered, then louder, sharper, "Jen—move!"

Brandon swung his flashlight beam like it was a weapon. "We need more light!" He yelled—and I couldn't tell if he meant it for Jennifer or Stacy.

Stacy pivoted, sweeping her beam wide—not graceful, not precise, but intentional—forcing the light into every pocket of shadow they tried to cling to.

"I'm trying!" she yelled, voice cracking. "They won't—there's too many—"

Another shape peeled out of the dark.

Then another.

I couldn't see all of them. Just pieces—a limb here, a shoulder there, flashes of motion intersecting with sound.

"Stacy!" Jennifer shouted again, frantic. "Keep me lit!"

Their calls overlapped, folded over one another, the space reshaping itself into something that listened back.

They weren't watching us.

They were listening to themselves.

"I almost got it! Keep holding them back!" Jennifer shouted.

My hands were shaking.

I tightened my grip anyway.

"As opposed to what!" I yelled, and lifted the pickaxe.

The first one dropped from the wall in a blur. It hit the ground on all fours and surged forward so fast my stomach lurched like I'd missed a step on stairs.

I swung the pickaxe down.

I didn't hesitate.

The impact rang up my arms, wrong and heavy, like striking something that wasn't meant to break. The blade bit deep—too deep—and the creature shrieked, the sound tearing through the tunnel hard enough to bleach my vision white.

It collapsed in a tangle of limbs.

Still screaming.

I raised the pickaxe again.

And that was when the light finally caught.

Not the whole body.

Just enough.

The beam slid across torn fabric—dark, thick, old. Wool. Something like suspenders fused into the body beneath, no longer separate from bone. The chest convulsed, splitting where I'd struck, and for one frozen second the past pushed through the present.

Canvas.

Miner's black.

A name tag, still stitched on, stubborn as rot.

J. CALDWELL.

The name hit me like a slap.

For one awful, silent second, I wondered if Marissa realized this, too.

"It's the miners!" I shouted, my voice tearing on the words. "Look at the uniforms!"

Brandon's face twisted—horror folding into something worse. Vindication. Like part of him had known and had been begging to be wrong.

"Jesus Christ," he breathed.

Another one shifted toward him.

A miner's helmet was welded to its skull, metal and bone grown together so seamlessly I couldn't tell where each ended. The lamp mounted at the front was long dead—glass clouded, casing rusted shut

—but it still faced forward, fixed in place like it remembered what it was supposed to do.

Its head turned.

One eye was missing.

Its hollow socket collapsed inward, dry and wrong, like whatever had turned to dust. The other eye caught Brandon's light and reflected it back, glassy and unfocused, offering no sense of sight.

Brandon swung the rod.

It pierced through the miner's torso with a sick, chalky crack. The creature shrieked, limbs scrambling uselessly as Brandon shoved it back, boots skidding on stone.

Then another shape lunged. And another.

Their skin was wrong. Too thin. Too tight. Translucent in places, stretched over bone that didn't look like bone anymore. Something crystalline threaded through it, replacing veins with rigid filaments that caught the beam and held it, glowing faintly only when the light struck just right.

And their teeth—

Their mouths hung slightly open, lips split as if something inside had pushed too hard, too long. The teeth weren't teeth anymore. They'd overgrown into jagged, orange-clear crystal, fused together in places, catching my headlamp like cut glass.

My mind leapt backward without permission.

Marissa's mouth.

The blood she'd swallowed like it didn't matter.

Our missing teeth.

Oh, God.

They kept coming.

Jennifer didn't look back. She couldn't afford to. Every ounce of her attention was wedged into the shovel, into leverage, into the stubborn physics of rust and refusal.

Stacy turned her head, her flashlight shaking.

And that was the moment she chose movement.

"I won't," she said.

It was barely louder than a breath—so small I almost missed it beneath the screams and the scraping metal. Then she said it again, steadier this time, like repetition made it truer.

"I'm not dying in a cave," Stacy said, voice shaking but clear, "I won't become one of them. If there's a way out—I'm taking it!"

"No—" Jennifer started.

Too late.

Stacy turned and ran.

"Stacy!" Jennifer shouted, but Stacy was already halfway down the corridor, her flashlight beam bucking wildly, scattering across stone.

For one suspended heartbeat, the creatures hesitated.

Their bodies stilled. Heads tilted. Listening.

Then two of them pivoted in perfect unison, mouths opening, teeth clicking as that focused sound poured out—not louder, not frantic.

Precise.

They didn't go for Jennifer's shovel.

They didn't go for Brandon's pipe.

They didn't go for my pickaxe.

They went for the one who was alone.

"Look," Brandon whispered, his voice breaking around the word.

"They go after the isolated," I said—and the realization tasted like swallowing glass.

"If we can get the lights on," Jennifer said, forcing the words through clenched teeth, "she might still—"

But she didn't finish.

None of us did.

CHAPTER FOURTEEN

WE THREW ourselves at the door.

At the idea that light might still matter if we moved fast enough.

"If we get them on," Brandon said, breath tearing in and out of him, "if we flood the tunnels—"

"—they won't touch her," Jennifer finished, already moving.

No one said what could happen if we were wrong.

Jennifer wrenched the shovel free and slammed it into the seam again, metal screaming against rust. "Guys—I cracked something!" She yanked it free, eyes blazing. "Here. Wedge here!"

Brandon jammed the flat edge of his pipe into the gap and leaned in like he was prying open a coffin. I followed, driving the pickaxe head into the widening split, every muscle in my back screaming as we put our weight into it.

The rust fought us.

The metal groaned.

Then the lock snapped with a sound too clean, too final—like a bone breaking where it was never meant to.

The door gave an inch.

Then another.

Jennifer planted her feet and shoved, hair spilling loose from beneath her helmet, her face twisted with effort, lit from below like she'd stepped out of some older story where women don't wait to be rescued.

The door swung open—

And stopped.

Something held it from the other side.

"Barricaded," Brandon panted, disbelief cracking his voice. "Why would—"

"Doesn't matter," Jennifer snarled.

We shoved again.

Wood splintered. Something scraped and collapsed inside. The barricade groaned, then slid, and the door finally gave way.

The smell hit us first.

Dryness. Old sweat. Rust.

And something beneath it—faint, sour, intimate—that made my stomach tighten like my body already knew what my eyes were about to confirm.

We squeezed through.

The generator room was small, tight, wrong. Crates lay toppled and broken, shelving ripped from the walls, everything shoved inward toward the door in a last, frantic geometry of survival. Tools, boards, a collapsed chair—someone had tried to build a bunker out of panic and bad equipment.

And beyond it, slumped against the far wall, was what was left of a man.

He wasn't fresh.

There was no rot. No wetness. No softness.

He'd dried.

The cave had done what caves sometimes do—it preserved the wrong things. His skin had shrunk tight over bone in places, darkened and leathery like paper left too close to heat. In others, it had pulled away entirely, revealing pale ribs, the hollow grin of a skull.

Not mummified in any clean, cinematic way.

Not wrapped. Not sacred.

Just... held.

His ears were stained dark.

And when our lights found his face, I saw it—the dried tracks from his ears down his neck, a crusted sheen where something had bled and never stopped.

A screwdriver lay near his hand, its tip darkened brown.

His uniform was still on him, stiff with age.

PARSE, stitched over the chest.

Brandon swallowed hard. "Jesus," he whispered.

It didn't sound like faith. It sounded like bargaining.

Jennifer moved first. She stepped carefully over the debris, reverent without meaning to be, and crouched beside the body.

"There's something in his pocket," she said.

She pulled free a folded paper.

A note—preserved by the same dry air that had kept him here like a warning no one listened to.

She held it up in the cone of her flashlight. Her lips moved as she read silently, then she looked at me, eyes wide in a way I hadn't seen since daylight.

"Read it," Brandon said hoarsely.

He'd already moved past us, crouched at the generator, hands gliding over the machine as if he were looking for instructions.

"Let's hope this thing was serviced," he muttered.

Jennifer swallowed.

Then she started from the top.

> 3-21-1933
>
> It's been three days since the cave-in took the boys, and the elevator with it.
>
> But they're still here. We heard them after.
>
> We tried digging them out, but something changed them.
>
> They looked like us, but wrong. Deadringers.
>
> The boys came at us. Reaching. Pulling us into the dark.
>
> The lights kept them back. They hate the lights. We've

attuned each breaker in the control room to hold them back,
and I've kept them on as long as I could.
    Still, they're picking us off... one by one.

Jennifer stopped.
"The switches," she said. "They're primed. We just need the generator."
Behind us, something scraped stone.

    I thought if I didn't let it go quiet, go dark, they couldn't find us.
    Now it's just me.
    They pound on the door when it's silent. One at a time. Like they're taking turns.
    The humming won't stop. You hear it even when you don't.
    It worms its way into everything. Even the very foundation, breaking it apart.
    Then it settles in your jaw. Behind your teeth.
    It wants in through the ears.
    I won't let it.

Jennifer's voice faltered on those words, and when she paused, the generator room didn't feel safer. It felt like we'd stepped into the cage of something that had already swallowed other people whole.

    If anyone finds this—don't let that damned mineral leave this cave.
    It spreads. It infects. It tells you lies.
    And if rescue never comes,
    I loved you, Winnie.

Every day.
Give all my love to baby Jim.
—Edward

Jennifer folded the note with hands that wouldn't quite obey her and looked at Brandon.

"It's the hum," she whispered. "The Eurydium. Its radiation. And... like some kind of parasite."

Brandon's eyes were glassy now. Red-rimmed. He nodded once, slow. "The frequency. That's what took Marissa. She listened too long."

He met my eyes—not with triumph, not with relief. Just sickness. Like knowing the answer didn't come with instructions for survival.

I looked at the dead miner—Parse—at the dried blood staining his ears, the note clenched in his pocket like a secret he'd tried to keep to himself until the end.

Jennifer moved.

"Get it running," she said, absolute. "Now!"

Brandon wiped his sleeve across his mouth. The machine squatted against the wall—rusted, massive, ugly. Thick metal casing. A heavy wheel half-buried in dust. Hoses stiff with age.

"There's gas," Brandon said, more to himself than us. He twisted a valve low on the side. It fought him, squealing like it resented the attention—then loosened. "Old, but—yeah. There's still something in there."

The smell hit immediately.

Sharp. Sour. Rotting fuel mixed with metal and wet stone. It burned the back of my throat and made my eyes water.

I grabbed the wheel with both hands.

"What do I do?"

Brandon flipped a small lever near the top. "I think you just haul it down."

"You think?" I asked, the wheel screeching to life.

Nothing.

I reset. Tried again.

"Come on," I muttered. Not to the machine. To us.

The generator coughed—a dry, angry sound, like something disturbed mid-dream.

Behind us, down the corridor, Stacy screamed.

"Again!" Jennifer shouted.

I threw my weight into it. The wheel spun. The machine shuddered violently, rattling hard enough that I thought it might tear itself apart—

Then it caught.

The engine roared to life in a brutal surge, raw and uneven, like something waking up furious about it. The generator bucked against its mounts. A belt screamed as it caught, throwing off a burst of gray smoke before settling into a hard, jittery rhythm.

The room vibrated.

The smell hit first.

Hot oil. Burnt dust. Metal heating too fast after years of cold. The exhaust pipe overhead rattled as it drew the worst of it away, the fumes ripping upward with a hollow, rushing sound—like the cave was exhaling something it had been holding onto for decades.

The lights came on all at once.

No warning. No mercy.

Yellow light flooded the tunnel outside, brutal and immediate, ripping shadows backward like they'd been dragged by a rope. Corners we'd only ever known as suggestions snapped into shape—raw rock faces, broken supports, scattered debris. The long stretch of corridor where Stacy had run was suddenly just... there. Ordinary. Exposed.

From somewhere beyond the doorway, the creatures reacted.

Not screams.

Something worse.

A sound like interference—like a signal tearing itself apart. Their harmonic calls fractured, collapsing into jagged noise that couldn't hold a pattern. Whatever order they'd been using dissolved. Something scraped frantically away into the dark, claws clattering, retreating fast and furious.

Then—

Silence.

Not the kind that promised safety.

The kind that confirmed we'd survived.

"They're backing off," Brandon said, awe bleeding through the fear. "The deadringers. They hate it."

Jennifer didn't look relieved. She didn't smile. "Good. C'mon—we have to find Stacy."

WE RAN. The generator bucked and roared behind us, vibrating itself angry and hot, the smell of oil and heat clinging to our clothes. The corridors were flayed open by light, the thrum of power chasing us like a second heartbeat we couldn't slow down.

The blue light Stacy had followed slowly came into view.

But now—with the floodlights burning—we could see what it really was.

The tunnel opened into a chamber wider than the others, collapsed long ago. Stone had fallen in sheets, sealing exits, crushing whatever hope had once been built into the space. Eurydium veins threaded the walls like frozen lightning, their glimmer radiant beneath the electric glare. Blood streaked the rock where someone had scraped it hard enough to leave skin behind.

And bodies were everywhere.

Frozen mid-motion.

Miners caught where they'd died—arms raised, mouths open, faces locked into the last shape they'd made before the cave ended them. Their skin had crystallized into brittle shells, translucent and pale, like statues pulled from ash.

A Pompeii of stone and silence.

The light slid across them in fragments as we moved—never long enough to take them all in at once.

A sleeve fused into stone, the cuff still dark with oil.

A helmet cracked clean in half, its lamp welded uselessly to a skull beneath it.

A jacket pinned mid-reach, fingers locked around nothing.

Names surfaced without permission.

HARVEY—stitched crooked over a chest that no longer rose.

JEFFERSON—half-buried near the wall, boots planted like he'd braced himself when the ceiling came down.

RICHARDS—collapsed near the center, one arm raised, palm open, as if he'd tried to shield someone smaller than himself.

They weren't piled.

They'd fallen where they stood.

Men caught in the act of choosing—run or stay, help or survive—crystallized mid-decision, the cave sealing them into its memory like it couldn't decide which version to keep.

I forced myself to look away.

Because the longer you stared, the easier it was to imagine the moment they'd realized it was already too late.

And Stacy—

She was near the center of the room.

Not running.

Not screaming.

Not moving at all.

She stood still. Her feet were planted in a narrow column of light that spilled down from a fracture high above—just a seam in the rock where daylight had found a way through mineral and time. The beam was thin, imperfect, barely enough to call illumination, but it held. It cut a pale line through the chamber like a rule drawn late.

The blue light she'd chased wasn't an exit at all.

Just daylight.

Filtered.

Distant.

She'd been right.

It was the sky.

For a moment, my body forgot how to move. Like the sight of her standing there—whole, breathing—had interrupted whatever momentum terror had built up in me. Relief tried to rush in, tripped over something, and fell apart halfway to my chest.

Jennifer didn't hesitate.

She took off in a sprint, boots slapping stone, breath already breaking loose like she'd been holding it in for hours. She was ready to throw her arms around Stacy, to grab her, to drag her back into proof—

And then she stopped.

Not skidding.

Not stumbling.

Just... halting. Like she'd reached the edge of something invisible. Like instinct had grabbed her by the spine and said *don't*.

"Stace," she said.

Her voice was steady, but her hands hovered uselessly at her sides.

Stacy's eyes flicked once.

Just once.

Enough to prove she was still here.

Her chest rose and fell shallowly, each breath measured like she was counting them out, rationing air. Her whole body shook—not violently, not in panic—but with the kind of tremor that comes from restraint pushed too far. Her hands were clenched at her sides, fingers curled tight around her flashlight, knuckles gone pale and bloodless.

She wasn't frozen from fear.

She was holding still.

I jogged closer, heart hammering, relief finally finding a crack to force itself through. "Don't worry, Stacy," I said, breathless, already half-smiling like that might make this real. "They're gone."

The words felt fragile the moment they left my mouth.

Stacy shook her head.

Small. Precise.

Her eyes never left the same spot.

The place she hadn't been looking away from since we arrived.

I followed her gaze.

And there—high above us, beside the chamber entrance—was an alcove.

Not a shallow cut.

Not a niche.

A hollowed space carved deep into the mining tunnel, wide enough to swallow light. The rock there curved inward like the inside of a lung, dark and expansive, shaped by something that had lingered.

And it wasn't empty.

Reflective, fogged eyes stared down at us, catching the electric light and distorting it. Too many points of shine. Too many angles.

Beneath them, crystalline teeth glimmered faintly, translucent and sharp, arranged in mouths that didn't quite remember smiling but remembered opening.

They hadn't crossed into the beam.

They hadn't retreated, either.

They were waiting.

Listening.

Stacy swallowed hard. I saw her throat work, the effort it took to make the smallest movement without breaking whatever fragile rule she'd figured out.

Her voice, when it came, was barely there.

"They're still here," she whispered.

CHAPTER FIFTEEN

NO ONE BREATHED.

The deadringers didn't move—but the feeling of them settling did. Like weight redistributing. Like a decision being postponed, not canceled.

My stomach dropped hard enough to make my knees feel hollow.

Jennifer didn't look at them again. She didn't need to. Her hand slid back until it caught Stacy's wrist, fingers wrapping tight—not yanking, not steering.

Anchoring.

"Okay," she said softly. Steady. Command without volume. "Nobody makes a sudden life choice. We just... stay together."

Stacy nodded once—too fast. Her eyes never left the alcove.

We moved backward as one shape. No turning our backs. No scrambling. Boots easing over stone like we were negotiating with gravity itself. Brandon's shoulder brushed mine, and neither of us pulled away. We stayed linked without admitting it.

Under each hanging light, we paused just long enough to make sure we were still all there.

Above us, the deadringers watched.

Their teeth clattered faintly, one by one. Heads twitching in unison as we shifted, crystalline mouths catching the light at angles that made my molars ache. One of them adjusted its grip on the ceiling—fingers flexing, toes digging in.

Listening.

Always listening.

We reached the mouth of the chamber.

Jennifer squeezed Stacy's wrist once. A signal.

Then we turned and moved.

The alcove vanished behind rock, but the pressure of it lingered—like something heavy pressing on the backs of my eyes. I didn't hear pursuit. I didn't hear anything at all except our breathing and the low industrial thrumming threading through the walls.

We didn't stop until the tunnel widened.

The chapel came into view.

Wax fused to stone. Offerings half-swallowed by mineral creep. The air felt heavier here—not hostile. Just... aware. Like memory had pooled and never drained.

We clustered without meaning to.

Stacy stopped first.

"I—I need my flashlight," she blurted. The words tripped over each other. "I left it. I need it. We need to go back."

"No," Jennifer said immediately. No softness. No edge. Just final. "We absolutely do not."

Stacy's hands clenched and released, over and over. "No, I need it. I don't have a weapon. I don't have anything. They're still here. They're still—"

"Stacy," Brandon cut in.

He stepped forward and pressed the rebar rod into her hands.

"Take this," he said, voice steadier than he looked. "Same rules as the flashlight. Point it where you mean it. Swing like you're offended."

She stared down at it, breathing hard. Wrapped her fingers around the metal like it might vanish if she didn't commit.

Then she nodded.

"Wow," Jennifer muttered. "Very medieval. Just like you said."

Stacy huffed once. "I'd look terrible in chainmail."

Brandon almost smiled.

Then he froze.

His gaze had landed on the wall.

The names.

Carved deep. Some crossed out. Some untouched.

"Hey," he said quietly. "Wait."

He stepped closer, breath shallow. "Harvey. Jefferson. Richards." He traced the stone without touching it. "They're listed. But none of them are crossed out."

I leaned in beside him.

"But Caldwell is," I said, following the clean, deliberate lines scored through the name.

Jennifer's jaw tightened. "They were tracking it."

"Tracking what?" Stacy asked, already knowing the answer.

"Who didn't make it," Jennifer said. "And who did... something else."

Stacy swallowed. "So this isn't—"

"It's not an infection," Brandon said immediately. Fast. Almost defensive. "Not random. Not automatic."

"It's conditional," I said.

The word sat there. Heavy. Unavoidable.

Jennifer nodded. "It needs permission."

We all felt it then—threading through the stone, patient as breath.

"You listen long enough," she continued, "you let it inside far enough... it gets a say."

Brandon shifted closer to Stacy—not crowding her, just there. "You and Jennifer didn't."

Stacy shook her head. "I heard it. I just didn't care."

Jennifer nodded once. "Same."

My throat tightened.

Marissa had listened. She had understood. She hadn't fought it... She'd answered.

"We need an exit," Jennifer said, already turning her focus outward. "Now. Alex—map."

My eyes went wide.

"Oh. Yeah. Right." I fumbled it out of my pocket, unfolding the paper carefully. The creases cracked where it had been folded too tight.

"Where'd you pick this up?" Brandon inched toward me.

"Survey office. Grabbed it when things were still pretending to be... *normal?*" I exhaled.

Brandon stepped in close, reading over my shoulder. His finger traced the lines slowly. Deliberately.

"...Okay," he said.

No disbelief. No panic.

Jennifer glanced over. "Okay... what?"

Brandon tapped the map with one finger, grounding himself in paper like it might push back. "This is us. Generator room. Chapel pocket. And here—" his finger slid, stopping on the thick red mark "—the cave-in. Before it decided to become an accident."

My chest tightened.

"It's still accurate," I said. Not hopeful. Just acknowledging a fact.

Brandon nodded. "Mostly. Time's chewed some of it down. Corridors narrowed. Pressure folded things inward."

"Not to mention cave-ins." Stacy threw in.

"Exactly," Brandon added, "But it's still usable."

He traced a route farther down the page.

"This corridor," he said. Softer now. "It's marked."

Stacy stiffened immediately. "Marked *how?*"

He rotated the map so we could all see.

A thin penciled line branched off the main passage. Not an exit. Not a shaft. Something else.

Bennington Memorial Site

Below it, smaller. Almost apologetic.

Ground loose, avoid.

Stacy stared at it. "I don't love that it's called a memorial," she said. "And I love even less that someone wrote avoid like it was optional."

"It means," Brandon said carefully, "that whoever drew this lived long enough to warn the next person."

"And that's supposed to make me feel better?" Stacy shot back.

"It means," he continued, undeterred, "that there's a place down here that wasn't meant for machinery. Or ore extraction. Or... whatever this became."

My eyes drifted to the wall. To the names. To the ones crossed out cleanly.

"Don't," Jennifer murmured.

I blinked. "Don't what?"

She met my gaze. Held it. Didn't soften.

"Don't stop," she said. "Don't listen. Not in here. We're close enough already."

She was right. I could feel it—how the hum sharpened when my thoughts slowed. Like it leaned in when you gave it space.

"She's right," Brandon said, and took the map from my hands.

That was when the blood came.

Not dramatic. Not sudden. Just a thin, red line slipping from his nose, tracking down his lip, his chin.

"——Brandon," I started.

He touched his face absently, then looked down at his fingers. Red. Wet.

A drop fell onto the headphones resting against his collarbone.

Jennifer clocked it instantly.

Her eyes flicked to the headphones.

Then back to his face.

"Put those on," she said. "Now."

Brandon blinked. "What?"

"The headphones," she repeated. No edge. No panic. Just fact. "If you're staying with us, you're putting them on."

His fingers closed around the cord like he'd just remembered it existed. He hesitated.

"I won't hear you," he said.

"That's the point," Jennifer replied. Calm as gravity. "If we need you, turn it low. But block out the hum. You just need to walk."

His jaw worked. Blood darkened his gums again, slow and persistent.

"You think it'll help?" he asked.

Jennifer didn't lie. "I think it's what we have."

She glanced at Stacy. Then back to Brandon.

"It starves it," she said. "Long enough."

Brandon exhaled through his nose. A breath that shook on the way out.

"Okay," he said.

He lifted the headphones and slid them over his ears. Careful. Deliberate. Almost ceremonial.

The wire trembled against his jacket.

He adjusted them once. Then again.

"Just in case," he said, already stepping backward, "I'm bringing up the rear."

Jennifer's head snapped up. "Brandon—"

"If this doesn't work," he said, meeting her eyes fully now, "I don't want to be between you and the exit. I can still guide us. I just... won't be in the way."

I held his gaze.

Then I nodded.

"Stay close," Jennifer said.

Brandon gave a thin, crooked smile. "I will."

And for the first time in a while, it didn't sound like a joke.

WE MOVED.

Beside Stacy, Jennifer didn't look shaken. She looked resolved. Because the act itself was the comment—the choice to keep walking, to stay upright, to refuse the cave the luxury of secrecy. If it wanted witnesses, it was getting them.

The station looked different now that it was lit. Less like a throat. More like a hallway in an abandoned plant. Bolted signage half-swallowed by mineral bloom. Concrete walls webbed with hairline cracks like veins. Rusted panels sunk into the stone, gauges fogged behind glass that hadn't reflected a human face in decades.

Structurally sound.

The only mercy we'd been offered.

The generator throbbed somewhere behind us, its pulse stretched thin by distance. Other than that, there was—

Nothing.

No screams.

No shuffling.

No harmonic calls carving space.

Just our boots. Our breath. And the frequency sliding under it all like a second layer of sound—close enough to mistake for thought if you weren't careful.

"There," Brandon said, pointing ahead. "That way."

He didn't linger on the other passages. Didn't second-guess. Just chose.

Every few steps, he glanced back, then forward again—measuring distance. Not from where we were going.

From where we'd been.

We continued our path under the hanging lights, staying close with bated breath.

"Keep moving," Jennifer murmured, like a spell she didn't want to break.

Then the tunnel dipped.

Not sharply—just enough that the floor darkened, the concrete turning slick, reflecting light in thin, broken sheets.

I noticed the sound first.

Not dripping.

Standing.

Water.

It pooled ahead of us, shallow at first—an inch, maybe two—spreading across the floor like the cave had decided to start holding its breath.

Brandon slowed. Stacy stopped.

Jennifer didn't.

She stepped forward, boot sinking with a soft, hollow sound.

"Knees at most," she said, testing the depth with her shovel. "We can cross."

Stacy swallowed. "Do we... have another option?"

She didn't look at Jennifer when she asked. She looked at Brandon.

Brandon checked the map, then checked the corridor behind us, then the water again.

"The map says forward," he said. "Unless we want to backtrack."

He didn't finish the sentence.

None of us wanted to go back.

Jennifer turned, eyes moving from face to face. Not commanding. Assessing.

"We don't stop," she said. "We don't wait. We don't let the cave decide for us."

Stacy let out a tight breath through her nose. "I hate that you're always right."

Then she stepped in.

No one argued.

The water crept higher as we waded—ankles, then calves—cold enough to bite through fabric, numbing fast. It smelled like dirt and clay and something older, like stone that had never expected to be exposed.

By the time it hit my knees, it felt less like water and more like resistance.

"Slow," Jennifer said. "No splashing."

"Like we're sneaking past God," Stacy muttered.

"God's not the one listening," Brandon said quietly.

That shut her up.

"Jennifer—take the map," Brandon said, lifting it higher. "Keep it dry."

She took it without breaking stride, raising it overhead. As she did, Brandon fished his portable CD player from his jacket pocket, lifting it awkwardly above the water like it was something sacred.

The normalcy of it hit me harder than it should have.

We were halfway through when the floor vanished.

One step.

Then nothing.

The cold swallowed me whole.

I went under hard—water rushing into my mouth, my nose, my chest—tasting like dust and rot and metal. My hands flailed, scraping stone, finding nothing.

I kicked.

Hit something solid.

Pushed.

When I broke the surface, I gagged violently, coughing muddy water back up in burning bursts, lungs seizing like they'd forgotten how air worked.

"Alex!" Jennifer shouted.

"I—" I hacked again, bracing myself against the far ledge. "I lost the pickaxe."

Jennifer was already holding the map higher, arms shaking now, paper trembling dangerously close to the waterline.

"Take it," she said. "It can't get wet."

Stacy waded behind her, white-knuckled around Brandon's rebar pipe.

Brandon stood behind her, water up to his chest, one arm raised high—CD player clutched like a lifeline.

I reached back toward Jennifer.

Fingers inches from the map.

And then—

Clink.

Soft. Careful.

Clink—clink.

It came from deeper in the station.

From the shadows.

From where the light didn't quite reach.

I froze.

My gaze snapped to the tunnel entrance.

And whatever breath I'd managed to steal back caught painfully in my throat.

Above us, the hanging bulbs dimmed.

Just for a moment.

Clink.

The lights sputtered back on, pulsing in and out.

"Everybody—move," I said through hoarse vocal cords.

Then the filament inside flared too bright, too fast—burning through the last of itself like it had been waiting for permission to die.

The bulbs went out.

Darkness rushed in to claim the space it had held. And beneath it all, we heard it.

Clink. Clink. Clink. Clink. Clink.

Splash.

CHAPTER SIXTEEN

THE DEADRINGERS THREW THEMSELVES FORWARD.

My headlamp let out a fuzzy, panicked cone of light slicing the black just in time to catch bodies peeling loose from the tunnel mouth. Limbs snapped outward. Joints bent wrong. Movements violent and overcommitted, like something lunging on bad math.

They weren't charging where we were.

They were charging where they thought we'd be.

"Alex!" Jennifer shouted.

I didn't answer. I surged.

Boots skidded on wet stone as I tore the map from her hands and jammed it inside my jacket without looking. My other hand locked around her wrist.

"Up—now!"

She stumbled, water sloshing loud around her legs.

The deadringers convulsed at it.

Heads snapped. Bodies jerked hard toward the noise. One lunged too far and slammed shoulder-first into the wall with a crack that echoed down the tunnel. Another pitched straight into the water, hit wrong, and shrieked as it thrashed blindly—glassy fingers scraping stone, legs firing uselessly.

Behind us, Brandon slipped.

"Guys—!"

Water surged up his chest.

Something latched.

He screamed once—sharp, startled—before it dragged him under.

The sound detonated the tunnel.

Everything reacted at once.

"Brandon!" Stacy shrieked.

She didn't hesitate.

She swung.

The rebar rod came down in a brutal arc and caught one of them across the side of the skull. The impact rang like striking a bell wrong —metal on glass on bone. The thing collapsed sideways into the water, convulsing, limbs spasming like wires shorting.

The noise was everywhere now—splashing, shouting, metal on stone, bodies hitting water—

And suddenly—

The deadringers lost us.

They lunged too hard. Too fast. Slamming into walls. Into each other. Into the flood. Several hurled themselves straight into the water, shrieking as they lost orientation, thrashing violently like insects trapped in a sink.

They weren't seeing us.

They were trying to hear through chaos.

"Jennifer—your shovel!" I yelled.

Jennifer didn't question it. She threw it to me and caught Stacy's arm, hauling her forward, both of them staggering out of the flooded stretch together.

Stacy nearly went down, boots skidding, but Jennifer held her upright through sheer refusal.

I didn't think.

I jumped.

The water swallowed me cold and filthy, tasting like dirt and clay and something ancient that had never planned on being disturbed. I kicked blindly, lungs already burning, hands scraping stone until they caught fabric.

Brandon.

His eyes were huge. Wild. One hand clawed at the thing latched to his shoulder, teeth snapping inches from his face.

I slammed the hand shovel into its mouth—bone too light, skin too tight—and its cheek tore, darkening the water around us. It recoiled with a shriek that vibrated through my teeth.

I grabbed Brandon and hauled.

We broke the surface together, both of us coughing violently as I dragged him toward solid ground. He retched hard, water pouring out of him, hands shaking too badly to help.

Behind us, the deadringers adjusted.

Not toward us.

Around us.

I saw it then—bodies peeling off the floor, climbing the walls and ceiling instead. Limbs splayed wide. Nails biting into stone. They moved like spiders avoiding a faucet, skirting the water entirely, crawling overhead without ever looking at us.

"They're—" Brandon gasped, choking. "They're not—"

"They can't see through the noise," Jennifer finished, breathless, the realization snapping into place mid-motion. "Sound scrambles them."

Static.

Signal interference.

"Oh my god," Stacy panted. "We're loud and confusing. It's like weaponized chaos."

"Don't stop being loud," Jennifer said. "Move!"

We lunged together down the corridor, boots slapping stone, water dripping, breath ragged and uncontained. My headlamp shook as I ran, the beam catching bodies clinging overhead—twitching, recalibrating, trying to triangulate us through the mess we'd become.

The tunnel tightened ahead.

A choke point.

The rock pinched inward, narrowing to something barely wider than a coffin laid on its side. Jagged stone pressed close enough that my shoulder scraped it as we pushed through, breath bouncing back into our faces, hot and panicked.

"This is bad," Stacy said, voice high and furious. "This is really bad architecture."

"Jennifer—Stacy!" Brandon yelled from behind us. "Go—go now!"

Stacy didn't argue. She lunged forward and threw herself into the gap, twisting sideways, the iron rod snagging for half a second before she yanked free with a curse.

Jennifer skidded to a stop instead, spinning back toward us.

"Brandon—"

"Go!" he shouted again. "Alex—after her!"

She hesitated.

Just a heartbeat. Just long enough to feel like time had teeth.

Then she turned and squeezed through, vanishing into the dark beyond.

I followed, twisting sideways, breath tearing out of me as stone scraped my ribs. The rock pressed close—too close—and for a split second my brain screamed *stuck*, screamed *this is where the earth wins—*

Then I spilled through.

I staggered forward, boots slipping on loose grit, sucking in air like I'd been underwater too long.

Behind me, Brandon slammed into the bottleneck just as something shrieked in the tunnel we'd left behind.

"Move!" he barked, forcing himself through, even as his shoulder clipped stone. "Move, move—"

The tunnel spat us out like it was done with us.

One second, we were crushed together by rock barely wider than our shoulders, breath ricocheting back into our faces—

The next, we were stumbling into space.

A hollow so vast my brain stuttered trying to understand it.

Cold air rushed over us, lifting the hair on my arms. A draft—steady, ancient. Like the exhale of something that had been holding its breath for a very long time.

My headlamp flickered.

Once.

Then again—longer this time, like it was considering giving up.

I slapped the casing with the heel of my palm.

"Don't you dare," I muttered.

The beam steadied. Shivered. Then pushed forward across the cavern in a shaking cone of pale light.

What it revealed didn't belong.

A shape.

Then another.

Then too many.

I took another step, and the ground crunched under my boots—soft wood splintering, soil shifting—and the sound crawled up my spine.

"Oh no," Stacy breathed. "Absolutely not."

It clicked.

Coffins.

Dozens of them.

Some crushed inward like soda cans, others split open along their seams, their insides spilling into the cavern like a history lesson no one had asked for. Wood splintered. Velvet rotted into dark stains. Hinges oxidized into rusted scars.

Skeletal arms protruded from pockets of soil overhead—curved, reaching downward, as if the bodies above had tried clawing through the earth before it swallowed them whole.

The ceiling wasn't a ceiling.

It was the underside of Bennington Memorial Cemetery. We were standing in a room the earth had made out of its own unresolved grief.

The ground above had slowly, relentlessly pushed them downward over decades. Gravity and rain and time conspiring until the dead cracked open and fell into the stomach of the earth.

"It's the—," Stacy whispered.

"Yes," Jennifer said.

There wasn't time for it.

Six feet above us, a thin sliver of daylight pierced through a crack in the ground. It painted the drifting dust in pale silver, like suspended snow.

For one stupid second, hope flared.

Then it died.

The light didn't reach far enough.

It didn't reach us.

My headlamp flickered again.

Harder this time.

"Alex, the light—" Jennifer started.

"I know!" I said, already moving it, already rationing where I aimed it.

"We don't have much time!" Brandon shouted, voice echoing too loudly in the open space. He frantically flipped the switch to his flashlight, but the beam wouldn't light.

"The battery's wet!" He yelled. "Stacy, throw me the rod!"

Stacy tossed it to him.

Brandon positioned himself at the entrance as the tapping grew to a roar.

My beam swept over the ground, the walls—anything that wasn't bone or broken wood.

"God—" Stacy cried. "It's in everything!"

At first, I only saw dirt.

Then the ground shifted—just slightly—and a faint orange pulse glimmered beneath the soil like a heartbeat under skin.

Eurydium.

Threaded through the dirt. Threaded through the coffins. Threaded through the bones.

Jennifer let out a sound that could've been a laugh. "So even death doesn't get to opt out."

She was right.

It was everywhere.

My headlamp sputtered.

Once.

Twice.

Then it went out.

And the cavern leaned closer as the dark swallowed us whole.

Stacy staggered back, the heel of her boot slipping on loose soil. Her breath hitched, sharp and ragged, and the sound of it punched panic straight into my throat.

"The light," she gasped. "The light—Alex, the light!"

I smacked the headlamp again. Harder. Once. Twice.

Nothing.

"Okay—phones!" Jennifer shouted. "Everyone—now!"

We flipped them open at the same time. But they were water-logged. Nothing lit.

Even if they had, they would've been fireflies lost in a cathedral of bone.

We instinctively closed ranks, shoulders brushing, backs nearly touching, like proximity alone could make us solid.

Stacy turned toward the seam of daylight above and screamed.

"HEY! PLEASE! HELP! ANYONE!"

Her voice echoed once—thin, desperate—then collapsed into the cavern like it had hit something soft and been absorbed.

The crack was too small.

Too high.

Too late.

"We're too deep!" I said.

Saying it out loud made it real. Made it something I could fight instead of pretending it wasn't happening.

Stacy slammed her fists into the dirt wall beneath the light, clawing at it like rage might rewrite physics. Soil sifted around her fingers, crumbling—then settling back into place like it had never been disturbed.

"This isn't working!" she screamed.

Then—

A small sound.

Soft.

Final.

Her tooth hit the ground.

Stacy froze.

"Stace—" Jennifer reached for her.

Stacy's eyes widened. Fury. Fear. Shame. All crashing together at once.

"No," she whispered. "No. Not me too. Not—"

Something squirmed through the bottleneck.

Thrashing.

Violent.

Then another.

Brandon's breath hitched. "Alex... I can't see anything."

My free hand found the camera at my belt.

Cold plastic. Familiar weight.

A last resort.

I lifted it.

Snap.

The flash detonated—pure white violence—splitting the dark open.

For a single stolen frame of existence, the entrance revealed itself:

Something standing at the far wall.

Humanoid. Almost.

Bent slightly. Head tilted toward Brandon, as if listening.

The flash died.

Darkness slammed back in.

Jennifer made a sound that wasn't quite a word.

Snap.

Another burst.

Five silhouettes now.

Closer.

Two climbing the walls.

Wrong in the way they held themselves. Wrong in the angles of their limbs. But there weren't just miners. There were others.

Gone again.

Snap.

They were in different clothes. One that could have been from the 1800s. Another from the 1960s. Then the 1980s. All frozen in a state between death. Corpses that failed to finish dying. Their bodies twitching like they were shaking off a dream. Their faces blurred under the intensity of the light—

The flash vanished.

And Brandon swung in the dark.

"PULL!" Brandon screamed.

I lunged for the nearest coffin lid. My fingers sank into the wood—and it gave way immediately, collapsing inward with a sound like paper tearing.

"I'm sorry!" I whispered.

The coffin split open, and whatever had been left inside slid free.

I dropped to my knees, grabbed the next one, hooked my fingers under rotted wood and ripped. It broke apart like soggy bread. Bones spilled out in pale arcs, clattering across the stone.

Jennifer didn't hesitate. She joined me, breaking each box that was left.

"What are you doing?!" Stacy recoiled.

"Making room!" I choked, hands plunging into damp soil. "If the coffins collapse, the dirt collapses—"

"What?!"

"And if the dirt collapses," I shouted back, voice tearing apart, "we climb!"

"This is insane!"

"Got a better idea?!" I snapped.

She dropped beside me hard, knees slamming into stone. She was shaking—full-body, no attempt to hide it—but her eyes were locked forward, jaw set like she'd made peace with something awful and was daring the universe to argue.

Wood splintered under her hands, sharp enough to slice skin. She hissed once—then kept going. Stacy followed her lead with a sound that was half a sob, half a curse, ripping boards free with a strength that surprised even her.

"God—this is so messed up," Stacy choked, flinging a skull aside. "I'm so sorry—"

"Later," I snapped. "Apologize later. Dig now."

Together, the three of us dragged skeletal remains free—parents, soldiers, children, people who'd once had names and futures and graves that were supposed to be final. We didn't look at their faces. We didn't let ourselves think about who they'd been.

I felt sick.

But not enough to stop.

The earth groaned overhead.

Not a sound—a decision.

Stone shifted. Soil loosened. The ceiling sagged.

Then—

Light.

A thin crack split open, fresh daylight pouring down like a blessing that didn't trust us to deserve it.

"Alex—now!" Brandon shouted.

And for the first time since we'd entered the caves, escaping didn't feel theoretical.

It felt possible.

But only if we moved right now.

I lunged upward, fingers clawing into damp soil that smelled like old rain and forgotten prayer. The slope wasn't really a slope—more like a wound in the earth that had barely decided to open for us. Every handful came away loose, collapsing behind my grip as fast as I could pull.

"Up!" Brandon yelled. "Jennifer—up, now!"

Jennifer didn't argue. She scrambled, boots slipping, hauling herself toward the opening with brutal efficiency. For a second her body blocked the light—then she was through, bracing herself above.

"Stacy!" she called down. "C'mon!"

"I'm moving!" Stacy shouted back, already scrambling, panic sharp but focused. "I'm moving!"

Brandon grabbed my shirt and shoved me toward the opening.

"You're next."

"No," I said immediately. "Brandon—"

"There's no time," he snapped—and this time the fear broke through, raw and unmistakable. "I'm taller than you—"

"That's not—"

He shoved me harder.

"You're next," he said again. Quieter now. Absolute. "Go."

Something in his voice told me arguing would waste seconds we didn't have.

I climbed.

The opening was tighter than it looked. Stone bit into my ribs. My boots kicked uselessly as gravity tried to remember me.

I got one knee up.

Then two hands locked around my boot and shoved.

I burst through into daylight.

I didn't stand.

I spun and dropped flat, arm plunging back into the hole.

"Brandon!" I screamed.

My fingers brushed something soft.

Plastic.

I grabbed and yanked.

Headphones surfaced into the light.

The cord dangled. Slack. Wrong.

"Brandon, I'm here!" I said.

Nothing answered.

Something moved below me, fast and wrong, and a hand—too cold, too sharp—clamped around my wrist and wrenched.

Pain exploded up my arm as something cut through skin.

I screamed.

Jennifer slammed into me from behind, then Stacy, arms locking around my chest, hauling back with everything she had.

"LET GO!" she screamed—at me or the dark, I didn't know.

My shoulder tore. My grip slipped.

The hand vanished back into the hole, taking a piece of me with it.

I crashed backward.

Stone slammed into my spine, knocking the breath from my lungs.

A headstone.

Carved letters bit through my shirt into skin.

Behind me, etched into granite I'd seen a hundred times on campus tours:

ELIAS W. BENNINGTON

1783–1852

I had climbed out of the founder's grave.

Jennifer collapsed beside me, gasping, one hand still locked around my chest like she didn't trust the earth not to take me again.

Stacy crawled up beside us, shaking violently. "Where's—"

She saw the headphones.

Stopped.

Below us, the opening went quiet.

No footsteps.

No breath.

No Brandon.

Just the headphones in my hand—warm from being worn—the cord slick with blood that wasn't all mine.

And beneath it all—

The earth still vibrated.

Patient.

Fed.

CHAPTER SEVENTEEN

THE GRASS WAS wet with dew, cold against my hand.

It felt wrong. Too soft. Too intact. Like it hadn't earned the right to exist after what we'd just crawled out of. For a long moment I didn't move at all. I let my face stay angled toward the muddy patch of spring grass and focused on breathing the way they taught you in health class —slow, counted, deliberate. In through the nose. Out through the mouth.

My body didn't care.

My lungs still remembered the cave air—heavy, metallic, close enough to bruise. Every breath felt borrowed, like I hadn't been cleared for this altitude yet.

The sun rested warm overhead.

Too warm.

It felt staged. Like kindness put on for an audience. Like the sky was only pretending it had been shining on this place the whole time we were disappearing beneath it. The world above us had kept going— campus, birds, footsteps, coffee cups—without ever glancing down at its own rot.

I leaned forward onto my knees and looked back at the break in the earth.

Half-expecting movement.

Half-expecting the ground to give him back the way it had given us back.

"He'll be right here," I said, the words slipping out before I decided to say them.

The hole breathed out damp air and dust. A slow exhale. No footsteps. No hands. Nothing that meant *alive*.

Stacy had stood up. Made it as far as a cedar tree a few feet away before her legs simply stopped listening to her. She folded down into the grass—not dramatic, not loud—just tired. Like her body had finally run out of instructions. Knees pulled to her chest. Arms wrapped tight around herself.

She shivered once. Hard enough that her teeth clicked before she caught it.

Dirt matted her hair. Mascara streaked down her cheeks in uneven black lines she didn't bother wiping away. She looked like grief had hauled her out of the ground by mistake and didn't know what to do with her once she was there.

A few feet away, Jennifer sat cross-legged in the grass, staring at her hands like they belonged to someone else. Her breathing was shallow and fast, controlled solely by willpower. She wiped her palms on her jean skirt, then on the grass, then froze—realizing she didn't know which was cleaner.

"Is this—" Stacy started, then stopped. Swallowed. Tried again. "Is this real?"

Jennifer didn't answer.

Neither did I.

Jennifer gagged suddenly—sharp, violent—like her body had tripped over something invisible. She turned away and retched into the grass. Nothing came up. She stayed bent forward anyway, dry-heaving, murmuring apologies under her breath like it was her fault for making noise.

"Sorry," she rasped. "Sorry, I just—"

"It's okay," I said, though I had no idea what okay meant anymore.

I pushed myself upright. Every muscle screamed in delayed protest. My hands wouldn't stop shaking. I tried to clench them into fists, but they trembled anyway, teeth chattering without the cold's permission. Dirt was packed beneath my fingernails, dark and stubborn. I scraped at it with my thumb over and over until the skin burned.

I couldn't remember standing.

My skin felt shockingly cold, like the cave had leeched all the warmth out of me and left something else behind in its place—something faintly electric, buzzing just under the surface. My shirt clung to me, damp with mud and sweat, like it hadn't realized we were done being buried.

The smell followed us up.

Wet soil. Stone. Old rain trapped underground.

When the sun hit my face fully, something inside me loosened. Not relief. Just... slack. Like a wire pulled too tight finally giving way.

The itching beneath my jaw faded.

Not all at once. It thinned. Retreated. Disappeared so quietly I almost missed it—like it had never been there at all.

Jennifer scrubbed her nose with the back of her trembling hand.

"It stopped," she whispered. "That hum. The—whatever it was." She hesitated, then looked at me. "Do you still... feel it?"

I rubbed my jaw without thinking, fingers brushing the tender spot.

"No," I said. Then, after a beat, "Maybe. I don't know."

A faint buzz stirred behind my cheekbone—so subtle it could've been memory. Or nerves. Or panic, finally catching up to me. It felt like the tail end of a nightmare—blurry, slippery, impossible to pin down once you were awake.

Except nightmares didn't leave gaps where teeth used to be. Or jagged claw marks still burning down your back.

Stacy hugged herself tighter. "I don't hear it," she said quietly. "I don't hear anything."

Jennifer's gaze drifted—not to the grass, not to us—but back to the crack in the earth behind us. She didn't say his name. Didn't ask if anyone else was coming.

She just stared at the opening like it might still answer if she waited long enough.

And the ground, for once, stayed silent.

We stayed like that for a long stretch of silence.

Time felt bent—elastic in the wrong places. I couldn't tell how long we'd been sitting there. Long enough for my pulse to stop racing. Long enough for the shaking to drain out of my hands. Long enough for the world to start pretending it hadn't split open underneath us.

Birds chirped overhead, bright and oblivious. A sprinkler clicked on somewhere across the lawn, its steady hiss scraping at my nerves. Near the chapel, a car beeped twice—sharp, impatient—like someone was late for something that still mattered.

Ordinary sounds.

They didn't belong anywhere near us.

I kept my eyes on the opening in the earth.

If I looked away, it felt like they would burst through.

I reached into my pocket and pulled out something small enough that my brain refused to name it right away. When the sunlight caught it, my stomach sank.

My tooth.

I turned it over in my palm slowly, like I was waiting for it to explain itself. In the daylight, it didn't look real anymore—too smooth, too clear, the edges unnaturally precise. Glass pretending to be bone.

"All of them," I said suddenly.

My voice was quiet. Even. Worse than if it had broken.

I kept my eyes ahead.

"Marissa," I continued. "Kevin. Josh. Matt." Each name landed flat, like I was reading them off a list I hadn't wanted to memorize. "Brandon." I closed my fingers around the tooth. "What was it even for?"

No one answered.

The question wasn't aimed at anyone anyway. It was aimed at the hill. The campus. The earth beneath it. At whatever had been humming down there, patient and hungry and incomprehensible.

Stacy shook her head once, sharp. "It wasn't a test," she said. "Tests have answers."

I huffed a breath that almost laughed. Almost.

"I keep thinking there's supposed to be a reason," I said. "Like if I can just figure out the rule I missed—something I should've said, or done, or stopped—"

I trailed off.

"That wasn't natural," Jennifer said. "None of it was."

Her shoulders sagged—not collapsing, just... lowering. Like she'd been holding them up on instinct and was finally running out of muscle.

"I keep waiting to hear them," she admitted. "Even though I know they're not—" She swallowed. "I know they're not coming out."

Stacy leaned back against the cedar tree beside her, staring up at the sky like she was daring it to comment.

"They didn't die for anything," she said. "That's the worst part."

Grief settled around us then—not loud, not sharp. Dense. Old. The kind that didn't ask permission.

Jennifer and I went and sat shoulder to shoulder with Stacy, facing the slope of the cemetery hill. The founder's headstone loomed nearby —clean, deliberate, a name carved to last. Beside it, the crack in the earth shed a little dirt now and then, like it hadn't quite decided whether it was done with us.

Jennifer leaned into me—not for comfort. For gravity. Like if she didn't, she might tip sideways into something she couldn't climb out of.

Stacy stayed close too, arms folded tight, jaw set like she was holding the world together by force.

"We're safe," Jennifer whispered, weak tears springing from her eyes.

The words hovered between us—fragile, hopeful in a way that hurt.

"Right?"

I looked out at the lawn. At the sprinklers. At students passing in the distance with backpacks and coffee cups and lives that hadn't cracked open yet.

"I think," I said slowly, "we're out."

I didn't say safe.

None of us did.

"That's... all I'm sure about."

Jennifer nodded once, like she'd expected that.

The sun kept washing over us—warm, patient, indifferent.

It softened the edges of the world without erasing what waited underneath it.

Morning had found us and gave us permission to grieve.

So had time.

I didn't realize how much of it we'd lost until the sound came.

A bell.

Clear. Hollow. Measured.

The campus clocktower rang once.

Then again.

Then a third time.

Each note rolled across the lawn, across the cemetery hill, settling into my bones like a countdown I hadn't known I was waiting for.

Stacy murmured. She squinted up at the sky. "Is that... noon?"

"No," Jennifer said. She was already standing. Already listening. "It's after."

The fourth bell rang.

Then the fifth.

My stomach tightened.

"Oh," I said quietly. The word landed wrong—too small for what it meant. "No. No, no, no."

Jennifer turned to me. Sharp. Immediate. "What?"

I didn't answer right away. I was already doing the math in my head, watching it click into place with sick precision.

"The tours," I said. "The afternoon ones."

Stacy's breath caught. "What about them?"

"The next group goes down at one," I said. "That was the schedule. Group B. South access."

The sixth bell rang.

Jennifer's jaw set. Not panic. Focus.

"Can we call it in?" she asked.

I pulled my phone out on instinct. The screen stayed black. I shook it once. Nothing. When it finally flickered to life, the display warped—water blooming beneath the glass like an oil spill.

"No signal," I said. "No service. It's fried."

Stacy checked hers anyway. Snorted when it did the same thing. "Cool. Now I have to schedule an appointment with a bag of rice."

The seventh bell rang.

Across the lawn, the world kept moving. More students crossed paths with coffee cups and backpacks. Someone laughed near the chapel steps. A groundskeeper waved to a jogger like this was just another Saturday.

None of them looked at the cemetery.

Jennifer dragged a hand through her hair. "Okay," she said. "Okay. Then we do this the old way."

Stacy stared at her. "Define '*this*.'"

Jennifer met her gaze. Didn't soften it.

"You go to the police," she said. "Now. You tell them everything. You don't downplay it. You don't try to sound sane. You make them listen."

Stacy blinked. Once. Then laughed—short, sharp, humorless. "You want me to walk into a precinct covered in dirt, missing a tooth, and tell them there are glass monsters under the cemetery?"

"Yes," I said. "Exactly that. Take my camera. It has proof."

The eighth bell rang.

Stacy hesitated. Just long enough to be human. Then she nodded, sudden and fierce.

"Fine," she said. "I'm not letting anyone else go down there." She pointed at us, her dirt-covered manicured nail shaking only a little. "But when this blows back on you two, I was never here."

Jennifer almost smiled.

"Go," she said. "Run."

Stacy took two steps, then stopped. Looked back at us—really looked.

"You better still be alive when I come back with flashing lights," she said. "I am not processing this alone."

Then she turned and bolted down the hill, boots slipping once in the wet grass before she caught herself and kept going.

The ninth bell rang.

Jennifer didn't watch her go. She was already looking past the chapel, toward the tree line, toward the paths that led back to the Geosciences building.

"We don't have much time," she said.

"No," I agreed. My body was already moving, already remembering the weight of stone, the sound of water, the way silence could kill. "But we might have enough."

The tenth bell rang.

Somewhere on campus, a door slammed. Somewhere else, laughter spiked and faded. The world above us kept its schedule.

Jennifer met my eyes.

"We stop them," she said.

Not try. Not warn.

Stop.

I nodded.

"Let's go," I said.

And together, we ran back toward the place the earth had opened—

before it could take anyone else with it.

CHAPTER EIGHTEEN

Walking back toward campus felt wrong in a way I didn't have language for yet.

Not wrong like danger. Wrong like gravity had shifted half a degree and my body hadn't adjusted. Like we were drifting through the world instead of moving inside it—two ghosts cutting across a campus that hadn't noticed we'd already died once and clawed our way back up.

The sun was out in that early-April way—bright but brittle. Too clean. Like it was polishing everything on purpose.

Students lounged across the quad, laughing about overdue essays, half-awake in sweats and flip-flops. Someone complained loudly about a midterm. A skateboarder zipped past and nearly clipped my shoulder.

"Sorry, dude," he muttered, already rolling on.

He didn't look back.

Everything was too normal.

Too loud.

Too alive.

Jennifer stayed close. Not touching, but close enough that I could feel the tremor moving through her like static. Her arms were wrapped tight around herself, fingers digging into her sleeves. Her teeth chattered—not from cold, but from something inside her that hadn't gotten the message that we were back above ground.

"You okay?" I asked quietly. Quickly.

She nodded too fast. Didn't look at me.

"Yeah," she said. Then, after a beat: "No. But walking is... helping."

The Geosciences Building rose ahead of us, exactly where it had been this morning. Same brick. Same windows. Same polite, academic indifference. But now I noticed the cracks—the hairline fractures spidering through the masonry, the slight tilt in the walkway like it had settled wrong years ago and no one noticed or bothered to fix it.

Under my shoes, there was a faint vibration.

I told myself it was the heating.

I knew better.

We threw open the doors and took the back stairwell two steps at a time. The concrete walls closed in fast, swallowing sound, our footfalls echoing too loudly in the narrow shaft. My breath scraped in my chest, every inhale still expecting damp stone and rot. The further down we went, the more wrong it felt—like we weren't heading toward help so much as circling back into something we hadn't fully escaped.

Voices drifted up from below.

Not panicked. Not afraid.

Normal.

We rounded the last turn and nearly collided with a cluster of students gathered in front of the elevator doors. Backpacks slung over one shoulder. Clipboards tucked under arms. Someone asked about why the cave ever closed. Someone else complained about the stairs. A guy in a beanie stretched like he had just woken up.

For half a second, none of them registered us.

Then Jennifer stopped dead.

"Don't," she said, the word tearing out of her before she could shape it. "Don't go down there."

A few heads turned.

"Jen?" a girl near the front asked, blinking like she'd misheard. "God, you look terrible!"

"You can't," Jennifer said again, louder now. Her voice shook, but it didn't break. "There's something wrong with the tunnels. People didn't come back. We—we barely did."

Someone laughed. Not mean. Just surprised.

"Is this like a hazing thing?" a guy asked. "Because that's actually kinda sick."

Another student frowned. "I need this for my GPA. I'll fail without it."

"They wouldn't run it if it wasn't safe," someone else added, maybe a grad student, already looking past her toward the elevator, as if she were an inconvenience standing between them and a deadline.

Jennifer stepped forward, desperate now. "Listen to me. I'm not joking. We heard things. We saw—"

"Jen," the first girl said gently, like you talk to someone having a bad day. "You're freaking people out. Did you take something? Are you on something?"

That did it.

Something in Jennifer collapsed—not all at once, but enough that I felt it shift beside me. She looked at their faces, searching for recognition, for fear, for anything that suggested they understood what was at stake.

She didn't find it.

The elevator dinged.

The doors slid open.

A staff member down the hall cleared her throat. "If you're not signed up, please step aside."

The grad student went in.

"Someone hit the call button in five. I'm going to do a quick check before we get started," he said.

Jennifer's hands curled into fists.

"Alex," she said, turning to me, eyes bright and furious and scared all at once. "We can't—"

I grabbed hold of her. We stumbled into the sign-up office as the door swung shut behind us.

The smell hit immediately—toner, old paper, burnt dust from

printers that had run too long without rest. The kind of smell that coated the back of your throat and refused to leave.

Then I saw the counter.

Three women sat behind it, each in a knitted sweater—soft pink, soft orange, soft green. Their hair curled the same way. Their posture mirrored. Their hands rested on the counter at the same angle.

And their smiles—

Their smiles didn't move.

Not when they blinked.

Not when they stamped forms.

Not when Jennifer and I stepped inside like two things dragged up from the earth.

The line of students stretched across in front of the door, notebooks tucked under arms. One of them was holding onto the same form I'd seen yesterday.

PAID RESEARCH OPPORTUNITY
GEOLOGY STUDENTS NEEDED
Document subsurface mineral formations.
Supervised fieldwork.
Sponsored by the
Bennington Subsurface Research Initiative.

The triangle burned logo seared into me like a hex.

Jennifer stepped forward before I could stop her.

"You can't send them down there," she said, voice breaking like someone had snapped it in half. "There's something wrong with those caves. People are dead. Do you hear me? They're dead."

The word dead hung there, naked and shaking.

Her breath hitched. Her shoulders trembled. She looked too small standing there in the doorway, like the building was already swallowing her back.

The woman in the blue sweater paused.

Just for a fraction of a second.

Her smile faltered. Her eyes lifted—actually focused on Jennifer this time.

"Oh," she said softly. "Did someone get hurt?"

Hope flared across Jennifer's face so fast it almost hurt to watch.

"Yes," Jennifer said, breathless. "Yes. They—"

The woman blinked.

The smile reset. Perfect. Painless.

"I'm sure it only felt dangerous," she continued, voice smoothing into something rehearsed. "That happens sometimes underground."

Something cold slid down my spine.

"No," Jennifer snapped, louder now. Sharper. "No, you don't get to say that. You don't know what happened. We went down there. We saw—"

"Line three needs your signature, sweetheart," the woman said, tapping her pen against the form.

She wasn't talking to Jennifer.

She was talking to me.

"Harry's boy, right?" She smiled.

Jennifer made a sound that didn't belong to language—half gasp, half sob—and stepped backward into me like she needed the physical world to keep her upright.

I caught her without thinking.

My eyes dropped to the counter. To the stacks of cardboard boxes behind it—plain university inventory boxes, taped shut, stacked neatly against the wall.

One label had started to peel.

Just a corner lifting. Curling outward.

Like it wanted to be seen.

I stepped closer to the counter, pulse thudding up into my jaw.

R. Prescott

VRX Laboratories

Outer Banks, North Carolina

My mouth went dry.

Ryan?

Like—cousin Ryan?

The name slid into place too easily, like it had always been waiting for me to notice it. I felt it then, clear and cold: a hand closing around the back of my neck.

I heard myself speak before I realized I'd decided to.

"Where... where are those boxes going?"

The woman in the green sweater didn't look up from her paperwork.

"Oh, it's for the geological samples," she said, voice light, practiced. Then, after a fractional pause, as if correcting a line in her head: "After today, they'll be sent somewhere they can be examined further."

Somewhere.

Jennifer's fingers dug into my sleeve so hard my shoulder jerked.

"Alex—no," she whispered, voice fraying. "The police. Please. Maybe we can help Stacy. We need to find someone who'll believe us."

She wasn't panicking. She was splintering. Holding herself together by the edges.

The woman in the green sweater stopped stamping.

She just folded her hands and waited.

That's when the door behind the counter opened.

And the room changed temperature.

Not colder—emptier. Like the air had been pulled out and replaced with something older. Heavier. Like the building itself had exhaled and forgotten how to inhale again.

The door creaked wider.

I didn't expect anything. Another secretary. A grad student. A TA with bad posture and a stack of forms.

Instead, a familiar voice drifted down the hall.

"Could someone print the latest seismic activity reports? I'd like them for the grant meeting."

I knew the cadence before I knew the words.

Dad.

My father stepped into the office with the quiet certainty he carried everywhere, like rooms instinctively learned how to arrange themselves around him. His hair had gone a little grayer since I last saw him, combed straight back and refusing to fall out of place. His shirt was pressed so sharply it looked painful—knife-edge creases, immaculate cuffs.

Clipboard tucked under one arm. Pen clipped neatly to the top.

A man who trusted systems.

A man who believed order could be imposed.

A man who thought chaos was just something that hadn't been categorized yet.

He belonged here.

And somehow, he still looked like home.

His eyes swept the room in a slow, methodical arc. Registered. Moved on.

Then they landed on me.

They softened.

"Alex?" His voice caught on my name, disbelief bleeding into relief. "Oh—thank God. Where have you been? Why do you look like that?"

The relief hit me so hard my knees nearly gave out.

He wasn't angry. Wasn't disappointed.

He was worried.

"Dad," I said, swallowing. "Something happened down there. Something really bad."

His brow knit immediately—the same expression he'd worn when I'd come home bleeding as a kid, trying to pretend I was fine.

"You're shaking," he said gently, already stepping closer. His hand closed around my arm, steady and careful. "Are you hurt? Did you fall? Your arm—"

Jennifer cut in before I could answer.

"There were things down there," she said, voice trembling but fierce. "In the tunnels. People—people didn't make it out. Josh, Marissa, Brandon, Kevin, Matt... they're all dead!"

He raised a hand, calm as a lullaby.

"Alright," he said, soothing. "Let's slow down. Both of you. Take a breath."

He leaned back against the desk, posture relaxed, authoritative without trying.

"What exactly is going on? One at a time."

"Dad," I said quickly, "there's something wrong with the rock. Eurydium. It's not just radioactive—it's... reactive. It changes things. People. We—we were the only ones to make it out of our group."

His eyes sharpened—not alarmed, but interested.

"You were in the first group?" he asked. "I saw your name on the afternoon list, but—" He sighed. Rubbed a finger thoughtfully along his upper lip. "I was concerned something like this might happen."

Then—to the women behind the desk:

"Has Christian returned from the integrity check yet?"

They shook their heads slowly, uncertain, suddenly very human.

"No one hit the button?" he muttered, more amused than annoyed.

He turned back to us, voice full of professional sympathy.

"Listen," he said kindly, "I know what you experienced must have been frightening. Underground environments can have an extraordinary effect on the mind. Seismic stress, disorientation, oxygen deprivation—it can trigger panic responses. Hallucinations. The brain fills in shadows with—"

"We're not making it up," I said.

Sharper than I meant to. Louder than I wanted.

The room went still.

Jennifer looked at me like I'd just said something dangerous.

My father studied my face—not angry. Not dismissive.

Evaluating.

"Alex," he said carefully, "I'm not saying you're lying. I'm saying the human mind is incredibly creative under stress. Today's earthquake, it—"

"People died!" Jennifer shook her head, tears finally spilling free.

His mouth tightened—not in grief, but in concern.

"We don't know that yet," he said gently. "And until we do, it's important we don't jump to conclusions that could cause unnecessary panic."

I was stunned by his assessment. That's what it was. Not a response, an assessment.

Behind him, the boxes sat quietly.

Address labels pristine.

Tape sealed tight.

He softened instantly—like he'd been waiting for my tone to crest, knew exactly when to press.

"Alex," he said quietly, almost fondly. "Fear does strange things to perception. Darkness amplifies it. Sound distorts. Oxygen drops."

Each word landed like a citation.

He squeezed my shoulder, firm and grounding, the way he always had. The way he'd steadied me before dentist appointments, before funerals, before things he thought could be explained away if I just stayed calm long enough.

"You're safe now," he continued. "That's what matters. We'll go down, send a team in for your friends—professionals. Trained. This is exactly what protocols are for."

For one treacherous second, I felt it—the relief trying to take root. The idea that this could still be contained. Filed. Fixed.

Then something twisted low in my gut.

I blinked. The thought slid in sideways.

"Wait," I said. "Dad... what are you doing here?"

It wasn't accusatory. It was instinct. The kind you don't argue with until it's too late.

He hesitated—only a breath, but I caught it. A man selecting the version of the truth that would travel best.

"I've been consulting on the geological expansion project," he said smoothly. "Helping with analysis. Verifying environmental safety. Why?"

The words sounded reasonable. Too reasonable.

My stomach lurched.

"So you're not—" I tried to laugh. Failed. "You didn't know what was happening down there."

His eyes softened at the edges. A tired father's patience.

"Alex," he said gently, "if I thought for a moment there was any danger at all, I would never have let students go underground. You know that."

And God help me—I did.

Jennifer shook her head, sharp and immediate.

"This isn't panic," she said, voice shaking but precise, like she'd sharpened it on the way over. "It's a pattern. And it's still active."

She lifted the camera. Her hands were steady now. Her eyes weren't.

"I have it documented. The tunnels. The structures. The—whatever those things are. It isn't finished."

He didn't flinch.

Didn't dismiss her.

He reframed her.

"This isn't the first time students have been frightened underground," he said softly. "Caves are liminal spaces. The mind fills gaps aggressively when deprived of stimulus."

He smiled, reassuring and complete.

"I'll go down myself," he added. "Check every access point. Every marker. If there's even a hint of instability, I'll shut the entire operation down today."

It was exactly what I needed to hear.

And exactly what terrified me.

He pushed open the door and moved through the throng of students.

Something clawed at my ribs.

"Dad—wait."

"I'll be back in ten minutes," he promised. "Try not to worry."

He pressed the elevator button.

Brandon's voice flashed through my head—*Go. I'll be right behind you.*

Then Marissa. Standing still. Listening.

My stomach tightened. Every nerve screamed don't.

The doors slid open with a tired groan.

There was no sign of the grad student—Christian. Just empty metal. Empty space.

"Dad!" I shouted.

Jennifer stepped forward. "He can't go down there—"

But he was already inside.

He wasn't being reckless.

He was being a father who didn't want his kid to be afraid.

And something in my chest finally snapped.

I lunged forward as the doors began to close, shoving myself through the narrowing gap. Metal slammed into my shoulders.

Dad's hand shot out on instinct. "Alex! What are you—"

Too late. The doors clanged shut.

Something struck the metal from the other side.

Not pounding.

Just once.

"Alex!" Jennifer's voice muffled from behind the door.

"Jen—" I said.

The elevator shuddered and began its descent.

And suddenly it was just me and him—

Dropping back into the dark.

CHAPTER NINETEEN

THE ELEVATOR GROANED as it descended, metal cables whining like they resented being asked to move at all. The incandescent bulb overhead flickered in an arrhythmic pulse, slicing my father's face into uneven pieces—creases caught in shadow, the dull gleam of his glasses, the weight of exhaustion pulling at his shoulders.

He didn't look angry that I'd forced my way inside.

He looked afraid.

"Alex," he said gently, too gently, "you shouldn't be here. You should be outside. You should be getting checked by medical, sitting down, drinking water—"

I laughed. It came out sharp and wrong, like a sound my body made without permission.

"I just crawled out of a collapsing cemetery," I said. "I think I missed the window for a juice box."

His mouth twitched—not amusement, not quite frustration. Something closer to pain.

He inhaled, long and slow. The kind of breath he took before a lecture that was going to disappoint everyone in the room.

"As I said, I didn't know you were in the first group," he said. "You weren't on the roster. I would have sent a search team after the tremor, but my contacts advised against it."

"That's your defense?" I snapped. "Paperwork?"

My voice rose before I could stop it. "Dad—five people died down there!"

He didn't flinch.

But something moved behind his eyes.

Concern. Calculation. And—worse—recognition.

"That shouldn't have happened," he said quietly. "The tunnel is stable. We reinforced every vulnerable section years ago. You shouldn't have been exposed to anything lethal. There shouldn't have been any—"

He searched for the word.

"—complications."

I stared at him.

"Complications?" My voice cracked. "Dad, we saw things. Things with teeth that—"

"There's nothing down there," he said, stepping closer—not as a scientist, not even as an authority, but as my father. His voice lowered, grounding, practiced. "Alex. Listen to me."

The elevator shuddered as it passed another floor.

"Eurydium emits low-grade radiation," he continued calmly. "That's why the cave closed in the 1960s. But we've reevaluated it, and it's nothing dramatic. It's enough to interfere with acoustics and visual perception, and we're aware that the long-term exposure disrupted the bat populations. Now, especially without them, sound behaves unpredictably. Echoes stack. Shadows misalign."

I felt something cold coil in my gut.

"Panic fills in the rest," he finished.

I looked at him. Really looked.

"You think I hallucinated all of it."

"I think," he said gently, "you were terrified. And fear does strange things when it senses displacement."

He paused, choosing his words with surgical care.

"The mind invents predators when it no longer belongs somewhere. Especially in environments humans were never meant to occupy."

For half a second—just half—it almost made sense.

Of course it did.

Fear always looks like something else once you give it a name.

The thought slid into place so easily I barely noticed it arrive. My chest loosened. My hands steadied.

This wasn't panic anymore.

This was clarity.

The cave had been loud. Overwhelming. Hungry.

I could almost picture it all in my mind.

Josh died from the fall.

Matt bled out in the cart.

We lost Kevin and Marissa in the dark.

Maybe fear had filled the dark with teeth because teeth were easier than admitting the earth itself didn't want us there anymore.

The thought made me nauseous.

But Brandon didn't go away.

Blood dripped down my arm.

"Dad," I said softly, "we were chased."

His eyes flickered.

Doubt? Or something closer to alarm?

"You're not hearing me," he said, firmer now. "Nothing down there is alive. The bat population fully collapsed in 2000. When they disappeared, the tunnels changed. Air pressure. Echo distribution. Human equilibrium."

Something about the way he spoke felt... rehearsed. Not lying. Practiced.

He'd had years to make this sound reasonable. Hadn't he?

You're giving him too much credit.

The thought startled me—not because it was cruel, but because it felt corrective. Like a finger tapping the margin of a page I'd misread.

He wasn't explaining. He was containing.

"I watched them die," I said. The words tore loose before I could soften them.

He heard it. His expression faltered—just once. The mask slipped.

Then he looked away, like the vulnerability embarrassed him.

"I was right next to one," I continued. "Holding him up—by the old mining shaft. We—"

"Your group reached the mining layer?" he interrupted, too quickly. His voice sharpened with interest despite himself. "No one was supposed to go near that area. But even then, we've been expanding the shaft slowly. It couldn't have been more than a foot wide. It was the safest way to access fresh ore pockets."

"Well, it wasn't," I said. "It was a rift. Big enough to swallow an entire research group."

The elevator continued its steady descent.

"Why?" I asked. "Why is this all so important? Why Eurydium? Why hasn't anyone researched it other than you?"

For the first time, he hesitated. Really hesitated.

He drew in a breath. This one trembled at the edges.

"My time with it started in 1985."

The elevator bounced once, then continued its descent, sinking deeper into the earth. The vibration settled into my bones—familiar, almost comforting, like the ground recognizing one of its own.

"I never planned for my research to involve you," my father said, quieter now. Not apologetic. Just factual. "That was never part of it."

The floor dropped again. And that's when I heard it fully.

The frequency.

Low. Subterranean. Threading through the metal like a second current. My hand slid along the panel beside the doors, fingers searching seams, buttons, anything that looked like a way out.

"What are you doing?" he asked.

Not sharp. Not alarmed.

Just curious.

"There has to be a stop," I said. My fingers shook as they traced the edges of the control panel. "A brake. An override. Dad—we have to go back up."

He watched me for a second too long.

Then he said, gently, "There's no reverse."

The words landed heavier than the elevator itself.

He frowned—not at the controls, but at me.

"Alex," he said, stepping closer, lowering his voice like I was spiraling instead of thinking, "breathe. You're safe. I need you calm."

If it was just fear, the thought continued, quieter now, *why does he need me calm?*

I swallowed.

Because panic spreads, I told myself. *Because he's my father. Because—*

Because calm people don't ask the wrong questions.

The elevator bulb flickered. My reflection fractured in the metal walls—my face split and reassembled, too composed for how this should feel.

His gaze drifted past the metal walls, unfocused, like the past had been etched into the steel and he could still read it if he tried hard enough.

"When I was working in Los Angeles," he said, "right after your mother died... I was out of my mind with grief," he continued evenly. "I wasn't sleeping. I wasn't eating. I was desperate for something—anything—that could make the world behave again."

He swallowed.

"And then something crossed my desk. A glass mirror—except it wasn't. Translucent. Warm to the touch. Reactive under certain frequencies. It shouldn't have existed."

My hand stilled against the wall.

"And after weeks of analysis," he said softly, reverently, "I realized what it was."

I already knew the answer.

"Ghost Glass," he said.

The elevator sank lower.

"I spent days running tests," he continued. "My colleagues said my data was flawed. That I was misreading results. That *fantasy* had compromised my objectivity."

He exhaled through his nose.

"The signatures didn't match quartz. Or calcite. Or anything on the periodic table."

His voice dropped.

"It was an element. A new one."

"And no one believed you," I said.

He nodded once.

"The papers rejected me. The university dismissed me. The headlines—"

He shut his eyes.

"Fraud. Data manipulation. Career ruined. They said grief had broken me."

He looked down at his hands.

"Maybe it had."

The bulb overhead flickered again. The light stabbed my eyes. I looked away, blinking hard, relief washing over me as the shadows reclaimed the space. Something warm slid over my lip. I wiped it without thinking.

Blood streaked my knuckle.

He stopped talking. Not because I'd interrupted him. Because he was watching me now. Really watching.

My breathing.

My hands.

The way I wasn't pacing. Wasn't shaking. Wasn't unraveling the way panic was supposed to look.

His eyes flicked to my mouth. To the blood. To my eyes.

"You're not disoriented," he said slowly. Not to reassure me. To himself.

"Radiation-induced hallucinations don't usually present this coherently," he murmured. "Exposure takes time. Years, typically."

A pause.

Then, softer: "Not... hours."

Something shifted. He wasn't looking at a frightened son anymore. He was looking at an anomaly.

He knows more than he's saying.

I frowned, just slightly. *Had I been thinking that already?*

"Still," he added quickly, almost defensively, "the brain seeks patterns under trauma. Perception organizes itself when overwhelmed—"

"Why did you bring us here?" I asked.

My voice didn't shake.

"To Bennington. Why did we leave Fairfax?"

He hesitated.

"We needed a place to start over," he said finally. "A site with a history of mining this stone. And when I found fresh traces here—"

He shook his head faintly.

"Everything made sense again."

He's lying. The voice told me.

I couldn't tell where I ended and it began.

"It had nothing to do with her?" I asked. "The missing girl on the poster?"

I hadn't planned to ask that. The question surfaced fully formed—clear, insistent—like it had been waiting for a pause.

His gaze snagged.

Just for a fraction of a second.

"Who was she?" I pressed.

"An early test subject," he said. Too quickly. "A mistake. One I've regretted every day."

The elevator groaned lower.

"Eurydium came into my life just after your mother died," he continued, voice softening, almost pleading now. "It made me do terrible things. But it was the only thing that felt like hope. The only thing that made me believe the universe wasn't cruel without reason."

My chest tightened.

"That maybe," he whispered, "there was a way to undo the past. Change the future. Give her back to you. To us."

The vibration pressed closer.

"You think you're Orpheus."

The elevator kept descending.

His breath hitched.

"I was so close," he whispered, like the words had been rehearsing themselves for years. "I was on the path back to her. I could feel it. I could feel her—just on the other side of understanding."

The elevator light flickered overhead.

The hum surged, threading through the metal, through my teeth, through my bones.

"I thought..." His voice shook. "If I could understand it—if I could unlock what it was trying to show me—maybe someday I could see her again. Just once. Just enough to know she wasn't gone without meaning," he paused. "And then she disappeared forever." He looked broken, pained, remembering and trying to forget at the same time.

I realized it then.

Jennifer and Stacy had turned away from the glow. From the hum.

But my father never did.

Even now, he still leaned into it.

Listening.

But it didn't talk back.

It didn't want him.

Dad continued, almost pleading with the space itself, "And now, with these newest samples—if I could prove we still had a base worth funding—maybe I can finally make it real. Not a theory. Not a fluke. Something repeatable. I could go back."

"Dad," I said, sharper than I meant to. "That's not possible. Mom's dead. She's gone."

The words felt brutal and necessary all at once.

"You're all I have."

He flinched—not away from me, but inward. "You don't understand, Alex," he said quietly. "You never will."

"If no one can understand you, then why are you sending ore samples to Ryan?" I asked. "Why drag him into this instead of me?"

He rubbed the bridge of his nose, thumb pressing hard like he could physically push the thought back into his skull.

"Ryan is conducting adjacent research," he said. "He was with me in '95. He experienced the same phenomenon I did in the eighties. VRX and BSRI share the same parent group, but my reputation still precedes me. So we share samples. Never theories."

"You should've told me," I whispered.

The elevator shook lower.

"All these years," I continued. "All the moving. All the secrets. Why were you always trying to go back?"

My voice cracked.

"Why wasn't your life with me enough?"

The question landed and stayed.

My father's face folded in small, human fractures. Lines softening. Shoulders sagging.

He stepped toward me. Half a step. Barely there. But real.

"Alex," he said, voice breaking clean through the center, "you were never second. Never."

His hands shook at his sides.

"I just didn't know how to be a father," he admitted. "Not when every night I went to sleep knowing I could bring your mother back. I was terrified I couldn't raise you without her."

My throat tightened.

He reached for me—

Only halfway.

A hesitant, trembling motion, like he wasn't sure he had the right anymore.

"Son," he whispered, "I'm so sorry."

His eyes dropped.

To my mouth.

To the blood on my knuckle.

To the way I stood there—still, grounded, not afraid.

Something in him shifted. Not intellectually. Not academically.

Personally.

"Alex..." he said, quietly now. Not as a scientist. Just a man who had run out of time.

"We can still—"

The elevator lurched.

I shook my head once.

"We can't," I said. And I didn't know why I said it. Why I felt that way.

Orange flakes drifted past the narrow window outside the elevator like burning snow. The noise inside me pulsed in response, familiar now. Intimate.

My veins burned faintly beneath my skin.

The elevator shuddered.

And somewhere below us—

Something screamed awake.

CHAPTER TWENTY

THE FREIGHT ELEVATOR rattled its way down the shaft, metal groaning around us like the structure itself had arthritis. Every bolt complained. Every cable sang its age. The sound wasn't just noise—it had rhythm, a tired persistence, like something that had been doing this long before we asked it to.

Dad stood beside me, posture stiff but deliberate. The stance he took whenever he was trying to project calm for my benefit. One hand braced lightly on the railing. Eyes forward. Jaw set.

He was breathing carefully.

Not naturally—intentionally. The measured inhale, the controlled exhale. The way he'd taught me to breathe when storms rattled the windows and I was little enough to think the house might float away if I didn't anchor it with my lungs.

Another scream tore upward through the rock.

Closer.

Higher.

Almost human.

Dad froze.

Completely.

The elevator shuddered, then clanged to a stop with a sound that rang too long, too loud, like it wanted to be remembered.

This time, he didn't explain it away.

"Someone's hurt," he whispered.

The words came out small. Fragile. Like he was afraid the cave might hear him and disagree.

The doors groaned open.

Dad leaned forward instinctively, peering into the dark beyond, his voice cracking as it carried out into the tunnel.

"Christian?" he called.

It wasn't confident.

It wasn't composed.

It was scared.

He stepped out first, shoes scraping softly against stone, posture cautious now—no longer the certainty of a man with a map, but the hesitation of someone realizing, too late, that the terrain doesn't care what you expect.

The darkness outside wasn't the tidy, measured dark of university blueprints.

It was layered. Breathing. Old.

The air pressed back against us like it resented being disturbed. Like it had been holding something in and we'd just cracked the seal.

Some small part of me prayed Jennifer would hit the call button.

That the elevator would reverse.

That this descent would end here.

That part of me was already dying.

Dad swallowed.

"Alex," he said quietly, without turning, "stay right behind me. If this is a structural collapse, we need to—"

Another scream ripped through the tunnel.

Not distant.

Not echoing.

Close enough that the elevator light stuttered like it had been slapped.

Dad jolted.

For the first time in my life, I saw my father—the man who had calmly talked me through thunderstorms, kissed broken bones, and held me at my mother's funeral—hesitate without knowing what to do next.

He turned back toward me.

And something shifted in his face.

Not panic.

Recognition.

Like the professor diagnosing a problem had vanished, replaced by a father realizing his son might be standing too close to something that didn't care about credentials.

"Alex," he asked softly, carefully, "did you... hear anything like that before? In your group?"

I nodded.

My throat wouldn't open.

Didn't need to.

He took a breath.

It came out uneven, stuttered.

Then—quietly, deliberately, like he was placing weight on a cracked floor—

"Alright," he said. "I believe you."

The words mattered more than he understood.

"Something's wrong down here."

The ground trembled beneath us.

Dust sifted from the ceiling, slow and delicate, like sediment drifting through deep water. It landed on his shoulders, his hair, the sleeve of his coat—marking him, gently, like the cave was making a claim.

Dad stared.

Whatever framework he'd been clinging to—protocols, explanations, the comfort of theory—split straight down the middle.

"This isn't right," he whispered.

He turned back toward the tunnel.

Stopped.

Then looked at me again.

Longer this time.

"Alex," he said, voice lower now, unsteady, "stay close to me."

It wasn't an order.

It was instinct.

I stepped toward him—

—and the cavern answered.

A shriek tore through the dark that did not sound human, or animal, or mechanical. It sounded hungry. Old. Primeval. Awake.

The elevator light dimmed.

Something shifted ahead of us.

Not rushing.

Not hiding.

Waiting.

Dad's breath caught.

"Dear God," he whispered. "What is that...?"

He turned back toward me sharply.

And this time, fear cut clean through his expression.

"Alex," he murmured, "let me see your face."

He stepped closer.

"Son—look at me."

His voice cracked on the word.

Everything else fell away.

Because the reflection in his glasses caught the light just right.

It traced my jaw.

My throat.

The edges of my eyes.

Orange veins pulsed beneath my skin—fine, branching lines curling under my jaw, threading upward like roots searching for something to claim. My pupils glimmered faintly, not bright enough to burn—

—but bright enough to promise they would.

My breath came out wrong.

Too hot.

Too sharp.

Like something else was using my lungs as a doorway.

And in the hollow left behind by my missing tooth—

Something pressed forward.

Hard.

New.

Dad staggered back half a step, his boots skidding on metal.

His mouth fell open.

A small, involuntary sound escaped him—half-gasp, half-sob—so quiet I almost missed it. He lifted his hand toward my face.

Only halfway.

His fingers flattened in the space between us, trembling, hovering —like if he went any farther, he'd lose the version of me he was still clinging to.

Then he pulled his hand back.

Too fast.

Like he'd been burned.

"God," he whispered. "No. No—Alex—don't..."

The vibration inside me surged.

Certain.

It rose up my spine like a tide that had always known where it was going. It matched the Eurydium threaded through the walls, through the rock, through the history of this place. Not a signal calling out— but a resonance answering back.

My teeth ached. Pressure built behind them, slow and deliberate, like something measuring the space it needed before taking some kind of action. Something bright and exact thrummed behind my eyes, lining my thoughts up into something clean.

"I feel it," I said, stumbling toward him.

My voice didn't sound like mine anymore. It vibrated—metallic, sharpened—like it had passed through a blade on its way out.

"I can feel it burning inside me."

He flinched.

Just a fraction of an inch. Barely visible. But it was there.

Then—for the briefest, most devastating second—he stepped toward me.

Small. Unsteady. Human.

"Listen to me," he said, his voice cracking once, like a fault line giving way. "Fight it. Alex... you have to fight it—"

The pain came fast enough to steal the air from my lungs.

I folded forward on instinct, hands braced on my knees as something sharp pressed up against my gums. I spat without thinking.

Blood struck the stone.

Too dark. Too thick.

One of my teeth worked loose.

It didn't tear free.

It pushed.

I sucked in a breath through clenched teeth and made a sound I didn't recognize. My fingers curled, nails biting into my palms as the ache spread—jaw, neck, chest—like pressure equalizing too fast. Like something inside me was learning how to take up more space.

My skin boiled.

Itched.

Veins stood out along my arms, pale and rigid, stiffening beneath the surface as if they were being redrawn. As if they were remembering a shape they'd once had and were relieved to return to it.

I knew I should have fought it.

That part of me still existed—somewhere quiet and distant—the part that remembered what resistance looked like. What it cost. The part that still knew the difference between standing and yielding.

I didn't move.

The hum didn't grow louder.

It didn't need to anymore.

Light hurt now. I blinked hard, tears slipping free before I realized I was crying, and stumbled to the ground beyond the elevator. The stone didn't feel cold anymore.

It felt... safe.

Like leaning against something that had been waiting for me to stop pretending.

Somewhere above me, Jennifer was alive.

That mattered.

It had always mattered.

I closed my eyes.

When I opened them again, everything felt quieter.

Not empty.

Settled.

Dad spun, slamming his hands into the elevator panel. Buttons lit beneath his palms—each one glowing uselessly as he pounded them like faith alone might wake the machine.

Nothing happened.

The elevator lamp flickered violently.

And in those broken flashes of light, I saw them.

Bodies bent at wrong angles.

Translucent skin stretched thin over bone.

Limbs jerking like marionettes with trembling strings.

And their mouths—

Their teeth glowed.

Bright orange.

Lit from within.

Fangs forged from molten glass.

A ring of jagged smiles surfaced at the edge of the light, circling the elevator like predators around a dying fire.

Dozens of grins.

Hundreds of teeth.

All watching.

All waiting.

And somewhere deep inside me—

Something smiled back.

One of them stepped closer.

The light caught the curve of its shoulder. The careful angle of its spine. The way it didn't rush, didn't lunge—just waited.

I knew that posture.

My stomach dropped—not with fear, but recognition.

Another shape leaned forward from the dark, moving slower than the rest, head tilted like it was listening for something only it could hear. The hesitation in the movement was wrong in a way that felt intimate. Familiar. Personal.

I didn't need to see their faces.

I knew them.

Brandon had always stood like that—a half-step back, weight shifted, watching the room instead of the door. Ready to react. Never first.

And Marissa—

The way she tilted her head when she was thinking. When she was deciding whether to speak. Whether something was worth saying out loud.

I looked away before the light could finish assembling the thought.

My father stumbled backward.

"Alex," he whispered. "Get inside."

This time—just once—his voice cracked with grief.

Not fear.

Not authority.

Grief.

A brief, devastating echo of the man he should have been. The man who might have saved us if he'd chosen differently. Sooner. If he'd listened instead of studied.

Then the creatures moved.

The deadringers surged at us in a shuddering wave, limbs jerking, bodies stuttering through space like signals fighting for coherence. Their breaths rattled, overlapping, tuning themselves—broken radios warming up to the same frequency.

The light behind me stuttered violently.

Flicker.

Blackout.

Flicker.

Each flash caught a still frame of terror—my father's open mouth, his outstretched hand, the silhouettes closing in.

He reached for me, hand extended, instinct flaring.

And then stopped.

Because the cavern inhaled.

And I inhaled with it.

The light faltered.

Once—

Twice.

And in that final heartbeat before the dark sealed over us, something brushed past me.

Cold. Damp. Curious.

The touch wasn't violent. It didn't grab or claw or pull. It tested,

the way you might test water with the back of your hand before stepping in. Measuring. Asking.

I didn't flinch. I didn't even turn.

Because the moment it touched me, its screech harmonized with
the pulse inside my skull—clean and exact, sliding perfectly into place
like the missing note of a chord I'd been holding my entire life without
realizing it was unfinished.

Not noise.

Not pain.

Resonance.

Recognition.

A welcome so complete it felt ancient.

Something in me settled. Clicked.

I realized, dimly, that I could still run.

The thought drifted past like a leaf on water—weightless, without
urgency. I knew where the tunnel curved. I knew where the cemetery
was. I knew how to move my legs fast enough to maybe get away.

I also knew I wouldn't.

And for the first time since the descent began—

I wasn't afraid.

Fear had been loud. Jagged. Exhausting.

This was quiet. Clarity.

Hunger.

Not the kind that gnaws or begs or panics. The kind that knows
exactly what it wants and understands that wanting is not the same
thing as need. The kind that waits.

My father made a sound then.

Not a scream—not fully.

It broke off halfway, cut short like a violin string snapping at the
peak of a note. A sound that had nowhere to go and no time to
become language. I didn't turn to see him.

I didn't need to.

All I heard was dragging and a wet *crack* against the stone
beside me.

Glowing grins overlapped in the dark, converging—orange light
flaring in jagged bursts. Teeth like molten glass. Breath like static.

Bodies bending, aligning, syncing to the same pulse now running clean through me.

And behind me—

with a final metallic scream—

The elevator doors slammed shut.

Sealing the light.

Sealing the exit.

And sealing whatever version of me had still believed this was something I could ever escape.

EPILOGUE

OFFICE OF
STRATEGIC RESEARCH AND DEVELOPMENT
INTERDIVISIONAL BRIEFING

FILE DESIGNATION: OSRD-GEO-9
CLEARANCE REQUIRED: LEVEL IV
STATUS: INTERNAL / RESTRICTED
SUBJECT: *Pendleton University Subterranean Event*
LOCATION: *Bennington, Vermont*
DATE OF INCIDENT: *April 12, 2002*
DATE OF REVIEW: *April 18, 2002*

SUMMARY:
On April 12, 2002, a sanctioned geological descent beneath Pendleton University resulted in a multi-fatality event, structural compromise of restricted tunnel systems, and the activation of previously dormant subterranean phenomena classified under Lazarian Parameters.
Initial response units reported catastrophic equipment failure beyond Sublevel 8. Visual documentation was limited. Audio feeds were inter-

mittently disrupted by sustained harmonic interference described as "sentient in nature."

Recovery operations were suspended after forty-seven minutes.

CASUALTIES:
Confirmed: ██████
Presumed: ██████
Unrecovered: ██████
Numerous biological anomalies remain active below the collapse zone.

SURVIVING PERSONNEL:
WEISS, JENNIFER
TRENT, STACY
Both subjects were recovered above ground with minor physical injuries and acute psychological distress. Each has been detained for questioning under standard OSRD nondisclosure protocol.
Statements are consistent regarding:

- auditory phenomena
- loss of spatial continuity
- biological alterations attributed to Eurydium

Neither subject has been cleared for public release.

MATERIAL ANALYSIS:
Trace deposits of Eurydium were identified and recovered throughout the lower tunnel system, embedded in surrounding rock formations and structural supports.
Exposure patterns and behavioral outcomes demonstrate partial correlation with ██████ (1943), ██████ (1952), and ██████ (1997).
Further comparative study has been authorized.

INSTITUTIONAL STATUS:
Pendleton University will no longer be receiving federal or private

research grants related to this incident. All subsurface programs have been permanently suspended.

The Bennington Subsurface Research Initiative (BSRI) is hereby terminated, effective immediately.

Contact with Dr. H. Mercer, OSRD liaison embedded at Pendleton, has been lost. His absence is under review. No recovery efforts are currently planned.

Mercer's ongoing research directives have been reassigned and will continue under OSRD subdivision VRX Labs, overseen by R. Prescott, operating under approved compartmentalized clearance.

SITE STATUS:

All known access points beneath Pendleton University have been sealed under joint authority.

Public explanation disseminated: *structural instability due to historical mining activity*.

It is the assessment of this office that full excavation is neither feasible nor advisable.

RISK ASSESSMENT:

The subterranean system remains active.

Observed phenomena appear responsive to light, sound, and proximity.

Containment is considered *temporarily* stable.

Long-term outcomes cannot be projected with confidence.

FINAL NOTE:

Historical review confirms this is not the first incident associated with Eurydium.

Containment has succeeded before.

It has also failed.

END OF BRIEFING
OFFICE OF STRATEGIC RESEARCH AND
DEVELOPMENT

AFTERWORD

Thank you for descending.

The Ninth Layer began with a simple image: a group of students stepping into the dark, believing they would return unchanged. I've always been fascinated by the idea that beneath every institution—every polished surface and carefully maintained reputation—there are foundations. And beneath those foundations, sometimes, there are things we were never meant to uncover.

This story is about fear, yes—but also about curiosity. About what drives us downward even when every instinct tells us to turn back. It's about loyalty tested in tight spaces, about the way pressure reveals who we are, and about the quiet cost of knowledge once it's been earned.

The dark in this book is literal. But it's also the kind we all carry—the unanswered question, the risk we take, the door we open because we need to know what's on the other side.

Some stories are about escape.

This one is about what happens after the ground shifts.

To every reader who made it to the surface—thank you. Your willingness to walk beside these characters through the claustrophobia, the silence, and the uncertainty means more than I can say.

If something in these pages unsettled you, lingered with you, or followed you into the quiet afterward... that was the intention.

Not to harm.

But to remind you that some places stay with us long after we've left them.

Some layers are geological. Others are buried in memory. And some are still waiting.

Respectfully Yours,

Lincoln James

ACKNOWLEDGMENTS

A special thanks to the fantastic people who helped make this book possible:

Adri

Ben

Bree

Cossy

David

Denise

Jack

Jessie

Kamran

Keaton

Lee

Mariah

Mason

Maureen

Mike

Mila

Nadia

Rob

Ross

Ryan

ABOUT THE AUTHOR

Lincoln James, your favorite author's favorite author, is known for his haunting love stories, vintage thrillers, and slow-burn suspense. His characters feel, ache, and bleed, often trapped between the past and the people who won't let them forget it. When he's not writing, James is a Communication and English professor in New York City and cherishes moments with friends and family, proving that the most thrilling tales lie in the love and laughter shared with those closest to us.